CW01395633

# Copyright & Thanks

# Acknowledgements:

*For my husband, kids, Tina, Nat, my sister, parents, in-laws and friends who I consider family, other family who genuinely know me; thank you!*

To Kirsty,
All the best!
Life isn't Predicted.
Go & grab it!
love Louise Murchie

# One

## Ellen

I can't help but grin from ear to ear, as envious as I am, as one of my lifelong friends declares her love and commitment for the man she now stands beside. Their tiny daughter is being held by her former nanny just a row in front and my friend's brother, the nanny's boyfriend, is helping take care of the little girl.

I glance back to watch Shauna and Harek as they are pronounced man and wife with a kiss even the Princess Bride would be jealous of. I know I am. Along with everyone else, I join in the cheers as we let the groom guide his bride to the huge outdoor marquee and the festivities can begin.

Ruth finds me later that evening. Along with her, Shauna and Helene, we have known each other since primary school days. We've grown up together, watched Shauna find the first love of her life, marry him, bear him two children, then tragically mourn him when he died in a motorcycle accident.

These women were there for me when my marriage failed, though failure is a relative term. He decided that he didn't love me anymore and as I looked into his cold, stone eyes as he told me that he never really had, I died inside. Whilst I enjoyed the physical attention at Helene's wedding eighteen months ago, I wasn't wanting a repeat performance this time.

"You can grab one, ya know, our bab," Ruth winks at me in a comical way. Her accent is a far stronger Birmingham one than mine, perhaps because Ruth talks an awful lot more than I do, or perhaps my Northern influence is showing through. Where Ruth is the epicentre of most parties (save perhaps this one) I am usually the one stuck to the wall, observing.

I shake my head at Ruth over the sound of the music, but smile as I shrug my shoulders. No one here takes my fancy and it took a lot of effort and fear-control the last time I was at Helene's wedding to speak with the few new people that I did. The alcohol and the quiet attention led to my last bedroom exploits. I don't see that man here.

I wring my hands together and then force myself to stop. The age-old habit I have when I am nervous shows through enough for Ruth to see. She doesn't say anything but offers me a hug. I fall into her embrace, smelling her perfume as it clashes with mine, but feeling the need for some comfort.

"I am not going to repeat the last Dutch wedding we were at," Ruth tells me as she speaks directly into my ear. The music isn't loud, but there is a lot of noise from the number of people here, as small as this gathering is.

"Dirk is here," I say, nodding across to where he is. It's been eighteen months since Helene and Fons married here in Rotterdam. It was why and how Shauna and Harek met, though their journey to this point wasn't without incident or angst.

Ruth just nods at me, making some of her strawberry red curls fall over her eyes. "He's not single though. He came with someone on his arm, so I'm leaving him well alone." She shrugs as if she doesn't care, but I recall that we didn't see much of her that weekend, save when we cared for Shauna after Hareks' attack. I know she does care but I'm grateful not to be left to my own devices for once.

I take two glasses of champagne from a passing waiter and hand one to Ruth. We dance, we hug Shauna and Harek, hold their daughter Aisla whilst admiring how handsome Shauna's sons now are, and compliment Carrie, Bryce's daughter. Harek has really stepped into the dad role and between them, the best man and his wife, Shauna's parents, Helene and Ruth, I do not feel alone.

## Two
### Ellen

Ruth joins me as we head back to Hull via the ferry. Ruth drove up to my parents as my daughter wanted time with her grandparents, rather than be at Shauna's wedding. I didn't mind, it meant less stress for me for one weekend.

We're on time for the ferry, thanks to Harek's considerate butler, Johan. We wave to him from the deck as the ferry leaves Rotterdam and we head back to our lives.

I sit and sigh as we leave Rotterdam behind. It is a beautiful city, not that I got to see much of it the first time I was here. This time, Shauna insisted that we take a tour, Helene and Fons offered to be our guides. Helene's little one was adorable and it wasn't long until Fons whisked him off back to their place for a nap, leaving the three of us to enjoy our day together.

"Missing the place already?" Ruth asks and I observe we're both dressed similarly. Tank tops, jeans, light-weight trainers and a jacket. Ruth hands me a coffee in a polystyrene cup, which is too hot to drink right now. I contemplate taking the lid off it but I know how clumsy I am. As I'm debating whether I should, Ruth pulls out a pack of hand-made caramel Belgian waffles, takes the lid off her coffee, and places the waffle over the top, letting the steam melt the hard caramel inside. I grin and copy her, knowing that the caramel being gooey is so much nicer.

"I'm not missing it," I say. "I am just not sure I want to go back to my life," I try not to look at Ruth, but she gets what I'm saying.

"I'm not looking forward to going back either. I want what Shauna has, again." Ruth has never been so set or dour about Shauna's luck in life.

"You want to settle down?" I try not to sound so astonished, but Ruth's quizzical look tells me I failed.

Ruth just nods. "Or a regular partner. I am so fed up bouncing around and some of the good-looking guys are shallow," she shivers at a memory that she hasn't shared with our group. "I've been the rebound girl too often."

"Someone reliable, who understands you," I offer. If someone would even take five minutes to work out I'm the shy, quiet one of our group, not just an afterthought or the tag-along, they'd have my interest.

"I want someone who gets me too," I offer quietly. I dare not voice that I want the protection I read about so often in the romance books I review and promote on Instagram. Ruth leans across and squeezes my hand for a moment, telling me she understands.

Ruth casts a glance at me from the waffle she's now devouring. I adjust my glasses and copy her. All too soon, we're back at the port, fetching my car from the long-stay car park and heading to my parents' house so Ruth can collect her car.

Ruth doesn't hang around too long when we're with my parents. It's late on Sunday and she didn't book Monday off from work, though it is still school holiday time for me.

"Take care, lovely. Let me know you're back okay?" I ask her as she gives me another bone-crushing hug. I forget that Ruth has a heart bigger than her breasts and a hug to match. She waves to my parents, my ignorant daughter Samantha, and then heads off for home.

I sigh, turn towards my parents' bungalow, and head in.


I look around the bedroom I share with my daughter when we visit. It has two single beds with a delicate floral pattern on the duvet set, a set of drawers for our stuff, and a small dressing table. The curtains match the duvet's every time we visit, no matter what duvet set is on the beds. I think mum secretly enjoys the quiet life up here; it's certainly much easier for them in my grandmother's old house than it was in their two-story back in Birmingham. The house I now occupy and have improved upon.

Gran dying left her bungalow to my parents, who then didn't need their house. With my divorce through, I bought it with the amount I was given in the settlement. That enabled them to improve this one as they saw fit and I got a mortgage-free life with my daughter and we didn't have to change schools.

Samantha huffs as she comes into the bedroom, my moment of solitude destroyed by a moody teenage girl, which is normal being a single mum.

"What did you ask for now?" I enquire gently. Samantha will go off like a bottle of pop, so much more like her father than me. I can tell by how she's acting she didn't get what she wanted. Life was so unfair at thirteen.

She looks around and blinks a few times as if she hadn't seen me sitting on the bed.

"When did you get back?" she asks, sitting forwards on her bed and leaning across to me.

"About half an hour ago. Ruth was here for a while, we had a cup of tea together," I replied. "Ruth waved to you when she left, you were at the window," Sam's wearing a black t-shirt with blue jeans and her hair looks like it hasn't been brushed in days.

"Oh," she says. "I didn't see you," she mumbles as she leans back a bit. "Was the wedding good?" she asks as she swings her legs up onto the bed and flops down onto her back. She closes her eyes but opens them again a few moments later when she turns her head to look at me.

Knowing that she is at least paying attention, I respond.

"It was beautiful. Michael and Andrew have changed a fair bit, Rotterdam seems to agree with them." I watch as she grimaces a little at the news of Shauna's eldest children, one of whom I'm sure Sam had a crush on. "Shauna was beautiful in her dress. Do you want to see?" I pull my phone out and Sam gives me a half shrug.

I scroll through the pictures I took on the day. The boys in their suits, the groom and best man in their Honour of Scotland kilts, the remake of Helene's Kransekage that Shauna says started their romance, their daughter and niece in their dresses. Sam fawns over the picture of the little girl and oos at Shauna's bridal gown. It was a very cream number, not as tight as the dress she wore in her first wedding to Matt. I must have scrolled through about a hundred images, some of which I will send to Shauna, others just show the fun of the day.

"Are we still going to the Street Life Museum?" she asks as she hands me back my phone. I pondered for a moment wondering where I put the tickets so that they were safe.

"Let me find the tickets, but yes, we are," I pull out the bag I left in Hull and find the ticket's quite quickly in the small pouch on the front. It's a fear of mine, losing tickets to something or somewhere. I always double-check where things are before I answer, which frustrates a lot of people. Shauna and the others soon realised my fear and learned to trust me with important documents.

"Good, I'm so bored," she drones. She's indulged and spoiled by my parents and I know she will have been waited-on hand-and-foot whilst I was in Rotterdam.

"Only the boring are bored," I reply. I'm not sure how much she'll push back. She looks at me but doesn't give me any verbal, which is a change for her. I hear my mother calling us for dinner, so we head out to join her and my father.

The following day, we head to the Street Life Museum, which is mostly indoors but some of the vehicle exhibits have been moved outside into the late August sunshine. Samantha and I walk around, taking in the old classic cars, cable buses, and other early nineteenth-century vehicles, bikes, buildings and exhibits.

We leave one exhibit of a red classic race car and turn a corner when Samantha is knocked off her feet by a huge lad, who instantly apologises for his clumsiness. She huffs and begins to start telling him off, but stops as another tall, good-looking man appears behind him.

"I'm sorry," says the youth again, holding out his hand to help my daughter up. She graciously accepts his help and looks at me with her eyes wide open. She seems to notice how good-looking he is, at least that's what I get from the sudden doe-eyed look she's giving him. I'm looking at his father with probably very similar thoughts. I toy with my hair as it sweeps off my shoulder and tuck my handbag tighter under my arm.

"Oscar, I've told you to stop rushing about mate," he chastises the young man with an accent that's strangely familiar to me.

"Sorry Uncle Nick," he grumbles. So, the man isn't his father, but his uncle. My heart soars and I have no idea why. He's taller than me, sure, but that's not hard, I'm five foot two. He has medium brown hair, which is shaved in at the sides, military-style, stubble that's a few days old. His light green eyes dance in my direction.

"No harm done," I pipe up, helping Sam check herself. I can only surmise that it's her pride that's taken a bruising more than her bottom.

"Still, I'm sorry," grumbles Oscar. "Did I hurt you?" he asks. He's fishing for her name, obviously.

"I'm…" Sam brushes herself down again. "I'm okay, thank you. I'm Sam," she rushes out. Oh dear, it seems my daughter is perhaps as introverted as I am.

"Let me buy you some ice cream," he offers. "There's a good stall over that way," and he points in a direction we've not managed to investigate yet. He turns to his uncle. "That's okay, yeah?" His accent is more Hull and Yorkshire than Birmingham-based. Nick simply nods.

"Of course it is," he looks at me and his lips curl up in a roguish way. "I'm Nick, this oaf is my nephew, Oscar. I'm sorry he knocked your daughter over," he says as he extends his hand towards mine. I take it and shake it gently.

"I'm Ellen," I offer. Since I know their names it is at least polite to offer my own.

I turn as Sam shouts "Come on mum!" to find that she and Oscar are a good twenty meters ahead of Nick and I. After casting a small glance at Nick, I shrug my shoulders and play with my hair a little more as we follow them.

"Are you up here for the day?" he asks but I shake my head. It takes me a moment or two to find the words I want to use. Looking at him gets me even more tongue-tied than usual.

"We have family in the area," I finally say. "We're visiting, but we're heading back tomorrow."

Nick nods, his eyes dimming slightly. "Where's home?" he asks.

"In the West Midlands," I reply. I hardly know this man, why would I want to give him my details? However, I'm drawn to his mouth, the shape of it and I pull my shoulders back a little more, standing straighter.

"Oh, really? I'm in Lichfield, in one of the new builds just outside on the way to Sutton Coldfield." I gape at him, then I remember my manners.

"That's not far away," I say. "We live in Amblecote," I offer as further evidence that I know where I live.

"Yeou propar spake?" he offers in the thickest, clumsiest, funniest Black Country accent I've ever heard.

"Spake proper," I counter without missing a beat as I try my hardest not to laugh at his attempts. He laughs as we finally catch up with our younger charges.

Oscar and Sam have already decided what flavours they want, which isn't surprising. Sam will have the same as I do; we always have the same. Mint choc chip. However, there are so many other flavours to choose from I decide I'm going to be bold.

"Which one would you like?" Nick offers, picking a coffee caramel mix for him in a huge chocolate wafer cone.

"A small lemon sorbet, please." I catch Sam's glare, she's not used to me choosing something different.

Nick has three scoops in his cone, I only want the one. Nick however has brought me a double lemon sorbet and cheesecake, which sounds super sweet. If he were handing it to Shauna or Helene, they'd be fawning over it. I accept it graciously and slowly lick the top layer, which is the cheesecake. It has shortbread in the middle with a light lemon flavour. Nick graciously pays and I remember to thank him, which prompts Sam to do the same.

The kids wander off together, talking about this and that, which makes my heart sing. Sam might not be quite as introverted as I am, which pleases me. My life was hard enough when I had friends who understood me. As an adult who is quite shy, it's harder to make myself get out there more.

"So what do you do for a job?" he asks. I've eaten one side of the first scoop and now I'm mixing two different tangs of lemon together. It's surprisingly nice.

"I work at the central library," I offer. "You?" I watch as he carefully eats his ice cream, not making a mess. He's so different from Mark.

"I help my dad run a steel manufacturing company. You know all those big metal joists they use on buildings?" I nod, I've seen them, they're huge. "We manufacture them." He straightens up as his pride takes over. He's clearly proud of what it is he does for a living.

"It's a solid profession. We're forever building things. I'll be glad when the building works on Broad Street are finished." They've been tearing down the old library and rebuilding that area for what feels like an eon, though it's probably only taken them a few years. However, the nineteen-sixties concrete was full of stuff that can be harmful, so the City Council has had to be clever and slow in how it's all taken down.

Nick nods. "Yeah, they've been doing that forever. It'll be good to walk from Broad Street down to New Street again." He knows the area.

"Do you go to Brum often?" I ask. Nick shakes his head.

"When I go out with the guys, sometimes. Lichfield isn't far by train, a few stops on the direct line that comes into New Street and I'm there in forty minutes or so."

"I wouldn't know, I never go into Birmingham on the train. There are no train stations near me, so I go in via the bus when I'm at the library. They can send me to cover other branches though, but that's usually agreed in advance, because of Sam."

I nod towards my daughter and it seems she's in a heated discussion with Oscar about something. I somehow doubt she's got him talking about fashion.

"I wonder what they're talking about?" Nick muses as he too watches the kids.

"Teenagers," I offer. "Who knows?" The truth is, anything is possible with teenagers.

We spent the rest of the afternoon chatting casually. I can feel Nick getting frustrated with me as I take my time to answer his questions and ask my own. I've never been very good at flirting or talking with new people. On occasion, I see Oscar looking at us both, then the kids are in a head huddle, probably talking about us.

"I see we're the subject of conversation, again." I offer as Sam is the one to take a glance back at us.

Nick huffs and digs his hands into his pockets. I wish I were more self-confident when meeting new people. It takes a little time for me to get comfortable around people, but I can't always explain that. I never have the words, even if I practice a phrase or a sentence, it never comes out the right way when I do say it.

Nick looks at the sky and I join him, seeing that dusk is falling. He checks his watch as we amble back to the entrance.

"Thank you," I blurt out. "For the company this afternoon." I rush to say what my mind is thinking whilst my mouth still works. I bite my lower lip as I run out of what I want to say, my mouth freezing up but my mind wants to ask him for his number.

"Perhaps we'll see each other again?" he offers.

I only nod and grab Sam. "Perhaps. Bye!" I drag her back to the car and away from Oscar and Nick, kicking myself the whole time.

# Three
## Nick

Ellen pulls Sam away as soon as we're at the car park and I wonder what I said to offend her. She was hard to get to know, but there was something there that made me try harder than ever. The fact that my dick was at half-mast for most of the walking and talking we did must have escaped her notice. She was tiny compared to me and I'm only five foot eleven. She often played with her long brown hair, twirling it up in her fingers or biting her lip and it was hard to get her to talk about herself. I could swim in her clear blue eyes for the rest of my life, but she doesn't seem to want me to. I was going to ask her if she wanted my number, but she ran off with her daughter before I could.

"I got her number," Oscar beams at me.

I nod. Darn! My teenage nephew got the daughter's number where I had failed to get her mums. At least I knew where she worked most of the time. I recall that library, its square shape is all glass and steel with lights and a swirling design on the outside. It's rather spectacular, it's got seven floors and has more space than the old one twice over. My company supplied a lot of the joists needed to build it and I'm proud we had a hand in helping to build one of the largest public libraries in the world. It's a busy place and I sigh in frustration as my thoughts run away with me. Oscar gives me a knowing glance.

"What?" I bark, a little too harshly. He recoils slightly. "Sorry, just…" I look at where Ellen and Sam went, just in time to see Ellen drive out of the car park in a small blue car.

"Sam said her mum is painfully shy. More so since her dad walked out on them," he offers. He's clearly done a better job at finding out about them than I did.

"Painfully shy?" I ask. My stomach sinks, she wasn't being rude. She just didn't know me and couldn't tell me this is how she is normally and I feel like an idiot.

Oscar nods as we get into my car. "Yeah, he walked out about seven years ago, Sam said, days before Christmas. Told her mum he didn't love her, or Sam. He didn't contest the divorce either. She moved into her grandparents' old house that her mum brought off her parents. It's all a mess, or it was."

I gape for a moment, then close my mouth. "Did Sam offer anything else?" I ask, hoping that the lad got more information. Like a typical talkative teenager, he did.

"Yeah, her grandparents live up here. Moved up to take care of her great-nan, Ellen's grandmother. When she died, the house switch happened, which is why Ellen has her childhood home and her parents live up here."

I smile, grateful for the inside knowledge.

"So she's painfully shy, huh?"

Oscar rolls his eyes. "Yeah, we've established that." He taps a few things out on his phone. "It says here," he waves his internet-enabled phone about, making his point, "that dating a shy person can be hard. You've got to gain their trust. Small gatherings are essential. Time is too. Don't expect a response straight away, or even a phone call back the same day. They'll play with their hair, wring their hands when they're nervous and don't like being in unfamiliar situations."

I absorb what he tells me as I drive him back to his parents. Ellen displayed some of those characteristics today.

Driving Oscar back, I think back to our family dynamic and why Oscar and I are even here. My older brother didn't want to join the family business of steel making and met his wife in York one day. They moved to Hull when he got a job with the police force and I have taken some leave to come and visit with them. They wanted a day off and I wanted to do something that wasn't just dragging Oscar around the old City of Culture.

"What else does your wonderful internet have about shy people?" I enquire. He shows me a page, then rolls his eyes as I start the engine.

"I'll send you the link Uncle Nick, though you're not going to like the second one that's on this list, 'cause you're terrible at it!" He bounces around as his voice increases and I can only guess what the second skill is in dating a shy woman. It's something I've been accused of a lot in my youth but something I am trying to improve upon. My listening skills.

My phone pings as I reach the car park barrier and before long, we're heading home to my brother's place. I'm staying here one more night before I drive back home to Lichfield.

# *Four*
## *Ellen*

Sam grins at me as I drive away from the Street Life Museum, then she yells at me to slow down. I breathe and calm myself and my driving. I slam the wheel in frustration, forgetting Sam is next to me.

"You liked him, mum, didn't you?" She's Captain Obvious and I cast her a sideways glance as we waited at a set of traffic lights. She laughs at me. "Would you like his number? I exchanged numbers with Oscar..." she shifts in her seat and brings one leg up to tuck it under her bum. I bite my lower lip whilst I ponder if I'd like Nick's number. He didn't seem to be like Mark, my first husband. Nick seemed more patient, but that might be because he's getting to know me, or wanted to. I sigh and Sam pipes up.

"Mum, just let me grab his number and you can text him. Or shall I have him text you?" I glance across as I turn us into the road my parents live on. Sam nudges me gently. "You know what Shauna would say if she were here. Or Ruth?" I glare at her a little, trust her to bring the girls into it.

"They'd say take a chance," I whisper. I turn the engine off and Sam pivots in her seat to face me.

"They would. Helene did, and she's happily married and Shauna is again. You deserve it, mum," she touches my arm and smiles at me as I sigh and just nod.

"Okay, give him my number." 'After all,' I think to myself. 'What's the harm in a text or two?'

# Five
## Nick

Oscar comes bouncing into my room without knocking as I leave the en-suite.

"Oscar, you need to knock mate," I tell him as I shut the bathroom door behind me.

"I did!" he beams, standing in the doorway.

"Did I answer?" I ask, getting cross with him.

He just shakes his head. "No, but I knew you were in here. Mum says dinner is ready, and uncle Nick, Sam's mum wants your number after all. Here's hers." He hands me a piece of torn paper with numbers that are badly formed.

"Oscar, what is this?" I ask. "Your writing is terrible mate," I say, grabbing my phone. "Read the number out," I tell him and as he does, I add it to my contacts and double-check it before I hit save.

"Tell Lisa I'll be down in two minutes," He just grins at me and swaggers off. I hear his footsteps thud down the stairs, and a smile begins pulling at my lips. I quietly close my door and think about what I want to say. I'd read the link Oscar had sent me on the way back from the Museum and I know I can't be pushy with her. She'll close up if I do, I need to be patient. That's going to be hard in itself, I hate waiting for things.

*N: Hi! Thanks for trusting me with your number. Here's mine. Hope we can catch up when we're both back home. You made today*

I pause. I could say that she made the day awesome, but that sounds cliche and too bold for such a shy lady. I smile as the word I need finally comes to me and I finish my text, then hit send.

*N: perfect. Nick.*

I suspect it's going to be hours if not a day or two before I get a reply, so I tuck my phone into my back pocket and head down to dinner with my brother's family, trying not to act like Tigger as I do.

# Six
## Ellen

My phone pings just after we sit down to dinner but I ignore it until we've eaten and cleared everything away. We're heading off tomorrow so it'll be mostly motorway driving for me tomorrow and I detest the M1 stretch at Nottingham. I sneak a look at my phone as mum, dad and Sam get engrossed in an episode of Game of Thrones. It's from Nick and I gasp, forgetting for a moment that I need to breathe.

I read his message twice. I can feel the heat in my cheeks and I'm sure my dimples are showing. Sam just throws me a wink and leaves me to consider what I'll send him back. I don't text him back until bedtime.

*E: Thank you. I'll be leaving early to drive home. I'll catch up with you next week?*

I sigh as I put my phone on silent and tuck it under my pillow so it wakes me up at eight am. I'm glad but surprised that I didn't receive a reply until the following morning. Nick wishes me a safe journey. That's all. My stomach goes all fluttery, light, knotted. He's not trying to push himself onto me. He responded and did not make any other suggestion that we meet up halfway home or anything else that's pushy. He's just... being there. I smile.

"Are you okay love?" asks my mother as she comes into the kitchen. I've put the coffee on for her and dad and poured myself a glass of water. Our bags are packed and waiting to go out to the car.

I nod. "Yeah, I..." I look at her. "We met someone yesterday," I begin and Mum's shoulders shake.

"Yeah, Sam mentioned," she replies, her eyes sparkling and the curve of her lip gives away that she's happy for me.

"Oh, did she?" I ask. I'll be having words with my daughter when I get her alone in the car, though I'll probably wait until we're around Doncaster when it's too late to bring her stroppy self back here.

Mum just nods. "We asked her how the museum was and she spent all the time talking about this boy Oscar. Then she just mentioned you might fancy his uncle as her phone went ping again." I chuckle. I'm guessing that Oscar and Sam got busy texting. I feel the need to tell her to be careful. She's developing, growing up. She's not the baby I once knew and the world is a scary place. Mum has pulled out two mugs and is busy making up the coffee the way she and dad like it.

"Oh," I responded and closed my mouth. What I was going to say, just doesn't seem right anymore.

Mum touches me on the arm. "If he gets you El, and you like him, be brave," she encourages as she takes a cup of coffee through to dad in bed.

Sam comes through about ten minutes later, dressed, slightly groomed, and yawning.

"Why do we have to get up this early mum?" she asks as she digs around in the cupboards for a bowl and finds the cereal that they've gotten in just for her.

"Because I need to drive us home and the motorways might be jammed later. I want to get going by nine," I say with a slight hint of determination. Sam groans, so I know she heard me.

"Have you packed everything?" I ask. She has a mouth full of cereal and gives me a thumbs-up in reply. "I'm going to go and check," I say, standing to head back to our room. Sam has packed, I can't find anything lying around she's likely to have forgotten. Now, I recall Shauna on a girls' weekend away one time, we were still finding stuff all over after she'd "packed" and she hasn't changed in that way since, forever. I'm grateful Sam's not like her.

I bring our bags out into the hall just as mum and dad emerge from their bedroom. They give me a huge hug and we go to sit down for breakfast one last time before we come up again at Halloween.

## Seven
### Nick

Ellen said she was leaving early and I've decided to copy her. The motorways are always jammed later in the morning and though I don't have to go quite as far as Ellen and Sam, getting home earlier in the day has an appeal, but so does staying longer. However, my brother Alex and his family need to take Oscar shopping for a new school uniform as he seems to have grown six inches in height over the summer months (though it's more like four in height and another shoe size) and I decide to leave them to it.

Once we've eaten and I've helped clear up, I pack up and head home, letting Alex lock the door behind me and leave him to his shopping nightmare.

It takes me until Doncaster before I decide to stop for a break. There were accidents on the motorway before this set of services that are going to make my journey home nearly forty-five minutes longer than I needed or wanted. I pull in and the car parking is mad, though I manage to find a space near the lorry park. Stretching my legs and back from the cramp after being held in traffic for twenty minutes, feels so blooming amazing.

I look around at the hundreds of cars, lorries, vans, and bikes parked up, the battle for the next available space, other drivers taking a break and I sigh. It would be nice to be here with someone you liked, to sit on the grass on the hill at the back. I roll my shoulders and chastise myself for the thoughts, then head off into the concrete building that's full of people.

The services are quite busy but given that a lot of people were probably trapped in their cars for longer than they usually would be, it doesn't surprise me. I head to the mens, do what I need to do, then join the queue of people for a coffee. A small tap on my shoulder turns me around and I'm face to face with Ellen and Sam.

Ellen looks pale but it's Sam that speaks.

"Err, can we ask you to get us some coffee too? Just, it's a bit busy," she glances at her mum and I get it. It's a little Grinch-like right now: too many people and Ellen is probably overwhelmed. I nod.

"Of course. How do you take it?" They give me their order (two latte's, one with mint chocolate syrup, one with caramel) and then they head off to the ladies, which I know is going to be as packed as a nightclub's toilets will be. They're going to be gone for a while.

I have all three drinks in a tray waiting by the door of Costa when they appear. I grab Ellen's hand. "There's space outside," I say and guide them through the throngs to the picnic area outside, and I find a table near the back where no one else wants to go. Ellen gives me a small smile and takes a seat, whilst Sam throws herself into the bench seats with gusto. I manage to hold the bench level and place my weight down firmly and slowly to counter her enthusiasm.

"Thank you," Ellen whispers as I hand her one of the lattes. She wanted the caramel one and I made sure that the lady labelled them up. I hand the mint one to Sam and take the black coffee for myself.

"It's a pleasure," I say and turn to Sam to give Ellen a few moments to just be. "Did you see the fire engines?" I ask her. She nods.

"Yeah, the roof of one of the cars was cut off too! What do you think happened?" She takes the lid off her coffee and Ellen jumps back. Sam doesn't spill anything but Ellen kind of glares at her for a moment, then mellows.

"I don't know, it looked worse than a rear-end shunt. There were two fire engines and an ambulance in attendance when I went past. I just hope no one was hurt," I replied as I glanced at Ellen. Sam stretches her arms and rolls her shoulders back.

"I take it you were behind me?" I suggest gently to Ellen. She lifts her head and I see her pool-like eyes shine back at me.

"Yes, looks like we were," she whispers. She's got one hand around her coffee, the other on the table and I reach out to gently just touch her, to give some reassurance.

"I'm glad you weren't a part of it," I say. Then I turn my attention back to Sam.

"Does your mother have to take you for school uniform shopping too? That's where Oscar is right about now. Either that or a pizza parlour. I'm not sure which one wins," I squeeze Ellen's fingers gently, then let go.

Sam checks her phone. "He's at McDonald's," she says and shows me a picture on his Instagram account. The boy is eating for lunch what I would eat for dinner and I know Alex is planning lasagne for dinner, Oscar's and my favourite. Kids with high metabolisms get it easier. I like to watch what I eat these days. Sam rises to put her coffee cup in the bin. I hadn't even seen her drink it.

"Are you okay? Do you need anything?" I ask Ellen. She throws me a small, warm smile.

"I'm better now, thanks to you," she says. Her voice is a little louder and a bit punchier. She's not playing with her hair or biting her lip, so I guess she's doing okay, but I have read enough to know that asking her will make her so not okay.

"I'm glad," I say. I want to ask her so many other things, but I refrain. I need to keep it to small conversations until she opens up, to trust me enough. I can't just jump in like I usually would. The fact she let me hold her hand whilst I talked with Sam about the accident, which I think freaked her out a little, was small in my world, but probably huge in hers. Her hair is in a loose plait behind her head and she has on a deep pink lipstick that I want to kiss off. Add in the baby blues and her small frame, I suddenly want to cuddle her, to protect her. What the hell!

"Do you think the motorway has cleared up a bit?" she asked me, pulling me back from my wandering thoughts.

"I have no idea, but we have about another hour before we have to pay for the parking. I hadn't planned on hanging around that long," I offer the simplest of explanations.

"I think we can give it another fifteen minutes and then head out," she smiles at me and looks around for Sam, who is sitting on a kids' swing in the play area.

"That sounds like a good plan. Shall I check the route ahead for us?" I offer. Her eyes go wide and she sighs, surprised perhaps that I even offered. She nods her head.

"Thank you, again," she murmurs and her cheeks go pink.

"That's okay. I need to know myself," and I put the phone down on the table to pull up the rest of the route home. The M1 and the connecting roads to the M42 and M6 look clear, though that can change in a heartbeat.

"You know, I could be in Rotterdam already if I'd gone from Hull. Even waiting for a ferry, I'd be at my friends' place quicker than I am getting home," she scowls as she speaks and I think it's because of the route ahead.

"You have a friend in Rotterdam? What's it like?"

She perks up and begins to tell me of the sites she's seen when she went to her friend's wedding. She tells me how her friend, Shauna, has married a Dutchman and relocated out to that city over a year ago. They've just tied the knot after having a baby he never thought he'd ever get to have. Her eyes dance and her confidence begins to show itself as she talks about her friend, who I am beginning to understand, I don't ever want to piss off.

"So yeah, that's Shauna. Then there's Ruth and Helene. Helene went over to Rotterdam first, but we've been friends since we were nine," she smiles at me, a huge beam of a smile that lights up her whole face.

"And you're only twenty-five," I tease. Though, I'm half teasing. Her daughter's age tells me she's at least the same age as me, but Ellen does look rather youthful. She giggles at my compliment but tangles her hair up in a finger. That made her nervous. How can she not take a compliment? I want more than a quiet word with whoever has made her feel ashamed of her being herself.

"I'm eleven years older than that," she says. That stops me. She's thirty-six? I check I'm not trying to catch flies and I have to think quickly about a reply.

"That doesn't bother me, if me being thirty-one doesn't bother you," I offer. She gapes like I thought I had, but composes herself quickly.

"You don't look like you're thirty-one," she counters with a shimmer of confidence. I lean in and smell her perfume, smelling her.

"And you do not look thirty-six," I smile at her gently, hoping I don't scare her away by giving her another compliment or two. Her cheeks flush pink and she purses her lips into a thin line.

"We'd best hit the road," I offer, standing up and gathering our empty cups so they can be thrown away. Ellen nods and I hold out a hand to help her up. She hesitates for a moment but I don't back down. She tilts her head to one side for a second, then straightens up and takes my hand.

I bin the empty cups and Ellen motions for Sam to follow, who was doing a great Gulliver impression on the only swing the tiny play area had. I walk them back to their car and ensure they're safe, then I head to mine and drive home, knowing that she's about a mile ahead of me the entire way.

When I get home, I open up a few windows and brew some coffee, then think about what I can eat for dinner. It's never bothered me about eating on my own before, but now I've met Ellen, it does. We've only spent a few hours together, but I want her company more.

I picked up the phone to check it but she's not text to say she's home. If she was ahead of me before I turned off for Lichfield, it'll be about another twenty minutes before she gets home. I sigh and see what is in my freezer, nothing appeals, but I do need to eat. Sighing, I grab something and reading the instructions, I turn the oven on to warm up, feeling the loneliest I've ever felt.

After clearing away my meal, I decide I need to learn how to cook. I could ask my mother, knowing I should learn a few things beyond the lasagne. I don't always want something so heavy or that large, so I look up simple meals for one on my phone. I found a reference to a cookbook and decided to order it on Prime, so it'll be here by Tuesday. Just as the confirmation of the order email arrives, so does a text from Ellen.

*E: we got back about ten minutes ago. M5 had accidents on it too!*

I had never considered that she'd have another part of the motorway to contend with. I replied immediately.

*N: Oh no! Are you okay though?*

*E: Yes, we are. Just making a coffee now, then grabbing some food. Thanks for being there today. It meant a lot that you just gave me space.*

I look at the text. It's the most words she's sent me since I got her number the other day. Was it only yesterday? The day before? One day is all it took for me to smile like a teenager.

*N: You're welcome! I'd like to take you out for a coffee, or lunch. In fact, either. You decide. Saturday?*

I sit back and wait. I've given her options, made the decisions about where and when, all hers. I know her responses aren't going to be immediate, she'll take the time to think things through and be comfortable with them before she shares her thoughts. I smile, grab a beer and call my brother.

An hour later, as I'm unpacking and hanging out my laundry to dry, I get a text back. I smile as I open the message.

*E: There's a good cafe on Brierley Hill High Street I know. I can meet you there for lunch on Saturday. I have this weekend off.*

There's another text straight after with the cafe's name, address and a google maps link. It's about an hour from me here in Lichfield, but that's okay. I look at the route and smile.

*N: I can do that. What time would suit you?*

I finish putting my clothes on the drier and move it to the conservatory. It'll dry in there quite easily as it warms up a lot during the day. I see a few shirts that I need to iron, so I plug the iron in and let it warm up.

In fifteen minutes, I ironed my five shirts, hung them on hangers, and took them to hang in my wardrobe, sorting things out how I like them for first things in the morning.

As I tuck the ironing board and iron away back into the corner, Ellen's latest text arrives.

*E: How does 12:30 suit you?*

Oh, she's giving me the choice now! The time suits me fine and I text back: *Perfect!*

Then I get ready for bed. I usually only wear my briefs to bed and I begin to wonder what Ellen wears. It's the last thing I remember as sleep draws me under.

# Eight
## *Ellen*

Nick isn't pushing for a date, well, he is but he's being respectful and letting me decide on several things, for which I'm grateful. I decide I'd like more than a coffee with him, it's too far from Lichfield for just a coffee date, lunch at least could take an hour or two, which he might be okay with given the distance.

I picked my favourite cafe just off the high street. The owners know me so if anything bad happens, they'll be able to at least call the police, or help me out. I unpack our laundry, thankful that mum did it for me before we came home. I called them when we finally parked on the driveway. It took nearly four and a half hours to get home from the Doncaster services which are an hour from mum and dads. Nick's text asking me out makes me smile and lifts my spirits. Perhaps today wasn't so bad after all.

Monday rolls around and I go into work with more of a bounce in my step. The head librarian gives us the sections we're working on and asks if I can help out with the library's Instagram account this week. I love doing that, so I accept it heartily.

"You always do well with it, thank you," he says as the meeting breaks up.

"You're welcome, Phil." I smile and head out with the others to grab the phone we use for the social media account. I'll take pictures of the library at weird but wonderful angles, the book piles we're putting away, the latest deliveries of books we have to catalogue, or new artwork that's around. Our aim is seven posts throughout the week, responding and interacting as necessary.

The phone is near flat so I head to the reference section and plug it in at the charging point, then photograph the trolley load of books I'm about to put back on the shelves. I lock the phone into the drawer and take the keys before I begin to place the books and tidy the shelves.

I check my phone at lunchtime to find Samantha has finally gotten up and let me know she's heading to her friend's house for the remainder of the day. I text her friend's mum to ensure that she is there and okay. I'm relieved when I get a confirmation text back to say that yes, they're messing about with hair and makeup, as teenage girls do.

I think about texting Nick, to see how he is. I pause. Does he want to hear from me? We texted each other yesterday, a lot. I bite my lip as I think, and one of the other librarians comes over to nudge me playfully.

"What's wrong Elle?" she asks. She's more confident than I am, taller too. Her heart is solid though, like Shauna and Ruth.

"I met someone, at the weekend," I begin. Lisa perches on the table and nods, making her blond bob dance as she waits for me to go on. "I don't know if I should text him."

"Has he texted you already?" she asks. Her voice is soft, quiet. No one else can hear us unless they're standing right next to us.

"We did yesterday, but not today." I bite my lip again.

"And you want to text him first today?" she asks. I nod. "So, why don't you ask how his day is going?" She suggests "Keep it simple." She pats me on the shoulder, then sits down with me at the table in the eating area.

I smile and text Nick the question she suggests, as it is better than anything I can come up with. I tuck the phone back into my pocket and carry on eating my lunch. A small-sounding ping comes back moments later.

*N: Day is going okay. Looking forward to Saturday, it'll be my treat. Will Sam be joining us?*

I blink. I hadn't thought about what to do about Sam, though I'm sure she'll make her own plans.

*E: Not sure what my daughter has planned, so perhaps?*

His reply is instant.

*N: We'll see on the day.*

He sends a winky smiley face to go with the message and I like that he's able to plan with or without my daughter being with me. He's letting her decide if she wants to join us, at least I feel that is what he's saying. I show the text to Lisa and ask her for her thoughts.

"He's leaving the ball in your court," she says, taking a forkful of salad and munching it.

"Yeah, he is, isn't he?" I agree and I squirm in my seat but smile broadly.

"You like him a lot," Lisa states. I purse my lips together and smile, then nod. "Enjoy it, he seems like he's a good one, at least so far." She takes a sip of her drink.

"So far?" I ask, suddenly getting worried.

She grins at me. "Elle, you've only just met him," she reminds me. "You've not had time to get to know him, but I do know you've not smiled this much since…" she cocks her head to the side and her eyes squint as if trying to remember something. "Forever," she adds. She touches my hand gently. "Give it time, he seems to be able to give you space to think and respond as you wish to. That is a rare thing."

Lisa reminds me of Shauna and I resolve to call my friend, or at least drop her a message about all this.

"Thanks," I whisper, ever grateful for her grounding me.

"Live a little," whispers Lisa as she begins to clear her lunch away. The day is overcast so I don't opt to go for a walk as I usually do. The decision turns out to be the right one ten minutes later as a downpour bounces off the ground, making the water fountain in front of the library rather redundant. I also know that the rain will make a moody picture, so I dart out, snap a photo and run back in again. Despite being damp, I'm back inside where it's warm. The library cafe barista smiles and hands me my usual caramel hot cocoa and I accept it gratefully, paying for it on my card and heading back up to the reference section to edit and post some of the photos from today.

Half an hour later, just as I hit send, my phone pings. It's a message from Nick. I carefully put the works' phone down and ensure I can't knock my cocoa over, before I quietly check what he says.

*N: I hope you're nice and dry, heavens just opened up here.*

*E: I will be: I ran out to take a photo for the library Insta account and managed to get it in ten seconds!*

*N: You took that? You're good! You should give lessons on using Instagram, I'm useless at it.*

*E: I use it for work, my card making and my book reviews.*

The dots flash across the top of the screen for a moment, then my answer comes back.

*N: You make cards? Birthday cards and all that?*

*E: In my spare time, yes. I'm not one for going out by myself.*

*N: Neither do I. I prefer going with other people, but not too many.*

He likes smaller groups of people, just like I do. Or does he? I get nervous as the dots appear again.

*N: Confession: I have trouble remembering names a lot of the time, so the smaller the group, the more chance I have to remember their names. I can remember my employee's names though!*

I smile and I get where he's coming from. Ruth, Shauna, and even Helene can remember where, when and who they met months after they've met them. I'm like Nick, it takes me a while to get to know people and therefore, their name. People you're in charge of are slightly different, you need to ensure that they feel included.

I make more of an effort with new colleagues than usual, for that very reason.

*E: You run your own company?*

*N: My dad owns it, but I do the day-to-day stuff, he does the background corporate stuff. It works well.*

*E: Sounds stressful.*

*N: It can be, but I have a good group of people to ensure it works.*

I notice the time and smile.

*E: Need to go, lunch break is over.*

*N: Be safe and stay dry!*

I pondered for a moment then sent him the link to my card-making Instagram account. He follows it and likes quite a few cards I've made before I blank my screen and get back to work.

The rest of the week flies by. Nick and I text each other every day, some days we have more to say than others. He never pesters me when I don't respond for hours and once it was nearly twenty-four hours before I did remember to respond. He didn't berate me or tell me off though, he just said he was glad I was okay and confirmed we were still on for Saturday. That was Thursday and today is Friday, the day before our lunch date. Lunch date. Those words fill me both with dread and excitement in equal measure.

After work on Friday, I head home. Sam has been good this week and she thankfully goes back to school next week. We purchased all her new uniform before Shauna's wedding, so I didn't have to do it the week I went back to work. She seems to have enjoyed her time at the various sports clubs during the week, or visiting friends.

"Mum," she whines at me and I know that voice: She's after something.

I glance at her so she knows I've heard her. "Yes, Sam?" I ask. She asked me to stop calling her Sammy when her father walked out on us a few days before Christmas. We did a lot of growing up that winter. I forgive him for it, but I will never forget.

"Can I go to Georgie's house tomorrow?" I think about which of her friends is Georgie, but I draw a blank.

"Who is Georgie?" I ask, hoping I've not forgotten someone important.

"A boy Trisha knows," she lowers her eyelashes and I stand up to my five-foot-two frame. She's as tall as me already, which annoys me sometimes.

"Have I met this boy?" I ask. She gives me the rolling eyes look and I can tell that I haven't. "Obviously not," I quipped before she could get a word in edgeways. I text Trisha's mum to see if she knows anything about it and she replies that Georgie is one of Sam's friends, according to Trisha.

I show her the text from Trisha's mum. "So, you are both lying. Whatever it is you're planning on doing, the answer is no. Trisha can come here or you can go to hers. You're not to leave whatever house you decide you're going to." I give her the look that I know will cause a fight, one she won't win. I get the opposite reaction though.

"Okay, thank you," she whispers.

Wait a minute, what? I gape an "O" then close my mouth.

"Pardon?" I ask. She sighs.

"One of the girls in school was pressuring us to go to her house party via our WhatsApp group, but she wouldn't take no for an answer. So now we can say we can't go because you and Trisha's mum have sussed out something is wrong and won't let us." She bounds over to me and hugs me. "Thanks, mum!"

My phone rings and it's Trisha's mum with a pretty similar story from Trisha. She says she'll watch the girls tomorrow at hers and I ask if I can drop her there at around ten am. Sam smiles and nods at me and I feel relieved.

"You know, you could just tell me what's going on and we can agree I'll be the "bad mom" Sammy, I don't mind." I use her infant nickname to show I'm not angry at her, but she needs to tell me if she needs my help for that.

She nods. "Okay. I want to leave that group on WhatsApp, I don't like who else is in there."

I nod. "So leave and if they ask, tell them I checked your phone and made you leave it. Do it tomorrow at Trisha's if you like, or here now, but let Trisha know?"

She nods and pulls her phone out from her back pocket to message Trisha. Thirty seconds later, Sam's smiling at me. "Done!

We've both left it at the same time, saying our mums have sussed out about the house party and that group."

"See, not so hard, is it?" I ask.

She shakes her head. "She's in the same year group as Trisha and I though," she sighs.

I cringe. "She's a popular girl then?" I ask.

"Loud and a bully, but she's hard to say no to as she does it so sweetly," offers Sam. I reach across and touch her hand.

"You and Trisha need to stick together and do other activities at lunchtime to avoid her. You can tell her to go away, however you need to and if she doesn't, we'll cross that bridge. Girls like her need all the attention, so stop feeding the trolls," I offer. I had that issue at primary school until Ruth befriended me. Then Helene joined our group that summer and Shauna when she arrived. One of the other three (though it was more Ruth and Shauna) was always upfront about standing up to the bullies and we were quite happy in our little group. I wish for something similar for Sam and Trisha.

Sam nods. "What are your plans for tomorrow mum?" she asks. I feel my cheeks going pink and warm. "Mum?" she asks as her eyes widen. "What have you got planned?" She starts bouncing in her seat. "Are you going to see Nick?" she ventures. I nod.

"He's coming over and taking me to lunch," I finish eating and place my cutlery on the plate as you should do. "He wanted to know if you wanted to come with us," I ask. She shakes her head.

"I don't need to be a third wheel on your first date mum!" she cries out incredulously, then she giggles. "You should invite him over for dinner one night," she suggests.

"And what will you be doing?" I ask her.

"I start studying for my GCSE's this year mum, I'll bet the homework is going to be insane, but you know how I like to do it as I get it," she shoves the last of her food into her mouth, chews a few times and then finishes her drink.

"It'll take a few weeks to start getting that lot," I recall how it was when I was at school, which is far too long ago now.

"I'll still pass though mum, thanks. You enjoy yourself. I'll be at Trisha's and be out of her mum's way."

She's clearing the table off for me and I come to as she asks if she can now leave.

"Sam, what should I wear tomorrow?" I ask.

Sam grins. "Let me help you with the dishwasher and then we can go and look, okay mum?" I smile as I feel proud of my kind-hearted daughter.

Half an hour later and I have a nice outfit ready. Cropped faded jeans, a gypsy floral top, a coat that comes to my knees, and two sets of low heels to pick from for tomorrow, depending on the weather. I hug my girl and she bounces off to her room. I set the outfit aside on my dresser chair and double-check what make-up I have and the location of my favourite coral pink lipstick.

My phone pings as I wipe the work makeup from my face before I moisturise. It's from Nick.

*N: Looking forward to tomorrow. I know it's cliche but what are your favourite flowers?*

*E: I like a lot of different ones. There's no need...*

I leave the sentence hanging. He doesn't need to, but I'd like him to. I look at my hands and decide to give myself a mini manicure since I have a little time before I go to bed. I grab my manicure kit, some nice nail polish that goes with the outfit, and head downstairs to the seat with the day lamp next to it. The one I like to curl up in and read a book. The light is excellent for reading and doing nails.

*N: Need, no. Want to? Yes. I'll find something as quietly vibrant as you.*

My heart swells at his reply, he's being so sweet. I can only send him back a heart emoji. A second later, another message appears.

*N: Can I call you?*

I pause. We're going to meet tomorrow and I've loved texting this week. It kept my spirits up. I bite my lip a moment and I hear Sam on the stairs.

"Just getting a drink," she says as I turn around to watch her. "You okay mum?" she asks and I show her the latest texts.

Sam chuckles and touches me on my shoulder. "Just say yes mum, it's probably easier for him, and wouldn't you like to hear his voice?" she asks as she makes her way to the kitchen.

I ponder for a moment and decide that yes, I would. I send back a thumbs up and Sam is heading back up to her room with a glass of squash as Nick calls.

"Hey," he croons down the phone at me.

"Hi," I squeak back. I hear him chuckle slightly.

"I just wanted to ask, is Sam going to be joining us tomorrow?" His voice is lighter, elevated as if he's hoping she's not. I'm glad she isn't, at least on the first date.

"She isn't. She'll be at her friend's house," I confirm. I'm glad in one way and not in others that she won't be there. Still, I've picked a place that knows me and I always have my book in case I'm left to my own devices.

"Okay," he replies. "I look forward to seeing you tomorrow. Sleep well."

"Okay, bye," I say and he hangs up. That was a short conversation. I hear movement on the stairs behind me. Sam is there, standing with her juice half drunk. She heard it all.

"That was quick," she offers. I simply nod. It was. She grins. "Gives you time to talk tomorrow and you can dream of his voice tonight," she says with a broad grin as she heads up to her room. I wait until her bedroom door is shut, then close the living room door and text the girls. It's Friday night so I don't expect an answer from any of them. Helene does.

*Ellen: Going on a date tomorrow.*
*Helene: Oh, with who?*

Shauna and Ruth don't respond, then I remember Shauna's probably still on her honeymoon (Harek was taking her to see the Northern Lights on his Catamaran, Iris Rose) and Ruth is probably out for the evening, as she does.

*E: With Nick. I met him after Shauna's wedding at the Streetlife Museum with Sammy and his nephew. The kids hit it off, literally (Oscar ran into Sam and knocked her flying) but he was gracious and apologetic for it. He brought us ice cream!*

*H: That's great! Does he know how shy you can be?*

*E: He's... working it out. He's looked up how to date a shy girl I think. Sammy told his nephew I was, as well as what happened with Mark.*

*H: Goodness, what did she tell him, exactly?*

*E: That he upped and left us six days before Christmas, telling us he didn't love either of us. Even the nephew thought he was... I can't use the word Sam says he used. It's not nice.*

*H: I'll bet it was colourful! Well, be safe! Where are you meeting him? Is Sam going?*

*E: At Cafe Rouge on the High Street, our old haunt.*

*H: Perfect! Good luck, let me know how it goes!*

*R: You go, Len! I'm off with work colleagues tonight, catch you tomorrow or Sunday!*

I smile as Ruth joins in at the last moment. I tell her to be safe, finish my manicure and then go tidy up before bed.

# Nine
## Nick

I intended for our conversation last night to be short. I wanted to hear her voice again before we met up again today but did not engage her so we ran out of things to talk about so soon. I head off for an early morning run, managing five miles before I head back, strip, shower, and change into clean freshly washed jeans, a casual shirt with an open collar, and a light jacket. The Docs are polished, just the way my RAF uncle would be proud of. I decided to keep the week-old stubble, rugged beard.

This is a first date, not a second or even third, and I am counting that far ahead. The most I want to do is to kiss her. But dear god how I've looked forward to kissing her. Her soft pink lips always seem to be covered in a light gentle lipstick and her piercing baby blues lose me every time. I wonder how she's going to have her hair. Over the shoulder? Pulled back? It's long and wavy, so anything is possible.

I make my way to the kitchen to pour myself a glass of water, brew some coffee and make some breakfast. A quick breakfast of scrambled eggs, freshly toasted bread, and black coffee sets me up for the day. I check my watch and decide I've plenty of time to visit the florist to pick up my order and fuel up the car for today and the coming week. I checked in with my brother Alex and mum and I spoke with my father yesterday, mostly about work. I did let slip to dad, intentionally, that I was going on a date today. I just haven't told them she's slightly older with a teenage daughter.

Mum responds with a "good luck for today" so I know she's talked with dad. Alex wishes me good luck, he knows what happened on that Monday and the drive home, we talk every other day and I needed to check in with him when I got back. Lisa, my sister-in-law, would have my hide if I didn't.

I check the time and it's nearly ten, so I head to the florists and pick up my order, then I secure it in the boot so it doesn't get squashed. I'm keen, I need to give myself an hour and we're not meeting until half twelve, so I don't need to leave until nearer eleven. I give up trying to kill time and set off just after half-past ten.

It was just as well I did, the M5 was again blocked at Junction 2. Thankfully, Sat nav brought me a rather convoluted way and I'm on the high street, parking up at just before a quarter to twelve. I sigh as I make it on time. I hate being late. I check where Google Maps says the cafe is and it's to my left as I leave the car park. I take the flowers gently from the boot, then I head to the cafe to meet Ellen.

She's already here, earlier than I am. I don't care that I'm early, I get to spend more time with her as a result, but I take a moment to observe her.

She's sitting sideways in her chair, back to the wall, her nose in a book. The Cafe isn't too busy and she has a cup of something before her. She reaches for it, puts it to her mouth, and grimaces slightly, so I'm guessing her cup is empty. This is a perfect moment to walk in and greet her. Her legs are encased in faded crop jeans, the top highlights her delicate frame whilst her auburn locks is half pinned back but loosely, so a few strands fall about her delicate features. I push open the door and the bell above me rings. I've never been in a place with a bell on the door like this, it makes me feel like I'm in the nineteen-fifties.

"Ellen," I stage-whisper as I reach her table. She jumps slightly, clearly engrossed in what she's reading and I read the title. "Lady Chatterley's Lover." It's an old title and not one I've ever read. "Hi," I whisper and she rises to meet me. I help her up and kiss her on the cheek, then present her with the flowers. Her eyes go wide and there's moisture in her eyes. I wonder when was the last time she was given flowers.

"Thank you," she mouths, there's hardly any volume to her voice. I picked a bright bouquet with lots of different colours. "They're beautiful," I hear her say. A staff member comes over and offers us a vase to use temporarily whilst we eat. I thank him and guide Ellen back into her seat.

"You found it easily enough?" she asks. I nod.

"The M5 was a nightmare again at junction two, but I got smart," I thank the same staff member as he brings over another tea for Ellen and asks me what I'd like. I give him my black coffee order and continue. "I followed the instructions Sat Nav gave me so I wouldn't be late," I watch as her cheeks go slightly pink.

"A man that listens to instructions?" her lips roll in, back out and her dimples show. She's teasing me and I... I realise I enjoy being teased, at least by her. Her face falls as it's taken me too long to reply. I lean forward.

"It had to happen at some point, even if it came from a smartphone," I wink and thank the staff member for bringing me the coffee.

"What would you like to order? Our specials are on the board," he turns and motions to the huge board above the counter. "Or you can order from the menu," and he points to a folded, laminated menu option.

"Could you give us five minutes, please Carl? Nick hasn't had a chance to look through it yet," Ellen smiles sweetly at him and he chuckles.

"Sure thing Elle. I'll be back in five," and he heads back to serve the next customer. I turn to her, admiring her bravery.

"Thank you," I say. She clearly could ask as she is comfortable here, which is what I wanted her to be. "So, what's good?" I ask, picking up the menu from the table. There's usual cafe fodder here, toasted sandwiches, paninis, and the like. I turn to the specials board and see fresh hot chili-con-carne, fried foods, and full-on lunches. I look around and there's a mixture of different age groups in here, some having afternoon tea but there are plenty others just eating and enjoying good food.

"I was going to go for my usual," muses Ellen, pulling me back to why I'm even here.

"And what's that?" I ask her. She's petite and slim so I can't imagine she'd eat what I could.

"French brie and ham panini with a side salad," she blushes and plays with her hair a little. I wonder why she's gone back to being nervous.

"That sounds great, but I think I'll have," I pause and look through the menu. There's a meat monster panini with beef, salami, and other meat goodies that takes my fancy. "The meat monster, with a side of fries. Would you like anything else with yours?" I watch as she ponders my question. "Onion rings or anything?" She shakes her head.

"Onions are not good for me," she whispers. I raise my eyebrows. "Tell you why another time," and she blushes more deeply than she did a little while ago. I nod.

The barista, Carl, is back and we place our orders, then he leaves us to talk.

"How often have you read that book?" I ask. It looks in pristine condition and the spine isn't broken. I did notice she didn't bend the book back, even though it's a hard copy she was holding.

"A few times. I usually keep a book on me," she is blushing again. How much stick did she get from every guy she's been with? I am curious as to why though, so I ask her.

"And what reasons might you have to bury your nose in a book when you work in a building full of them?" I ask.

She giggles a little. "You know I'm…" she plays with her hair. "Not all that confident," she whispers. "Books, they let me hide. They let me be present but not "in" the full thick of things unless I want to be." I ponder what she has said.

"I hear they're a great weapon, especially those with hard spines," I offer. I've never been hit on the head with a book, or anywhere, but I have stubbed my toes on a few that have been left lying around my nephew's room.

Ellen thinks what I said was funny and she's chuckling away, so I recount a drama at Oscar's house.

"Honestly, I nearly broke my toes when I kicked a book," she gasps. "It was in Oscar's room when he was younger. He was more terrible at putting things away then than he is now," I roll my eyes for effect. "I'd gone up to fetch him for dinner as he hadn't answered his mum. I walked into his room, into a pile of books, some of which were these little hard things. I was only wearing my socks," I remember how it happened. "Oscar thought it was funny that I not only skidded on a book but stubbed my toe on about three before I could even reach his bed. I couldn't dance for a week!" She's laughing quietly, her shoulders rolling in fits as she tries to keep her amusement in check.

I shudder. "I still can't think about a book without my toe aching," at that comment, she can't hold the giggles back anymore and there are tears of laughter streaming from her eyes. It takes her a few moments to compose herself before she can ask;

"What happened to all the books?" She's drying her eyes with a paper napkin and I wish suddenly I had a fabric handkerchief on me. But, I don't and I resolve to buy some.

I chuckle. "His dad, my older brother, and I spent the day buying him a huge bookshelf, then assembling it and mounting it to the wall." I pick up a fork and stab a steak fry that's been double cooked. Oh my, these are really good! I tell Ellen and she pinches one with a wink at me.

"He still has that bookcase, though it's not as tidy now as it was back then."

She nods and smiles. "I've never heard of books causing toe injuries before," she is still smirking and one of her dimples is showing. It makes her look so cute and much younger than her thirty-six years.

"It hurt," I quietly growled. She hides her snickering but I hope she can tell I'm teasing!

"What books do you like to read?" she asks. We talk about the few books I have read when I've had downtime at my brother's, mostly Jack Reacher books.

"So you like Lee Childs then?" she asks.

"My sister-in-law is a huge reader, loves books. Sure, she'll watch a movie with Alex and Oscar, but she loves curling up with a good book. The Reacher books are more for Oscar and Alex, she's more into romantic comedies or thrillers."

Ellen smiles. "She likes many different tropes and types, like me." She smiles and seems to be pleased that she's not the only one who can read a whole library of books, though I think even Lisa would struggle with the Central Library's collection.

"She does. Me?" I shrug as I eat some of the panini. "I read occasionally, I always seem to be doing other things, especially since I live alone, and I am out with the guys regularly."

"I hardly ever go out," she whispers. I smile at her.

"I would like to start enjoying quiet nights in with you," I hope she gets the message. She really interests me and I'm grateful that Oscar knocked her daughter flying. She looks down and plays with her hair. Okay, she got the message but it's made her uncomfortable. Time to change the subject.

"How's Sam after Oscar knocked her flying?" I ask. Her hands stop playing with her hair and she looks at me intently.

"She's okay. She hasn't complained about being sore or anything," She takes a bite of her panini and pinches another of my steak fries. We stop talking and eat up whilst the food is still warm, then when all the plates are cleared away, I ask for another round of drinks. I don't want to stop being with Ellen.

"Favourite movies?" I ask. We go through the movies we like and I'm surprised, for a moment, that she likes the marvel movie collection. Until she mentions Chris Hemsworth and his Thor-like body. I grin.

"I'll have to work a little harder in the gym to get that heavy look," I wink at her as I watch her eyes glance across my chest. She can't see what I look like under the shirt, but I do look forward to giving her the chance another time.

She licks her lips and I somehow swell up. How can that one, simple action, which probably isn't aimed at licking me, be so seductive? Or is she planning on licking me? Now is not the time to ask.

Ellen finishes her drink and I swallow mine, then I go and pay the bill.

"But, you drove all the way here," she protests, which is true. I just shrug.

"It's my pleasure," I tell her and settle the bill. I give the guy a tip for looking after us, especially as he helped to make sure Ellen was safe and that we had all we needed. He also didn't hassle us and I'm grateful.

"What would you like to do now?" I ask as I shrug my jacket back on and gently hand the flowers back to Ellen.

"Why don't we go home and I'll put these in water. I need to go to Hell," she says and motions with her head to somewhere beyond the High Street.

"Hell?" I ask, allowing my face to show my confusion.

"Merry Hill," she replies, grinning. "It's the local shopping area, it's huge and just down that way," she motions in the same direction again and I realise she's holding the flowers.

"Did you walk to the cafe?" I ask. I have no idea how she got there. She nods her head.

"Yeah, it's a short ten-minute walk for me," she smiles.

"Let me give you a lift back, then we can go to Hell?" I suggest. She nods and I escort her to my car. My Series 3 BMW is quite good at eating up the motorway and it's quite good at short distances too. It was why I picked it, and it looks decent.

We are two minutes in the car and we're outside Ellen's house. It's set back from the road in a quiet back street. I take note of the semi-detached, 1960's two-story house that looks like it's using the roof space as I can see Velux windows up there.

Her front garden has a line of flowers down the side of the drive, which is block-paved and free of weeds. The garden isn't spectacular but it is tidy and well maintained with some sort of tree in the middle. Her front door & garage is a deep red and I'm instantly enthralled with it.

# Ten
## Ellen

It takes us no time at all to get back to mine. I watch as he takes in my 1960's home and I suddenly wish for Shauna's immensely packed front garden. The fact I even have bulbs coming up in the spring around the pink magnolia tree is down to her.

I grab the flowers carefully and fumble for my keys, then manage to open the door. The sound of the keys in the lock makes Nick turn to me and he smiles.

"You do better with your garden than I do. My front is all driveway." For what seems like the hundredth time today, I relax. He's never criticized me for my choices so far and he did buy me these gorgeous flowers, paid for lunch, and escorted me home. I dig out a vase, or at least, I try to. I don't quite recall where they are.

I find one at the back of a cupboard and Nick helps fish it out for me as it's behind heavy cut crystal bowls and dishes. He moves everything out, then hands me the vase, then puts it all back in.

"You might want to leave that at the front," his eyes and mouth suggest that he's teasing. "I plan on you getting a lot of use out of that," and he stands up without having to hold onto anything. I feel my cheeks going pink and rush to wash the vase out before I make up the water with the liquid feed.

He leans against the fridge in my kitchen and watches me as I dry the outside of the vase and then make up the solution. He doesn't say anything as I trim and rearrange the flowers into the vase so that they take up the whole thing, not just look like they've been plonked into it.

"I never realised there was an art to arranging flowers," he says. His eyes are soft as if he's impressed that I've taken care and time to rearrange the flowers he took time and money to buy, just for me.

"Bouquets aren't always made up to go into a vase. I took flower arranging classes one summer," I offer. I softly explained how I picked the single odd flower, the huge peony, and made it the central piece, then arranged the flowers around it and under it to support and show it off.

"That's an art I never thought I'd appreciate seeing," he smiles a genuine, warm smile and I wonder if this is how Harek made Shauna feel? I wonder if this is what Helene feels with Fons? If it is, I want more.

I smile softly in return. My phone pings and I check it. It's from Trisha's mum Rachel, asking if it is okay for the girls to go down to Hell. I reply, telling her it's fine and then we head out to Merry Hill.

The place is busy but for some reason, it doesn't bother me. Partly because Nick is with me, but also, I know this area. I'm comfortable here. I look at him and he looks a little overwhelmed and I feel for him.

"Which shop did you need?" I ask.

"Err," he looks at me and then seems to gather himself together. "I was looking for Next," he says as we climb out of my car.

I smile. "That's down the other side," I point. "If you can help me pick up some new crockery, we can wander over that way." He smiles and nods. We take in the home furnishing stores at the top side of Merry Hill and I find two vases that I like which will go with the rest of my display pieces. Nick helps me carry them back to the car, then we trundle through the complex to find the store he wants.

"I'll let you browse in peace," I say. "I need to find some things for Sam here."

"I just need a few extra shirts, I won't be long," he says. He kisses me on my cheek. The kiss sends tingles through me and before I can respond, he's vanished into the men's section. I grab what I know Sam needs or wants, then I spy her. It seems she has the same idea.

"Eugh, mum, no!" she groans at me. Trisha giggles.

"What's the matter?" I ask. She points to the bra items that I'm holding for her.

"Not in that style, please," she begs me. I smile.

"Okay," I say, putting back the items I've picked out. I forget she's a teenager, not a little girl. She's slowly blooming right before me and I forget to check in regularly. "What do you prefer?"

She picks out something slightly prettier rather than plain and functional and I chuckle.

"Is that your size?" I ask her. She stops, then grabs the next size up. "Try both on," I strongly suggest. She nods and heads off to the changing rooms with Trisha. Nick catches up with me and I smile.

"Need to finish helping Sam," I nod towards the changing room and he notices we're in the ladies' underwear section. He nods and winks at me.

"Would you like another tea?" He nods towards the coffee shop in the store and I nod.

"A herbal tea?" I ask and he smiles warmly, his eyes lighting up as if I've just saved him.

"Sure thing," he says and heads off just as Trisha is coming back to grab my attention. For ten minutes I help Sam pick out new bras and my pocket is too light by the time she heads off. I have her purchases to take home, the rest she can get with Trisha by her side. The girl lives for clothes shopping. I spy Nick at a table and he looks bored.

"I'm so sorry!" I gasp as I finally meet up with him. He grins.

"I'd have stuck around, but..." his cheeks flush a little and I just nod.

"I know," I gush, embarrassed that my daughter distracted me. "I didn't know she was going to be at this store or that she was coming shopping for underwear," I offer. "Teenagers," I offer by way of explanation. I stop talking when he doesn't stop me by talking, but by chuckling, perhaps at me?

"Oscar does that with his mum all the time," he explains. Ah, he's seen his nephew do things like that. Thank goodness! "She goes out for one thing and comes home with new shoes and clothes for him as he springs on her that the shoes are too small, the jeans are too tight. They grow like weeds at this age, I remember." He pushes tea towards me in a travel cup that has a lid on it. He didn't expect me back for a little while. "Your tea might be about ready to drink. We can carry on browsing and window shopping when you're ready," he stands but leaves his bag behind.

"I'll be back, gents," he explains, motions to the toilets, and I smile. He saved us a table and brought me a drink, as well as lunch. I quickly drink my tea, which is now at the perfect temperature, and then suddenly, Nick is back with a smile on his face.

We spent another hour just walking around Merry Hill, talking. He indulges me in a little ice cream from a booth and we window shop. Sam catches a glance at us once as we're walking around, but neither of us intrudes on the other after the clothes shopping meet-up. I check the time and discover it's later than I thought. I should let Nick get off home.

We're walking back to the car, bags in hand and we're about to cross one of the access roads when we witness a rear-end shunt. There was no reason for the car in front to stop, it's after the lights and there was no traffic. Nick throws me a look that matches my thoughts. What did we just see?

## *Eleven*
### *Nick*

The sound of metal crunching into metal was unmistakable. I was watching the road and the car in front was just stationary with no hazards on, no brake lights showing, nothing causing him to stop suddenly when there's a turning into the car park to take. I look at Ellen and scowl a little, imagining the worst.

"I need to go see if they're okay," I say. She nods, her curls creeping down to surround her face as her head moves.

"I want to know that too," she huffs as her short legs manage somehow to keep up with my strides. The guy from the car in front is now out of his car, cursing the woman behind him for driving into him. I notice right away she has a small child in the back.

"Hey, you can stop that," I command as I get close enough now to be heard. Others have stopped to look but no one else is joining in to help out the woman. "That's no way to speak to a lady or another human being." The guy is smaller than me but sizes me up anyway. He backs off a little and his companion gets out of the car. Ellen catches up to me and another passer-by, a woman as tall as me, joins us.

"She crashed into me," says the driver of the vehicle that had stopped.

"Only because you had stopped for no reason," says the other woman, who is helping the distraught driver.

"I had a reason," he says.

"Really?" I counter in a clipped voice. I'm not giving him any more ammo and I whisper to the taller lady not to say anything else to him. "Swap details and let the insurance work it out. Or shall I call the police?" The guy waves his hands, jazz style, and backs off a little claiming he doesn't need the police involved. 'I'll just bet he doesn't I think. Ellen and this other woman have the female driver and the child in a calm situation.

"Write down your details," I say. The man backs off and gets into his car, saying something to his companion in a language I do not understand. He pulls away just as two of the shopping centre security vehicles turn up. I hear sirens sound in the distance and I ignore them to speak with the security staff. One of the security cars follows the man who was hit.

Ellen, the tall lady who wasn't the driver, and I explained to security what we saw. A few moments later, the police are here and we're giving statements. I look at Ellen who has her arms folded across her body as if protecting herself. I curse. She doesn't need this. I catch her eye and she gives me a wry smile before turning her attention back to the officer who is taking her statement.

I give mine, then security and the police talk for a moment. I get the gist that the insurance fraud incidents have been on the rise here for a few days, always with a different car, hence why the police were here so quickly. They talk to the woman driver and the police advise her to inform her insurance and give a crime reference number that they've generated whilst on the scene.

Security escorts the lady, her car, and toddler to a parking space and sees that she's okay while she waits for her husband to arrive. She's hugging Ellen and shaking the tall woman's hand in thanks. We wait until her husband is with her before we head back to Ellen's car, then her house.

"Oh my gosh," gasps Ellen as we make it back to her car and put our purchases in the boot.

"Yeah, I didn't expect that," I say, my voice rising as I speak.

"I thought that guy was going to punch you at one point," she tells me. I stop. I had thought that myself.

"Did you tell the police how he behaved?" I ask. She nods and hugs herself. I breathe out, relax and move to hug her. "They have our details, as does her insurance. How was she?" I ask. I don't even know the lady driver's name.

"Sue was fine, once she realised she didn't have to face him alone. Chris, the other witness, was helpful. She plays hockey some evenings," Ellen seems to admire that about the other witness.

"Have you ever played hockey?" I ask. Grass hockey is one sport I'm sure applies to all females in secondary school. Ellen nods.

"Not that I was any good at it. Ruth and Shauna were on the school team and they were good. Helene and I," she smiles and sighs. "We preferred gentler pursuits," she says with a coy smile and dancing eyes.

"Oh?" I ask as I let her go and we climb into the car.

Ellen nods. "I read, I was forever in the library. Helene would be helping the biology teacher with something that needed growing or studying plants in the library next to me."

I have this image of four very different but very bonded women taking over the world, one activity and diverse aspect at a time.

"Your friends sound like they understand you," I offer. She seems more confident when she thinks or speaks of them. I already guess I'm going to have to meet them and be assessed. That thought would normally scare me, but for some reason, I'm looking forward to it.

"They do," she emphatically states. Yep, I'm going to be meeting her close friends in the not too distant future.

We make it back to hers in no time flat and we unload my bags from her car into mine. I help her take the new vases into the kitchen to be washed before they're stored. Most of her fixtures are of a certain style. What she's picked fits that and adds colour. The chimney wall and sofa are in a deep blue come green kind of colour. There's a rug on the floor that matches the light grey of the rest of the walls. Every plant pot is in a teal or grey ribbed design, though she only has a few of these. There are lamps in the corner and a huge single chair in a complimenting colour that has a few books next to it.

"You have a lovely home," I say. She does and it makes me think about my place. It's a little cold with a hardly lived-in feel to it. I need to take a look online and change things around a little. Then I think about my sister-in-law and think of asking her for advice sometime later.

"Thanks, Nick," she says, smiling up at me.

"Can I," I want to ask if she'll let me kiss her. She nods and smiles, understanding what I'm asking. I bend down and kiss her lightly, delicately, on her lips. I go to pull away but she pulls me in and kisses me back, opening my mouth with hers so her tongue can dance with mine.

She pulls away first and bites her lower lip a little.

"Wow," I breathe as she looks up at me, her blue eyes the brightest and clearest I've ever seen. "Damn girl, you can kiss," I state. My voice raises a little, then I gently caress the side of her face and beam down at her.

"Can we meet up in the week?" I ask. I can't wait for a whole week to see her again, not if we're kissing like that!

She nods. "If you can get into Brum, sure. I might be off one day next week and I could pop over to yours?" I smile.

"I'd love that," I say. "What about Sam?" I ask.

She smiles. "If I come over during the day, can we have lunch again?" I love how she asks. "Sam will be at school," she explains. I get it.

"Sure. If you want to do an evening, I noticed a huge cinema in Hell," I take note of the fact even I am calling it Hell now. She nods. "Let me know what evening is good," I tell her, leaving the decisions up to her. Her choosing the date and what we see, if Sam is with us, is important.

I bend to kiss her one more time before I get into my car and drive away. I can't help but feel I'm leaving something behind and it doesn't sit well with me.

I text her that I'm back, the way out of Ellen's was easier than trying to get to her. The accident on the M5 had been dealt with and cleared. She texts back to say thank you again for a lovely lunch date, the flowers, the afternoon.

I unpack the new shirts I needed and set about giving them a quick wash. The weather is decent so I think I'll hang them out. Then I get on with tidying up my living room. I look around and I resolve to call Lisa now. Ellen's house has this cosy, warm feel to it which I now notice, mine is sadly lacking. My beige walls and dark grey sofa look uninviting. I called my sister-in-law for a quick chat.

"Nick," my brother answers the house phone and I grin. "What can I do for you bro?" he rumbles.

"Have I caught you in the middle of something?" I ask, closing the laundry room door to deafen the sound of the washing machine.

"Just busy in the garage," he replies.

"Ah, well, as much as I love you, I'd like to speak to my sister-in-law, I need some advice about my living room." Alex chuckles and hollers for Lisa to pick up the other land phone they have. She does and Alex leaves us to chat.

I explain what I want and Lisa asks that I set up a Pinterest board with her, adding pictures of what I have at the moment. It takes me ten minutes to work out how to do that and she had to walk me through it. Then, suddenly, ideas of bachelor pads come back at me. Then, Lisa calls me on my landline.

"So," she says as I scroll through the twenty or more images she's pinned for me. "You can either do a quick repaint of a wall or two, then add that colour into your soft furnishings. I think that's the cheapest way to get the more homey feel you're after." She pauses as I work my way through some of the images, but one catches my eye and I tell her which one.

"Yeah, that's quite easy to achieve. Some time at the DIY store, spend some pennies and you can have that look in a day. Especially if you go early for the store opening.

"Thanks, Lisa, you're a star," I stood and checked the time. The local DIY place will be closing in fifteen minutes, there's no time tonight. "Could I use the same idea in the bedroom?" I ask. Decorating isn't my thing, but Lisa's a whiz at it.

"Sure you can. Just do the same as we did. I can pin some more ideas if you set up another private board with me."

"Lisa, you should charge for this service, it's invaluable," I say. She hums at me, contemplating.

"I hadn't thought of doing that," she says. "Thanks, Nick! Anything else?" she offers.

"I'll send you some bedroom pics when I've tidied it up a little," I offer. She lives with my brother, she knows what a slob he is. Or was.

"You're being a slob again..." It's not quite a question, more of an unstated document of fact. I mumble something in reply and she chuckles.

"Just like Alex," she says, happily. "Take the shots, create a new private board and add me, I'll help you there too. Bedrooms can be a little bolder and still be calming, which is what you want if you're bringing a lady back?" Now that is an unspoken question.

"The chance is there," I reply. I can hear Lisa's happy, quiet sigh down the phone.

"Okay, Romeo, let's see what we can do about the bedroom too," she offers and I thank her. We hang up and half an hour later, the private board is created and shared. Lisa has pins for me to view and decide on before I've finished hanging out my new work shirts. There are a few more ideas here that I hadn't thought of and I call her back.

"How did they get that look in this?" I have a new build, the panelling doesn't exist. She tells me how she did it with no more nails and cut edging.

"Lay it out on the floor to check your angles though Nick," she advises. By the time she's chasing Oscar to bed, I have my ideas, a list of things I'd need that is as long as my arm and boards full of ideas on Pinterest.

"Thanks, Lisa," I say. "This place is going to change a lot this week." I'm stating a fact.

"You're welcome! I want to see it when it's done!" she commands.

"Sure thing boss," I tease. Truth is, I'd be struggling to make this house half of the home Ellen has without her.

"Night Nick!" She calls and hangs up. I've had about three hours of her time and I text her what I think she should charge for three hours' worth of design service. She doesn't reply for ages and I wonder if she's talking about the business idea with Alex. She's wasted at her job, this could be something she can do from home, via the internet. She has a good taste and if customers just need some inspiration and advice, rather than someone to do it for them, single blokes like me, she's onto a winner.

I settled in and sent Ellen a text. It's a Saturday night and I wonder what she's doing. For the first time ever, I want to go to bed early so I can be up early to get this project started. Lisa gave me some ideas of which walls to put the paneling and colour changes on. I move the sofa away from one part of the wall in preparation for it tomorrow and I text my dad, asking if I can borrow his dust sheets and some of his painting kit. He calls to ask why and I explain my ideas.

"I'll come over tomorrow, give you a hand," he says. This isn't a request but I don't object. If he comes over, he'll bring mum, who will cook and look after us while we work and I'm far less likely to get the cuts wrong.

"That'll be great dad, I appreciate the help." I'm feeling fabulous and I want to share it with Ellen, but this is a surprise. If she's bold enough to come over, I want my home to be my home, not just a building with four walls that I happen to reside in. Dad checks what I need, where I'm going, and says he'll be here by nine the following morning. I can hear my mum in the background, already offering to bring the bacon and crusty rolls over.

"I have eggs in already," I say, checking that I have. I say goodbye, tidy up the kitchen, and head to bed. This is the last night my house is going to be the blandest thing on the menu.

Mum and dad arrive exactly when they said they would, which is typical of my dad. I'll bet he was up an hour before mum, double-checking everything before he arrived. He hands me a set of painter's dungarees and I laugh, then pause. I don't have a set of clothes just for painting, but if I'm going to do this, I will make use of them.

"Thanks, Dad," I shake his hand and let mum loose in my kitchen while dad and I head to the DIY store.

"So, tell me about this girl then," he demands when we're out of earshot of mum.

I look at him and he just raises his eyebrows.

"Who have you been talking to?" I ask, suspecting Lisa or Oscar.

"Your brother mentioned you had Lisa's attention for hours yesterday about decorating plans, even gave her the idea she can do this consulting thing from home over that damn internet," he scoffs. Dad's not one for the Internet, he gets the idea, but not how it works.

"Lisa hates her current job," I begin. He scoffs again.

"I know," he sighs. "But consulting about decorating aspects?" he asks.

"You have no idea how much she inspired me yesterday," I point to myself to drill the point home, "or how she gave me the confidence to even tackle what we're about to start. Or what tools I'd need if you weren't helping me."

Dad looks at me as we sit at a set of lights heading out of Lichfield. "You? Need confidence?" he asks.

"About decorating, making a huge change to impress someone? Yes." He shuffles in his seat and it's a few moments of peace and quiet before he speaks again.

"So you like this girl enough to go out on a limb?" he asks. We get to where we're going, the huge DIY place just outside the City limits.

"Yes, I do," I say. I'm not usually shy, or backward. But with Ellen? There's something there… some… connection and I want more of it. "Her, I want to impress," we slam the car doors shut and make our way in. "More than I have ever wanted to impress a woman before."

Dad nods. "What's her name?" he asks. I grin and grab a trolley and offer it to him to push around. Not that he needs a walker or anything, but I offer it anyway. He declines and so, we head into the store and I talk about meeting Ellen, thanks to Oscar. Dad chuckles as I share the story of how Oscar did sweep Sam off her feet, the drive home. I recount yesterday's scene about the 'accident' and dad pats me on the back when I tell him what happened. I think about the lady driver and text Ellen to see if she's heard anything from her.

We start by picking up a rug, some cushions of the same colour, then a throw. I know the sofa is a dark grey, so we head to the paint section to find a colour that ties the beige, the grey, and the now coffee colour accessories. Dad finds the ideal shade and I buy a huge tub of it, as well as all the masking tape. Then I pick a colour for my bedroom before we head to the wood section to buy enough internal architrave to construct the false paneling.

It takes dad and I an hour to get what is on my list, plus a few more things. Mum didn't come with us, saying we'd need the space and I have to admit, she was right. I pay a small fortune for everything, including ordering new bed covers online and we haul it back to mine.

When we get back, we're pulling the purchases out of the car when Ellen calls me.

"Hey," I say and she sniffs. "What's wrong?" I ask, stepping away from dad for a moment.

"I got a phone call from the police, asking about the incident yesterday, but something felt off, so I hung up. What do I do now? I can't reach Roo," I can hear her voice rising, her breathing becoming quick and shallow; she's in a panic.

"Hey, breathe. The police haven't contacted me," I double-checked my phone. Nothing, no missed call. "Do you have the reference number they gave us?"

"Yes, I do," she whispers. I close my eyes and think for a moment.

"Was it a hidden number that called you?" I recall a girl at work getting calls from an unknown caller. When someone answered it, it was the local police force.

"No, a mobile number," she says.

"Okay, call 101, give them the reference number and ask if anyone has called you in regards to that this morning? If it's a genuine call, they'll have a record of someone trying to call you, I'm sure. If not, you can then block the number that called you so they can't call back."

"And the number that called me?"

"Give it to the police and then block it," I tell her again. She really is in a panic which given she's super shy, I read was a regular thing.

She sighs. "Thanks, Nick," she sniffs again but not as deeply. "I just can't reach Roo and…" I smile.

"It's okay. I'm glad you trust me enough to call me when you need it. That means a lot," dad raises his eyebrows at me as he walks past with a mitre block and a Japanese wood saw. I haven't told him Ellen is super shy until she gets to know you.

"Roo will be in touch when she can. Did you leave her a message?" I ask.

"Yeah," Ellen sighs. "She was going out on Friday night and usually, I've spoken with her twice by now." I can hear the gulp. "We always check in with each other after a night out, especially since Shauna and Helene are in Rotterdam."

I check my watch, it's still early. "It's ages before noon on a Sunday babe, not everyone is crazy like us and up already," I offer. I hear her chuckle, faintly.

"Yeah, you're right," she says. "Thanks, Nick," she breathes. "Bye," she barely whispers and the line goes dead before I can say it back.

"Was that your girl?" dad asks as he hands me the two huge tubs of paint I purchased. I nod.

"Yeah, she got a call from the police about yesterday and it freaked her out a little, she's not sure it was the police. She's super shy in general," I put down the two tubs of paint in the living room on a dust sheet mum had already laid out on the floor.

I hug mum in thanks and carry on talking. "She can't reach one of her friends to talk through her thoughts, so she called me." For some reason, that makes me feel amazing. That she trusts me enough so soon is beyond my expectations.

"That's good! She trusts you already," says mum.

I chuckle. "Just what I was thinking," I reply as dad hands me the painting overalls again.

"Put those on and we'll get the walls measured up and the wood cut." I follow my dad's instructions and for the next few hours, we work on the panelling, then painting the wood before we nail and stick it on. Mum provides us with food and drinks regularly. By the end of the afternoon, the second coat of paint is drying. It's a warm day so it's not taking long. Whilst the paint does what it needs to, dad and I measure up the panelling in my bedroom, then we get it stuck up on the wall. It's late evening by the time I tell dad he's done enough for me for one day.

Mum taps me on the shoulder and I turn. She's been quiet while we've been upstairs and I can see why now. She's ironed all my new shirts. There's an old one that is no longer suitable and I go to tear it up. Mum stops me, cuts the buttons off first, and puts them into a small plastic tub I kept from the Chinese take-away the other week. She labels it in a marker pen and hands it to me.

"Every man needs a basic sewing kit, Nick. Have you got one?" A memory of her giving a lecture to Alex about this very thing years ago hits me.

"Yes mum, look." I go to the sideboard and pull out a small box, the one I made in woodworking class at school. I've sanded it down and painted it since, I even replaced a hinge recently. As mum opens it, her eyes fill as she sees four different thread spools, some sewing needles, scissors, and other tools I took out of a kit I bought at the supermarket one time months ago.

"Now you just need to use it," she quips with a smile on her face. I chuckle.

"When I need to, I shall," I say. I go to put it back, then decide to move both items to the laundry room, near where I keep all the cleaners and iron.

Mum nods in approval and I help dad finish packing up all his tools. Thanks to him, the panelling is done and the living room is ready to be reset tomorrow when I get back from work. For now, I want a beer and to enjoy my home.

I then kiss mum goodbye and hug dad, whispering a thank you. I watch as they drive home.

# Twelve
## *Ellen*

I call Nick when Roo doesn't answer my calls and he calms me. She gets in touch, eventually and she insists on making it a video call with everyone. My chest tightens as I wonder what she could possibly want to tell us.

I text Nick to say she's gotten in touch and he replies that he's glad. No, I told you so, just, that he's glad. Why couldn't Mark get me like that?

Ruth and Shauna are the first two onto the video chat room, Helene follows a few minutes later.

"You wanna tell them, Roo?" Shauna sits back and looks at her screen with some concern. I can see Helene's reaction too, she hasn't a clue any more than I do, but I can tell Shauna knows what's occurring.

"You know I went out on Friday night with the girls from work?" Ruth begins. We nod. She walks us through something that would make me never leave my house again. Her drink got spiked. Not only hers, but her colleague's too.

"Please tell me you're okay?" I gasp, reaching for my shoes.

"I'm fine, thanks to Shauna and a guy called Daniel," Ruth leans in and breathes "Who I have to say, is hot," she fans herself and we chuckle. She tells us how he stepped in, involving the bouncers but because of the local derby football match and issues at a sports bar down the way, the police couldn't step in until today to take statements and everything else.

"Did they do a drug test?" I ask.

Ruth nods. "Yeah, Daniel and The Regency Hyatt staff had the sense of mind to make me and Lou pee in a container as evidence. He and his sister were absolute heroes."

I've never heard Ruth call anyone a hero before, except Shauna when she chased off Harek's attackers in Rotterdam. Though, Shauna doesn't quite count, she is a bad-ass.

"I'm glad the Regency stepped up," Shauna states. She's remarkably calm. She's never usually this calm.

"Why did they?" I ask.

Ruth blushes, her cheeks nearly matching her ringlet strawberry blond hair.

"He tried calling the last number on my phone, which was Lou, who was next to me in the same state. Then he called the next previous number I had dialled. Shauna's."

Shauna smirks. "Be glad I was able to get you guys somewhere to crash who would look after you. I need to send their concierge a thank you. They went beyond what I asked of them."

"What did you even tell them?" asks Ruth. "The breakfast the following morning and the pee bottles…" I see Ruth shiver, which makes my stomach knot and sink.

"That my friend and her work colleague had been drugged. They needed a safe place to sleep and that someone had stepped in to help her out. I needed their help." Shauna takes a sip of tea and replies something to Harek in Dutch. Then she continues. "Daniel didn't want to take Ruth home because he didn't know her but felt responsible and called me. I offered The Regency Hyatt as a suggestion and would they kindly help, with me paying for it?" There's a sound of something else being said to her in Dutch and Shauna laughs. "Yes, okay, Harek paid but gratefully," she beams, smirking at her husband who is out of camera view.

"From Rotterdam?" I asked, my voice rising. I couldn't believe what I was hearing.

Shauna nodded. "Yep. From here," and Shauna gives us that sly smile she always has when she's stepped up but doesn't want the thanks.

"You saved my bacon, thank you Shaunie! I can't believe I fell victim to that," moans Ruth. Okay, so she works in the legal department for Social Services at Birmingham City Council, so she's used to having her head on straight.

"This wasn't your fault," I say. "I saw a documentary on rape drugs, there's no way to tell you've been hit at the moment," and if someone is going to be that sneaky, I want to set Shauna off on them. She'd rip them apart, I know it.

"I still should have been more careful," Ruth says. I sigh.

"Well, yeah, but you didn't ask for this. At least you had someone step up to do the right thing," Helene points out as she burps her son.

"I'm so glad you're okay Roo," I say. I'd hate to be the one to comfort her if the worst had happened, but I would do it.

Ruth beams. "So am I. I need to thank Daniel and his sister for their help. But what do you get for a guy who owns his own tattoo parlour, is six foot four, and would give Thor a run for his money?" Ruth raises her eyebrows and Shauna hides a smirk and I know what's coming.

"Does he have a longboat?" asks Shauna. Helene laughs, I try to smother my smirks but Ruth... she glares at Shauna, then lets out a belly laugh.

"I deserved that!" she sings, aware that Shauna is teasing her. I relax, Ruth's okay but that must've been a frightening experience for her. However, thanks to a saint, she's okay, unharmed, and lives to tell a cautionary tale.

We get onto news of other things. Shauna tells us she's pregnant again, though she's not sure when she's due as she is sure she was pregnant before she got married, but not by much. She always knew quite early on, though I never worked out how. It took me eight weeks to notice and feel different.

Aisla is only six or seven months old now. "I ain't getting any younger," protests Shauna. "I need them closer together, I can't be doing this when I'm forty. I want to be over the pregnant part by then, I just want to enjoy my babies and watch them all grow."

It seems totally incredible that Shauna would go through that again, but she knows her body. We congratulate her and she tells us she doesn't want anything for the new baby, she has all of Aisla's things already and what she's outgrown is in storage.

We chat for a while longer and I wonder about telling them about Nick. Helene catches that I might want to speak up and gives me the floor space.

"I think I've met someone," I begin. The girls don't crowd me, they sit quietly and let me speak, tell my tale. So I bring them up to speed on where we're at, who he is and where he lives.

I look at Shauna. "You told me it would happen in the North. And it did," she smiles broadly at me but shrugs her shoulders. She doesn't take praise for her skills though giving her a thoughtful gift is good. I make a note to send her something for her, not the babies.

We all decide we're in a pretty good place in general terms and set a date for the next chat. I offer hugs to Ruth and tell her she can pop over whenever she wants. She says she'll contact me, but she needs some time to recover. I get that. We all tell her we're here if and when she needs us.


We sign off and it hurts that Ruth is hurting. I check on Sam and she's chilling. Ruth is less than half an hour from me, fifteen minutes if the roads aren't clogged up. I check the route to hers on Google Maps and smile. It looks like a clear run.

"Do you mind if I go and spend time with Ruth?" I ask Sam. Sam lifts her head and takes out her earphones. I repeat the question.

"I don't mind mum, no…" she puts her earphones back in and I tap her again.

"Stay in then, okay?" She nods and goes back to the textbook she's reading. She's using music to associate with subjects and I wonder what band or genre she's picked for history.

I grab my bag, pull on some boots, and drive to Ruth's.

It's late when I get back, though it's still light. Sam is still up and I make us some supper, though she said she had pasta earlier. I hadn't intended on staying at Ruth's for three hours, but it turns out she needed someone to sound off at and just be there. I gave her that space and let her just brain dump at me. I am all tea'd out though, I don't think I can face another cup, not even tomorrow. I get a text from Ruth with a huge thank you in caps and pink hearts all over it. I send a smile back and the message: *'that's what friends do.'*

I text Nick when Sam's gone to bed and ask if he's free to talk. He calls almost immediately and I smile.

"Hey lovely," he breathes as I pick up. It's so nice to hear his voice.

"Hi," I huskily replied. "My friend got in touch, it seems she had a harrowing weekend," I waited for him to say something, but it seems he's waiting for me.

"Do you want to talk about it?" he finally asks after a few moments of silence.

I sigh. "I don't know... I want to, but then again, I don't? Things could have been really bad for her," I tuck my legs under me and pull down the throw. "Thankfully, they didn't because someone else became vigilant."

"But she's okay?" he asks. There's concern in his voice, even though he's never met her. I've talked about Ruth a lot though.

"She is... I think she's going to take a few days to rest up. Filing the police reports was not pleasant," Ruth is used to talking to the police, but as she said, she'd never been a victim before. It was strange for her and unsettling. I am glad I went.

"Did you go to see her?" he asks. His voice is raised, he's still concerned.

"Yes, I did. I had to when I learned what had happened," I told him about her hero calling Shauna in Rotterdam and getting The Regency Hyatt to help out.

"She got that done, from Rotterdam?" he asks.

"I know!" I exclaim back. It seems we're both a little beside ourselves at how Shauna got involved. "But, she was the second last number Ruth had called. The other was the girl she was with, so…"

"Ah… He was smart. I'm glad your friend is okay." I can hear him sighing and he omphs a little, so I guess he's now sitting down.

"What were you doing?" I ask. His breath hitches and I frown.

"I've been moving things around, tidying up," I can hear the elevated pitch in his voice.

I go very quiet, I can't quite ask what is now on the tip of my tongue.

"Ellen? Are you there?"

"Yes," I whisper. I'm terrified he's with someone else.

"I've had my parents here helping me as I needed the extra hands to move it all and do other things. I will show you if you still want to come over during the week?" He pauses. "I'd like you to," he breathes, his voice almost commanding, not begging.

He's genuine now and I think he was not going to tell me that he's tidied up. Was it just for me? It might be. It seems the most obvious explanation.

"I'd love to. I'll know more when I get into work tomorrow," I reply, slightly louder than I answered him before. The shifts could have changed over the weekend, though they tend not to. The fact that he says "will show", if I want? It's my decision.

"I am going to let you get on with your evening. I want to finish putting all this stuff away so I'm not tripping over it tomorrow as I'm trying to get ready for work." His story about stubbing his toes on book edges makes me curl my toes.

"Have you made that much of a mess?" I ask, teasingly.

He chuckles at me and then I hear a clatter as things drop onto the floor.

"I have now," he deadpans in response.

"Sorry," I mutter. "I should go," I quickly state and I can feel my voice tensing up, but he stops me.

"Ellen? What's going on? Things were great on Saturday, despite the accident. What's changed?" He's a little more demanding now and I can't blame him. After what Mark did to me, told me with our daughter as a witness, I find trust is a hard thing to give out.

"Nothing," I reply, a little too quickly. I don't want to share what's going through my head.

He grunts at me in that non-believing way men have. "I have been busy and I would like to show you. Say you'll come over so I can explain? It's nothing bad, I promise."

I pause then reply as I sigh. "Okay," I change my voice to sound upbeat. "I'll look forward to it."

"Okay, great. I'll text you my address, okay? It's a new estate so it can be a little hard to find on the SatNav."

I groan and he chuckles. "There's an established corner shop at the top of the estate, SatNav will take you there, then my house is two roads down out of the way. It's quite easy to find," he adds emphatically.

We end our conversation but my stomach still has knots in it. I sigh and text Ruth my concerns.

*E: He just called. He says he was busy moving things around & tidying things up. What can a single man have to tidy away?!*

*R: Everything? He might live like a slob! Have you seen some of the "men" out there and how they live?*

*E: Really?!*

*R: Trust me, that's why I do hotel rooms most of the time!*

I breathe. Maybe he was being genuine and I am over-reacting. Maybe.

# Thirteen
## Nick

Ellen seems worried after I tell her I was tidying up. I missed out the word decorating because I didn't want her to think I was making a special effort, though I am. I've never wanted to impress a girl as much as I want to impress her. I tidy the last of the decorating stuff away so I don't trip over it. I can be clumsy, I've already told her how I nearly broke a toe on Oscar's books, so she has some ideas.

I sent her a text and I hope it's not too much. *'Good night, beautiful. Looking forward to Wednesday'*. I don't get a reply until lunchtime the following day, which kills me but I get it. She's shy, reserved and the tidying thing somehow freaked her out.

I reply about an hour after I get her text as I'm busy with the accounts people, so I don't feel bad that I didn't respond right away. I grabbed the chance when I was between meeting accounts and production. It's a full day, especially when one of the pressing machines develops a fault and we have to stop production of the joists to go in and fix it. It takes a few hours, but my guys know what they're doing. It was six pm when I left and I hadn't noticed she'd text me back.

*E: Hope you have a good day!*

*N: It was horrendous! Busy as anything, but that's steel production for you.*

*E: Oh no! What do you do to chill out?*

*N: I'll grab a snack and then head to the gym. I'll get a proper meal later on.*

*E: Okay, be safe!*

I spend a few hours at the gym after a quick snack of scrambled eggs. I go through my usual weights, then rowing, and finally the treadmill set at a brisk walk to cool down. I grab a shower at the gym, change into fresh clothes, and head home.

I quickly cook up a Chinese stir fry that I look up online and snap a photo, sending it to Ellen on a whim.

*E: That looks lovely!*

To be honest, it looks better than it tastes and I tell her that.

*E: Did you add the soy sauce or any flavouring to it?*

I pause and think: I didn't. *N: Oops!*

She sends back a smiley face and a suggestion that I add some sweet chilli to it over the top. I do and it tastes a lot better.

*N: Thanks! Must have missed that step out somehow.*

*E: Easy to do! Enjoy. See you on Wednesday. I'm going to bed now. Good night.*

Just like that, I have visions of what she wears to bed, what she looks like without any of it on and I wonder how petite the rest of her is compared to her height. I imagine that she's perfectly formed and I nearly choke as my mouth forgets to chew my food. I resolve to wait until our next date, after Wednesday, before I even begin to find out.

Wednesday arrives and the fairy lights I ordered still haven't arrived, so I head to the local home styling store and order two side lamps, then I spy what I want and grab them too. I'm at home when I get the strangest text from her.

*E: I'm at a petrol station in Lichfield. I think I'm being followed. What should I do?*

I responded right away, asking where. She gives me its name and I know where she is.

*N: Stay there. Call the police but I am on my way.*

# Fourteen
## *Ellen*

 $T$ he same car has been following me since I got onto the Wolverhampton Road and I'm scared. I tried to breathe, to stay calm but as I got into Lichfield from the A38 and Sutton, I couldn't take it anymore and stopped at a petrol station. Nick's text back gives me something to do, but do I call 999? The car passes me and I note down part of its licence plate. It seems familiar somehow but I can't work out why.

I spot Nick's car and I breathe a huge sigh of relief when he pulls in next to me. I jump out and grab him, then I realise I'm shaking.

I'm five foot nothing, I'm not burly like Nick or fierce like Ruth and Shauna. Nick's arms around me are warm, strong and they make me feel safe. He might be younger than me but he's so much taller and broader. I nuzzle into him and his hands are stroking my hair.

"Are they here?" he asks me quietly. I shake my head then murmur a no.

"They drove on, but I got some of their licence plate," I pulled away and headed to the driver's door to pull out the piece of paper from the pad I kept there. I show Nick and he just nods, his mouth thin and his jaw twitches.

He looks around. "Did you call the police?" I duck my eyes and shake my head.

"I wasn't sure what number to call," I began. He sighs.

"Come on, follow me to mine," he says and he opens my car door to usher me inside. I wait until he's ready and then I follow him back to his.

His directions were spot on. He gets to the corner shop and he really is two streets away from the busy-looking shop. He pulls into a driveway and right up to a garage door. He jumps out and motions for me to pull up onto the driveway too. I manage it and I take in Nick's home. We're just outside Lichfield, near the countryside. His home is a modern three-bed semi with a garage to one side. I imagine the door in the middle leads to the kitchen off on the other side, with bedrooms and bathrooms above. He smiles and holds his hand out for me and I take it, following him in.

I take in the modern building he calls home. The ceilings are lower than I am used to and I can smell fresh paint. He gives me a guided tour from the integral garage, laundry, and downstairs facilities to the fitted kitchen. He shows me the living room and I feel rather calm. The grey sofa is covered in accented cushions, with fairy lights not quite in place.

"I was doing that when you texted me," he says. I notice his cheeks going pink. I smile and offer my hand out to him.

"You were adding to this?" I ask, looking around. It's homely but clean. The smell of paint is very faint but still there.

"Yeah, it was bland before," he shrugs and turns from me.

"It's not bland anymore," I offer. The room is cosy, warm, inviting. I want to sit down and snuggle into him whilst watching a movie on that huge TV he has mounted on a wall with the panelling. The whole room is light but warm. "It's... stunning," I offer. I can't think of a better word and my vocabulary is quite extensive.

"You like it?" He seems unsure and I wonder why. He stands nervously and looks around. I nod in reply.

"Let me show you the rest," he says and he takes my hand, leading me up the stairs so I can view the three bedrooms and functional bathroom. He had the bath removed so it now has a walk-in shower. "It was one or the other," he says as my eyes light up. I'd love a walk-in for my bathroom, but Sam likes her bubble baths.

"You have a very tidy home," I comment. Again, he blushes and his eyes dance.

"It wasn't tidy or as organised when we met," he admits. "I did some decorating last weekend, dad and mum came over to help."

"You did a lot in a day?" I ask.

He nods. "Dad's good at the whole DIY thing. I'm not too bad at it, but if it were just me, I'd still be at it," he chuckles and leads me back to the living area. Off by the stairs is a little home office desk. I notice that he has no books at all in this house. I glance around and I wonder about asking him.

"I don't have books at home as you do," he says. "I hardly read at all," he looks ashamed.

"Not everyone can be a book dragon," I say. My phone rings but I don't recognise the number and divert it to voicemail. Nick gives me a questioning look as I quickly tuck it back into my bag.

"What happened with that call you got last week?" he asks as he half fills up the kettle and puts it on. He picks out some herbal teas and a selection of coffee for me to choose from whilst he waits for my answer.

"Which one?" I ask. I get a weird call a day now and I divert them all to voicemail. No message is ever left.

"The one you called me about on Sunday when you couldn't reach Ruth," he replies. I shrug.

"I called 101, but they didn't have a record. They told me to block it and I did. Then I get all these calls coming in each day. I divert them to voicemail but I never have a message left." He scrunches his face up so that he has frown lines between his eyebrows.

"That's not good. Is it the same number each day? Are you blocking the number every time?" he asks. I purse my lips together as he hands me a tea.

"I don't know, I just ignore it and get on with things," I reply. I don't want to tell him it's been a concern. He holds his hand out for my phone and I fish it out of my bag. Our fingers touch for a moment and I forget I'm supposed to be handing him my phone. He looks at it, then to me.

"Would you unlock it for me, please?" He breathes as the phone is held between us. I nod and unlock it, then hand it back to him.

He frowns and hmms… then picks up his phone. I watch as he Googles the number that's been calling me. "It's a scam, according to these sites." I can only watch as his fingers dance across my screen, then he hands me back my phone. I so want to be my phone right now.

"I've blocked it," he smiles and sips his coffee. "You shouldn't be dealing with them." He almost growls and then he perks up. "Let me show you, Lichfield. We're not far from town and some fresh air will help calm you," he says. I am not sure if I heard, felt, or just understood the "and me" statement of his at the end.

We head out into the sunshine, it's a warm day with a light breeze and it should be heading up into the high twenty-celsius range by mid-afternoon. Nick smiles at me and I wonder if he has noticed the summer dress and nearly nude sandals I have on. He hasn't paid me a compliment but then, I remember I didn't turn up at his door, he had to rescue me from the petrol station.

Lichfield is an old city, though it's small. I love the old Tudor-style buildings that are close together, the cobbled streets, and the library. Nick was surprised that I would find the library above all other buildings in the City, but then, I smiled and he remembered that I'm a librarian, card maker, and book blogger. I know Lichfield is the birthplace of Samuel Johnson, an eighteenth-century writer, poet, critic, biographer, and goodness knows what else about the English language during his seventy-five years of life.

I breathe in the City and Nick takes me to the Dr. Johnson's museum. For a few hours, I bathe in Dr. Johnson's literary genius, learn about his life, his loss and I'm buzzing when we emerge into the sunshine. Nick smiles at me and he takes me by the hand to guide me to somewhere in the City to eat. I have totally forgotten about this morning's misadventure and being followed.

# Fifteen
## *Nick*

Ellen being followed to mine worries me and I distract her with what I hope will be a great time at the Dr. Johnson Museum. I had no idea he created a standard of writing about one hundred and fifty years before the invention of the Oxford English Dictionary.

Ellen is positively buzzing in excitement and I hope that a pub lunch in my old haunt in the centre of town tops the deal. There's a nice courtyard garden in the back and we're just going to be on time for our reservation.

We get seated quickly and I let Ellen decide what she wants. I am going to be spending time at the gym tomorrow and I decide what I'm having quite quickly. Ellen catches up with me and I place our order via the pub's app.

"You're paying again," she admonishes quietly and she tries to slip the money for her half into my hands. I give her a look and gently give it back to her.

"You can pay towards the cinema next time, how's that?" This is my treat and I smile as she puts the money away. Our drinks arrive quickly and the staff give us both a warm smile and a nod. We talk about what we learned earlier and Ellen goes on to explain a few things I had missed or didn't understand about Dr. Johnson's life. Whilst we're talking, the food arrives and we tuck in. For being small, Ellen can pack her food away.

"I need to maintain a certain weight," she says as she catches me watching her. "If I go too below my ideal, I suffer from fainting fits, or worse." I nod. This is all news to me, but she's in her mid-thirties and I'm sure she's got a handle on it. I notice she only eats half the bread bun and I snaffle it from her plate, making a mental promise to work the excess off tomorrow.

"Where do you put all that food?" she asks as I half fill the top of the bun with the chunky chips, then fold it in half and eat it.

I try not to laugh with food in my mouth and I chew quickly. "I'll work it off tomorrow night with the PT," I say. I know if I tell her what I've eaten, she'll have me do extra anyway.

"You have a personal trainer?" asked Ellen. I keep forgetting I've not done anything more than kiss her.

I nod. "Yep. I'd never go otherwise. The sessions being booked in and paid for make me go." I finish off the extra chip wrap I've made and my meal just as Ellen finishes hers. She stacks the plates together, leaving everything neatly for the waitress to clear up. I notice she slips a fiver under a plate and I smirk. I take her hand and we slowly walk back to mine, talking about everything and anything as we amble home.

When we're back at mine, I aim to finish getting the fairy lights up but they somehow end up tangled. Ellen gently takes them from me and has them sorted out in five minutes, her little fingers nimbly untangling them without frustration. Then she helps me weave them around the panel framing dad helped me put up. When they're set how she tells me to, I close the curtains to get an idea of the effect, using the two side lamps alongside. When it's bright as it is, it's not clear how it'll look, but I can imagine at around ten or eleven at night when it's dark.

"This will look so much better at night," she says as she turns the lamps and the small fairy lights off. I smile.

"It'll be even better if you're here to share them with me," I suggest. She giggles.

"I can't tonight," she responds quickly, her eyes going wide. I hold my hands up, palms to her.

"I wasn't suggesting tonight, but another time," I sat on the sofa and pulled out my phone, showing her how the room looked on Saturday. She looks at me, then the phone, and then around as she flicks between what is on the screen and what's before her eyes.

"You did all this?" she breathes, handing me back the phone.

I nod. "Your home felt warmer and more inviting than this one," I hoarsely replied. "I wanted the same kind of feel and look, but something that was me. My sister-in-law helped with the idea, dad helped do it and mum cooked us lunch, did my ironing…" I let that hang. My mum will do chores if she is around, but thankfully, she gave up coming around daily when dad asked her to back off and let me find my own feet. Being the youngest can be a bind at times.

"Your mum comes to do your ironing?" She sits back and folds her arms. "I hate that chore. Thankfully, I haven't had to do it during the holidays as it's mostly Sam's uniform I've got to iron, especially her shirts. The rest of her stuff, and most of mine, doesn't need it."

I nod. "I hate it too, but the shirts are the only thing I insist on, especially since I'm the boss's son and I need to set an example."

She nods. "I know, I get it," she sighs happily and I wonder what she will taste like after the lunch we just had. It's nearly time for her to start heading back, especially since she has Sam to look after.

"Pick a movie and night and we'll go to the cinema to watch it," I offer. "I'll come over to you on Saturday afternoon? How's that sound?" I stand and offer her a hand to help her, then I pull her in and kiss her. She lets me in and her hands fumble at my shirt. I let her pull it out of my jeans and she places her hands beneath the fabric onto my skin. Her hands are small, soft, searching and she pulls back.

"You really do work out?" her voice rises and falls in heavy, breathy tones and I pull back a little, then whip the shirt off and toss it aside.

"Oh my!" she gasps as she looks at me. She licks her lips and I realise that she did that on the first date. This time, she does mean to eat me.

"Yes," I say, stepping into her and pulling her to me again. "I really do," and I capture her mouth as her gentle, little hands press against my pecs.

I don't know how long we're kissing for, it could have been ten seconds or ten minutes. She breaks away with a heavy sigh. If I thought she'd be willing to go further already, I'd let her. I don't know if she is, so I let her back off.

She gives me a small, warm smile and I grin back as I throw my shirt back on and tuck it back in, adjusting my now hard dick into a more comfortable position. She pulls her lips together and eyes my groin so I have to stifle a moan. She giggles.

"I'm sorry," she mumbles and I shake my head.

"It's okay…" I hold my hand out to her. "When you're ready, I will be too." I smile at her as her cheeks go a lovely shade of pink. I love that she hardly wears any makeup and what she does wear, enhances her soft features. Her eyelashes are a dark brown, not the fainter colour I suspect they naturally are. Her lips were glossy, but now they're a deep, slightly swollen pink from my kissing and nibbling. Her eyes though, I can't escape. They're the colour of the Greecian sea now, I hadn't noticed her eyes changing colour.

"Nick," she whispers and I hug her one more time.

"Do you want me to follow you back to the motorway?" I ask. She shakes her head in reply.

"I'll be alright, I'm sure. Sam has a key so she can let herself in. She often does when I'm working," she's biting her lip again and I sense that she wants to clarify something.

"We could," she glances up to where my bedroom is and I smile.

"Not today, not yet. I want," I look at her. "No, I need you to be okay and not have to run home right after." I pull her to me and hold her. "When we finally do sleep together, I'm not going to let you go right after." I feel her relax against me, the nervous tension she suddenly had, dissipates.

"Thank you," she mumbles and breaks away from me, grabbing her bag from the armchair on her way out to her car. I help her climb inside and watch as she starts the car and leaves. I keep watching until the car has turned the corner and is out of sight.

## Sixteen
### Ellen

The drive back from Nicks' was uneventful. He texts me in reply when I tell him I'm home and safe.

*N: Spoke with my brother. He suggests you call 101 and update the police with being followed by that car today.*

*E: Do I have to call them?*

*N: Easiest and quickest way. Let me know when you've done it please, okay? I was worried about you.*

I smile.

*E: Appreciated, thank you!*

I hear Sam moving about upstairs and I go to check on her. We talk about what we want for dinner and if she'd like to come to the movies with us on our next "date". She shakes her head.

"I can be at Trisha's for the night," she offers. I purse my lips together and sigh.

"You know, he is trying to make friends with you too," I say, sitting on the edge of her double bed. She looks up at me.

"I know mum, but it's you he's interested in," she says. "There's going to be plenty of time for him and I to get to know each other. I want you," she shuffles forward and places her hands over mine. "To work out if he is what or who you want." She smiles.

"You've talked this over with Trisha?" I ask. She's about the only other person she'd confide in apart from Trisha's mum.

Sam nods. "And with Trisha's mom," she confirms with a smile. Her books are around her, papers about chemistry are scattered out on her bed.

"I'll speak with Trisha's mom," I offer, smiling at her and standing up.

"She's expecting your call," sings Sam as she picks up a piece of paper she's not yet worked on.

I glance back at my rather mature teenage daughter and I wonder how come I got to be so lucky.

The call with Trisha's mom, Rachel, goes rather well. She's been waiting for my call. and expected a weekend sleepover request, at least on Friday night. I thank her and make arrangements, then I go and tell Sam.

She's still buried in chemistry papers as homework but the done pile is stacked up neatly, the to-do pile is scattered, but less so. At the foot of her bed, her usual overnight rucksack is packed and ready to go. I grin.

"You know already?" I ask her and she nods with a grin across her face.

"You don't need me hanging around, mum," she winks at me and I can tell her mind is in the gutter. Mine isn't that far behind though, especially after I felt and then saw how Nick takes care of himself.

"Well, okay," I say, not hanging around. "I'll get dinner started then," I state and she nods.

"I need about forty-five minutes?" she asks. I nod, wink, and then leave.

Whilst dinner is cooking, I look up the police website and see that I can update the crime number directly, so I do that and let Nick know what I've done. He sends me back a thumbs up and I get on with making dinner.

Dinner is cleared away and Sam vanishes off back upstairs. I can hear her talking and she sounds happy, so I guess she's called Trisha.

I text Nick now that the kitchen is tidied and we have the Friday night free.

*E: Sam is choosing to stay with her friend for Friday night. Is there anything you'd like to go and see?*

I can see the dots appear and his reply is instant.

*N: anything you want. You choose. I'll come to you, okay?*

I check the movies that are listed but none of them takes my fancy. I check the other local cinemas too, as the smaller one in Halesowen sometimes shows older movies that I didn't get to see on the first release. I'm out of luck there too. I'm humming as my phone rings with the ringtone I assigned to Nick.

"Hi," I say, breathing into the phone.

"Hi yourself," he says, his voice is light and bouncy.

"I can't decide what to go and watch," I sigh as I browse through the listings again.

"Do you have Netflix?" he asks.

"I do," I reply and then I turn the TV on so I can check what's there. There are more movie choices there than at the Cinema. I tell him what I have available and he chuckles.

"So why don't we stay in?" he asks. "If you want to," he quickly adds.

"I'd prefer that," I reply.

"Great," I can hear him shuffling something, then I hear him curse quietly and grunt as he stoops to pick something up. "What do you fancy to eat for dinner that night?" He asks.

"I'm not sure," I hesitated. "I'm good at cooking," I pop open cupboards and I can tell I can make a lasagne quite easily. "I'm happy to cook if you can bring dessert," I suggest.

I can hear him sighing contentedly. "That would be perfect," he offers.

"Lasagne?" I offer.

I hear a hearty, happy moan from him and I grin.

"Perfect. I know the right dessert to bring too," he offers. I wonder what it could be and we agree a time so that Sam will be at Trisha's house. I look around and decide that the housework can wait until after work tomorrow. We hang up and I'm happy about the weekend plans, then I open up my Kindle app and get stuck into a book review I'm a little behind on.

# Seventeen
## Ellen

The week flies by. Sam helps with the chores between homework assignments, saying that she needs a break from some of the maths homework she's been assigned already. In two hours, the house is spotless, the laundry is on and I've caught up on my book review. I post the review and send some hints back to the author. Not all authors want feedback from their reviewers beyond the five stars and an honest paragraph about the book, but this lady is new and was open to suggestions for improvements going forward. I send her a couple of paragraphs of notes, then hit send, being as kind as I can.

She wrote over seventy thousand words and I feel for her as she doesn't seem to have an editor or any advanced readers who would have picked up on the small errors. I'm putting laundry into the drier when I get a notification that she's replied. I pause and hold my breath as I read her reply, but she is grateful and because she is self-published, she can make the changes I've suggested and get it updated.

I smile and send her a good luck message, suggesting that she post about ARC readers being wanted on Instagram and what hash-tags to use, then I get on with my evening. I send Nick a text when I've curled up in my favourite chair with a chamomile tea and my Kindle, asking how his day has gone. It takes him a chapter or two to reply.

*N: Been at the gym, all sweaty!*

A picture message comes through right behind it and it's a selfie of him looking very hot, bothered, and totally gorgeous in his gym gear. His face is red, the sweat is pouring off him but I can see the sparkle in his eyes.

*E: Hot on two fronts*

I tease him a little and I wait for a while. Then I get a message back with just him in a towel in the showers at the gym. I gape at the image of him in the showers and I'm still holding the phone when Sam appears over my shoulder and gawks at him.

"Is that Nick!?" she asks, trying to get my phone off me as she places dirty plates on the coffee table. "Mum, he's hot!" She fans herself and smirks at me whipping out her phone and sending a message, I assume to Trisha. I send back a face with hearts for eyes and close my phone down, but it pings again and Sam giggles as I unlock it and see that Nick has sent back a laughing face.

*E: Sam is looking over my shoulder at you. Be careful what you send to me!*

*N: Nothing more than that. Everything else is private viewing only.*

Sam sees the last message, gags in a comical way then heads up to her room again with a drink and her phone pinned to her ear.

I see Sam forgot to take her dirty plates to the kitchen, so I slowly uncurl myself, allowing my circulation to come back, then I take them through and wash the plates by hand. Then I leave them to drip dry and head back to my chair to reply to another of Nick's texts.

*N: How was your day?*

I notice he never tells me he misses me, he's never pressured me to give more of myself than I'm willing to give and the more he just spends time with me, the more I want him.

I reply with how my day has gone, which seems boring but he asked. I ask about his day and he tells me work was okay, the gym was hard because his PT has put him through the wringer but he seems upbeat, happy, content.

We talk about Friday night and him staying over, which makes me giddy. When we finish texting, I text Ruth and ask for advice.

*R: What do you need advice for? You've got this! Enjoy it, okay?*

*E: Are you okay? We've not spoken much since that weekend.*

*R: Things are fine. Daniel and I have an arrangement, of sorts.*

*E: Of sorts?*

*R: Yeah... I have work functions to go to, I drag him along. He has some award ceremonies to go to because of his parlour, so I get to go to them with him.*

*E: And you're okay with this?*

*R: Yes. Friends with benefits.*

*E: Benefits... are you sleeping with him?*

It takes Ruth a few moments to come back. The dots start flashing, then vanish and reappear.

*R: Yes.*

*E: You're okay with that?*

*R: Yes, you know I don't want a relationship at the moment. I don't want to be tied down.*

I look at the screen and gasp. This is not what Ruth said when I went to check on her after that weekend. Nor was it what she said she wanted on the way back from Shauna's wedding. I bite my lower lip and ponder how I'm going to respond to Ruth, text can be so cold. It takes me a few moments.

*E: Are you sure?*

*R: Being honest... No.*

*E: Oh, Roo! Have you fallen for him?*

It takes Ruth a good half an hour to reply to me. By which time I've showered and gotten ready for bed.

*R: Trying very hard not to. That was the agreement.*

*E: The heart wants what it wants*

*R: Tell me about it. He's just come out of a long-term relationship. I don't want to rock this longboat just yet!*

I can still hear the humour in Ruth's reply, though it seems more veneer than normal. I sigh.

*E: What can I do to help you?*

*R: Be there when my heart breaks, okay?*

*E: As you would for me; always!*

# *Eighteen*
## *Nick*

Friday morning sees me at my desk just before seven am, suited and booted. I am early, partly because my kettle blew up on me this morning and I need the coffee. The other is because of Ellen. My secretary and PA, Hayley, is in just before eight am but I'm caught up on everything, apart from the timed meetings. She gives me a raised eyebrow and I smile.

"Leaving slightly earlier, around four," I tell her. She nods and sits at her desk, turning her computer on. She goes and does what she normally does before I get in and I feel strangely alive this morning. I check my diary and I see I have no meetings today until I catch up with the sales division at just before noon. A working lunch. I smile. I grab my phone and send Ellen a good morning text, knowing she'll be on her way to work just about now.

She replies quickly and I'm guessing she's on the bus now, heading into Birmingham. Hayley gently puts my morning coffee on the coaster on my desk and I nod in thanks, then get on with answering my father's enquiries about certain aspects of our production. One question has me taking a walk on the product floor to find the staff member with the answers I need, something I do every day anyway when I'm in the office. I find it easier for the employees, and my team, to ask me things if they can see me.

The sales meeting is short and sharp, our sales manager has a good handle on things and some of his team are given the floor to pitch possible supply lines, new products for us to make that haven't made it to the UK in general yet, especially car supply parts made of steel. I give the go-ahead for them to investigate the new chances. The sales manager hangs back after the meeting to discuss an order that looks fraudulent. Taking a look at his notes and observations, I agree and we cancel the order on the system and production. The rest of the day is busy tying up loose ends, scheduling final production for next week and by four o'clock I'm leaving the building, knowing that the production staff will close up and secure it all for the weekend.

By half-past four, I'm at home and in the shower, then I dress, grabbing all I have planned to take with me to Ellen's. Carefully packing it all into the car, I head to Ellen's at around six, expecting the motorways to be hell on Earth.

There must be a motorway god after all! I found myself outside Ellen's ten minutes before I said I would be there. She smiles as she opens the door and my heart stops as my cock tries to escape my trousers. She's simply gorgeous. Her skirt comes to just above her knees, pinched into her tiny waist. It's black but pleated, almost like a school skirt, but far sexier. Her top has the shoulders missing as if it's designer and its striped pattern only highlights her small boobs. Her hair is half up in a clip and I take in her total look. She looks amazing and I see she's drinking me in as much as I am her. I just hope she's not noticed me being a prowling wolf.

I smile at her as I carefully remove the dessert and take it over to her.

"Hi gorgeous," I breathe at her, trying not to act like a teenager in lust.

"Hi," she breathes back. She takes the glass dish from me and gives me a puzzled look.

"It needs to be in the fridge," I say. It's still semi-frozen, but fresh tiramisu sets better in the freezer than in the fridge overnight.

She nods and vanishes in the house as I head back to the car to collect the wine, the flowers, chocolates, and my overnight bag. She's back at the door by the time I am and I gently hand her the flowers.

"Oh Nick, they're gorgeous!" She looks at me with eyes of wonder that hold a tear or two.

"Not as gorgeous as you," I reply and she blushes, then glances at the floor. She turns and guides me into her home. This time, I know I won't be leaving until Sunday.

As we get into the kitchen, I let her arrange this latest bunch of flowers into the new vase. I watch as she focuses on her task, not looking at me. I get she might be nervous, it's been seven years since her husband took off days before Christmas. Has she been celibate all this time? I try to recall if she's said anything about any other exploits but she hasn't, not to me. I stand quietly and go to her as she finishes placing the last of the white floaty thing that adds volume but in my view, not much else.

"Ellen," I whisper and she jumps. She turns to me and she blushes again, pursing her lips and lowering her eyes, then closes them. Hell, is she that nervous?

I place the side of my index finger under her chin and raise her face. "Look at me honey," I whisper. She flutters her eyelashes open and sighs.

"As slow as you need, beautiful," I lean in and gently kiss her mouth. It eases the tension in her as her hands find my biceps, her fingers dig in slightly. I swallow her sigh as she relaxes another notch and I up the speed, kissing her, claiming her. I know I have to do it with care, for her sake.

The timer on the cooker goes off and she jumps back, then giggles slightly.

"Show me where things are," I tell her. She indicates where the cutlery and placemats are kept and I set the table just for us. The sun is still shining and she has the patio doors wide open, allowing bird song, the distant sound of buses and cars, and the sounds of her neighbour's water feature to reach our ears. This is perfect and I tell her that it is.

"Thank you," she replies, just loud enough for me to hear her.

She places two cork mats on the table and then brings out a decent-sized lasagne dish, brimming with melted cheese. It smells divine and I grin at her. Then I fetch the wine, find two glasses, and pour us a glass each. We sit down and begin to eat in comfortable silence.

I push my knife and fork together on the plate, having cleaned it of all the food Ellen piled onto it. Between the Italian salad, garlic bread, and superbly made lasagne, I'm stuffed.

"That was fantastic," I declare, then I have to cover my mouth as I burp. Ellen laughs and smiles broadly.

"I'm so glad it met with your approval," she stands with her eyes shining brightly, her smile going from one ear to the next.

"It certainly did," I say. "Do you have room for dessert, or shall we chill out with a movie and have dessert later?"

I'm trying to gauge how stuffed she is. Her portions were far smaller than mine were, but then, she's tiny compared to me. There's enough lasagne left over to be frozen. It's near impossible to make a small lasagne.

"Movie, then dessert," she says and her cheeks pink up. I nod and stand, helping her clear the kitchen. "You don't have to," she says.

"You cooked," I say. "You don't get to do all the tidying up too." She stops, then she starts wringing her hands together. I remember from the first website Oscar shared with me that shy, introverted people sometimes do this. I go grab her hands and smile at her gently.

"Ellen, it's okay," I tell her. Whatever it is that's going through her mind, I know it isn't okay. "I'm me, I help. My mother would give me such a telling off if she ever learned I was anything but a gentleman in a lady's house," I lean in. "Until I'm told I can be naughty," I wink, and she giggles.

"I'm sorry, I'm just not used to guests helping," she apologises and bites her lips. I sigh and pull her into me for a hug. She melts against me and sighs.

"I'm more than just a guest though, aren't I?" I ask. I feel her head nodding against me. I pull back a little and raise her chin so she looks at me. Her eyes are a pale blue, not the Grecian sea blue I've come to crave. This is a scared, pale blue.

"I'm not going to hurt you, I'm not expecting you to wait on me hand and foot, or at all. Whatever you've been expecting, and I think it's not good, it won't be coming from me," she smiles weakly, and a tear forms. Another appears and I pull her to me. Then I decide the dishes can wait, I need to know what's going on inside her head. I need to know why.

I move to a chair and sit down on it, then pull her into my lap and pin her to me. Her sobs aren't heartbreaking, but she's hung up on something.

"Tell me, Ellen, talk with me." I stroke her hair and remove the clip that's catching my hand. It looks worse than a crab claw and I somehow manage to get it out without hurting her or damaging myself. My Scottish aunt, my dad's brother's wife, would always ask us to talk with her, never to her. It's a phrase that's stuck with me since I was little.

"Mark," she begins and reaches out for some tissues. I let her go but pull her back as soon as I can. "Even after all this time," She blows her nose gently, then grabs a fresh tissue to dry her eyes. She sighs and looks up at the ceiling. I rub a hand over the small of her back, whilst holding the other hand across her lap.

"He used to control me and I would do anything to please him," she spits that information out at one hundred miles an hour as she scrunches the paper hankies up into a ball in her tiny hands. I move my hand over both of hers, clasping them gently and they settle. So does she. "When he walked out," she sighs but doesn't look at me. "I thought I'd never... Shauna told me I would. I thought what she said was a pipe-dream, her picking up on what I wanted," she sighed again. "Beyond one time in Rotterdam at Helene's wedding, I haven't..."

I get it. She's hardly been with anyone else. I've not been a saint, but it's been a while for me too.

"It's okay," I move my hand to turn her to face me. "It's been a little while for me too, nearly a year," I see acknowledgment flash across her beautiful face. "I'm nervous too," she leans into me, her head against mine. "And excited, but I really want to spend time with you too." She smiles and I reach for the box of tissues to offer her another one.

"One step at a time, okay? And I will help tidy up." She looks up at me with a faint smile on her face. Her mascara hasn't run and I suddenly see her pretty little mouth is open. I guide my hand behind her head and draw her mouth to mine, kissing away the salty tears. I try to keep the kiss gentle, at least for now. Thinking about devouring her, tasting her is now getting me hard but I don't want that, yet.

"Tidy up time," I say, pulling back. If I don't stop now, I never will and she's not quite in the right place at this moment. She nods and I let her climb down, then I help her tidy away and get the dishwasher going before we settle back down on the sofa with Netflix and a movie of her choice.

She picked something that wasn't boring that had Chris Hemsworth and Jason Statham in it. It was quite a good movie, I hadn't seen Statham play a bad guy before. We're snuggled up together on the couch, an arm is wrapped around her shoulder and her legs are curled underneath her. I stroked her shoulder and upper arm throughout the whole movie, not once did she complain. My most recent ex couldn't, or wouldn't, stand for my touching her in displays of affection unless we were engaged in intercourse and even then, it was short-lived. The fact she wasn't too heartbroken when we split up shows just how different we were.

Ellen sighs and slowly uncurls her legs from underneath her. I'm surprised she can feel them, she's been sitting like that for hours.

"Getting your feeling back?" I ask, helping her to sit up. She nods.

"I forget and then I go numb," she giggles and I hold onto her as she slowly gets the feeling back in her legs. She sits back and I move to her feet, taking one in my hands and gently massage the foot. She moans in pleasure as I apply a little pressure, then I work my way up to her calf. Her breath catches and my insides do a happy dance. I keep a stoic face on me but glance up at her quickly. Her mouth is open, her breathing has quickened and she's pushing her breasts forward with her hands behind. I take the other foot and do the same, evoking the same reactions.

# Nineteen
## *Ellen*

I've been curled up too long on the sofa, leaning into him, breathing him in. Chris Hemsworth and Jason Statham usually do it for me separately, but together? That was an excellent movie. It hurts when I uncurl myself but Nick doesn't seem to mind. He helps me sit up and when he grabs a foot to massage some feeling back into it for me, I gasp. His hands send electric shocks through me and as he works the back of my calf, I involuntarily moan. Since when was that an erogenous zone?

He glances up at me, his face showing no expression but his eyes are hooded, clouded in lust. I hardly notice that my mouth is open and my breathing has quickened, not until his face is right before mine and he steals a chaste kiss. He pulls back to look into my eyes and I can hardly see the colour of his, they're so dark. The sidelights are still on, enough to see him if we got naked. He pulls back from the kiss but I snake a hand up around his neck and pull him back down. I swallow his sigh as he swallows mine and I move so that I'm laying on the sofa with Nick on top of me. He's supporting his weight, so I'm not smothered or crushed.

The kissing lasts forever and as it continues, I pull his shirt up and feel his abs, his chest, and pecs. I saw them when I went to his house and now, I want to touch and taste him. My previously manifested fears from my now ex-husband are gone, he's no longer in my thoughts. Nick consumes my very presence and I arch up as my top is untucked from my skirt, his large rough hands are exploring my ribs and stomach, snaking their way up to my breasts. He's gentle, considering how big everything is on him. He doesn't roughly grab my tiny breast with his hand, he teases the nipple through the lacy fabric of my bra, the one I indulged in buying one lunchtime from town on an extended break.

"Off," he says, stopping to take his shirt off. I follow suit and remove my top and as I go to remove my bra, he helps. Then suddenly, his warm mouth is teasing, licking, sucking, and biting at me in the most erotic way. He teases my other breast with his hand whilst his mouth devours the other. Then switches and I hear him groan. Or was that me? I dig my fingers into his biceps, or I at least try to. He's solid, everywhere. I move my legs so that he can lay right between them and in seconds, I can feel his hardness pressing into me.

There's very little between us. Three, maybe four layers of clothing are all that separate us from joining. Nick stops and looks at me, his face flushed. He rubs his nose against mine, Eskimo style.

"Bedroom," he whispers, then he detangles himself from me and holds out a hand to help me up. He's grabbed our clothes and as I head for the stairs, he grabs his bag and follows me.

In my bedroom, Nick tosses our clothes onto my dresser chair and drops his bag behind the bedroom door as he closes it. I feel self-conscious for all of one second and then Nick has me in his arms as he begins kissing me again. I sigh and reach up, but I'm not quite able to reach his head. He's lowered himself down to my height as it is. I'm spun around and then I'm on his lap, facing him as he sits in a commanding position at the foot of my bed. He's placed me on one of his huge, strong legs with an arm around my waist but not pinning me down. The other is holding the side of my head to him and the kisses are exploring, tasting, commanding, teasing. Nick is the one in charge here and I'm happy to let him.

His hands once again find my small breasts and I shudder about what he thinks of them, only for him to moan as he sucks a nipple into his mouth.

I moan quietly, forgetting that Sam's not around to hear me but I can't keep quiet when Nick's fingers graze the inside of my thigh and tease me at my core. I'm already soaking wet for him. He stands me up then strips my knickers from me, lifts my skirt, and kneels. His head is between my legs, at my entrance, licking and sucking. My knees collapse and he spins me around so I'm on the bed with my skirt raised to my middle. He doesn't stop, never misses a beat and before long, I'm crying out and holding his head in my hands, encouraging him to stop and continue in equal measure.

"You're amazing," he whispers as I hear him undo his jeans. I lift my arse and take off my skirt, throwing it aside somewhere.

"Condoms," I whisper and he picks his jeans back up, fishes something out of the back pocket and rips it open. I watch as he rolls it on, then I can see the glint of mischievousness and a look of lust in his eyes.

The quilt is removed from under me, thrown to the bottom of the bed and it's kicked onto the floor. I think about closing my legs for one second, but before I can move or even doubt myself, he's laying between my legs, kissing me. I taste myself on him and I'm unable to tell him what I think of that. He's holding himself up over me with one hand and guiding himself to my entrance with his other.

"If you want me to stop," he whispers as he nibbles my ear, "tell me." He waits a moment for me to respond, but I reach up and catch his hair in my fist.

"Don't you dare stop," I breathe, then kiss him as he firmly pushes into me. It's been a while but he feels so damn good, filling me up. I hear him curse, I can see in the low light that his eyes are screwed closed.

"You're so…" he kisses me as he starts to withdraw and then he's pushing into me again. "Fucking hell," he pulls back from the kiss and he watches me as he finds his rhythm. I can't keep my eyes open, his thrusts fill me right to the brim and his length is rubbing me in ways I had long forgotten.

"Ellen," he breathes and I open my eyes, then I wrap my arms around him as my legs follow suit, pinning him to me. His forehead is against mine, our breathing ragged but still his thrusting never stops. I can feel the pressure building in me and I throw my head back as the first penetration climax since Helene's wedding in Rotterdam, takes over me. I shudder beneath him and as I convulse it sets him off. His pace increases and in seconds, he's coming with me, stiffening within me, both of us crying out the other's name as our orgasms take over.

I'm not sure how long I'm under him after we've climaxed when the chills hit me. He kisses me and withdraws, then the quilt is over me and the bedroom door opens.

"Bathroom, down the hall," I point in the direction of the only bathroom this house has. He nods and vanishes through the door. He's back in moments, diving under the thin quilt and cuddling up to me. He pulls me to his chest and cradles me in his arms.

"You're fucking amazing," he says as he kisses the top of my head. Then he lifts my chin and kisses me deeply and firmly.

"You're pretty amazing yourself," I whisper, tracing his abs and pecs with a finger. He's not stopped touching or feeling me all night and I get that he's intimate. The big brawny guy likes to touch.

"Do you need anything?" he asks.

"No," I whisper back, snuggling into him. With him beside me and the quilt over us, I'm now dozing in his strong arms and I feel like I belong for the first time in too long.

I'm not sure what time it is but I wake and Nick is beside me. He's not cuddling me anymore, he's on his back, an arm draped over his head and the other is beside me. I reach over and gently touch his hand. His hand twitches and he turns towards me, throwing an arm over me. I trace his pecs as I snuggle back into his embrace and I can sense that he is silently watching me

.

"Like what you see?" he asks, lifting my head so he can kiss me. I mumble a kind of yes into the kiss and before I know it, I'm on my back again.

"Condom," I whisper. He reaches across to the table by his side and he pulls a condom out of the box he placed there, goodness knows when. He rolls it onto himself and then he's kissing me deeply, slowly. I open my hips a little wider and then he's inside me again, balls deep and I moan in pleasure.

"Like that, do you?" He asks huskily into my ear. His thrusts are more gentle this time, slower. Perhaps because of the time of night, or because our earlier session was frantic and full of nerves. Now, he's making love with me, to me and I gently scratch his back as his thrusts hit me deeply but slowly. He moans when my nails scratch a particular point and his mouth finds mine. We take our time to enjoy each other and I arch back to lift my hips closer to him, to take in all that I can.

Our tongues dance as he thrusts deep into me and again, I can feel the pressure building within me. His well-built V is hitting my clit as he thrusts and he moans as I come undone beneath him again. His thrusting doesn't stop, he keeps the same pace, the kisses keep their pace but I'm coming undone again, quicker than the first time. I arch up against him, crying out his name, and then, he's coming with me, growling my name into my ear as he shudders and stiffens within me.

He's kissing me as I come to. I'm draped alongside him, half over him and he's on his back. When did we switch positions? He's stroking my hair, my shoulder, whispering that I'm safe in a soft voice I can just about hear.

"Are you back?" he asks as I shift to get more comfortable. I mumble a reply and he chuckles. "Never blissed a woman out before," he chuckles.

"Never?" I ask.

"Nope, not ever," he replies.

"I feel sleepy," I mumble.

"Rest, sweetheart," I feel another kiss on my head. "You're on top next time," he whispers and I smirk slightly as sleep claims me.

I awake to find the bed empty, though the sheets are still warm. I can hear movement downstairs, clattering in the kitchen as drawers are shut. I stretch out and gawk at the time, it's gone eight am and I'm usually up and functioning. I hear the stairs being climbed and I quickly grab my nightshirt and get it on before Nick comes back into the bedroom. He's found a tray and he's got coffee.

He smiles as he enters and he places the tray on the end of the dresser, then closes the bedroom door.

"Morning sweetheart," he says. I blush and purse my lips together, trying to hide a smile. His endearment is new to me, Mark never said anything like that.

"Morning," I mumble, sheepishly. I look up and watch him as he carefully hands me a mug of coffee and kisses me on the cheek. I feel my face going red.

"Let me know when you're ready to talk," his voice is quiet, hesitant but his eyes are lit up, sparkling.

"Talk?" I ask, blowing on the hot beverage.

Nick nods. "You don't seem to have been given many compliments before, or at all. I don't want to push, but when you're ready, I'd like to know." I freeze, not wanting to explain about Mark but guessing I have to at some point. I sigh, contemplating what to tell him.

He touches my knee gently and I lift my head to look at him. "When you're ready, okay sweetheart?" I give a small nod and blow on my coffee.

I'm halfway through my coffee when I just begin with my story.

"Mark, my ex, never really gave compliments unless it was in front of others when we were in private he never said thank you but expected me to do so when he would do something mundane for me he got better when I was pregnant and when Sam was born and I thought we had turned a corner but we hadn't for six years he never told Sam he loved her unless she said it to him first even though her first word was dada." I stop for a quick breath, then carry on. "When we got close to

Christmas we were due to spend it with my parents who were with my nana in Hull he dropped the bombshell that he didn't love me or Sam and he was leaving six days before Christmas he'd been moving out quietly for weeks and I hadn't noticed all his tidying up and not telling me."

The whole story rushed out of me like a dam bursting. The coffee cup was removed from my hands but I hadn't noticed until Nick's hands were in mine and his arms were hugging me from behind. I leaned back into him, closing my eyes, letting the tears fall.

"He's an asshole," he growls into my ear. "Does he even pay maintenance for Sam?"

I shake my head and dry my eyes with the back of my hands. "CPS are after him every given opportunity but it seems he gets cash in hand jobs, or when he is on a salary, he says he can't pay for her as he has to live and has debts to pay. We manage though," I offer.

"I have no doubt you are, sweetheart. He's not worthy of you, you're better than he will ever be," he kisses my ear and grips me tightly. "I'm going to be giving you compliments a lot Elle, so you'll have to get used to it. My family hugs a lot, we're stubborn, we dig in, we get things done. We also love fiercely and we do not back down."

I sigh at his words as they hit home. "You've been on your own for a long time, but you don't have to be anymore." I turn to him and his grip lessens to let me.

"I've forgotten how to," I begin and then his lips are gently touching mine. His lips are not forcing me, nor claiming me. He's just there, with me. Just the same way the girls have been until recently. If I called, they'd come running. But Nick is here right now.

"We'll work it out," he tells me as he pulls back a little. "Last night was amazing. You," he looks into my eyes, and his eyes are a mixture of green and amber, almost gold. Wait, his eyes change colour? "are all I am ever going to need." I smile at his words and I lean in to kiss him. He pulls me onto his lap so I'm facing him and we kiss.

Slowly at first, then I nip at his bottom lip slightly, remembering that he said I was on top next time.

Feeling bold, partly because it's just us in the house and partly because of what he's just said to me, I strip my top off. He's not quite naked under me and I move to yank his hipsters down and off him. He helps and in seconds, he's standing at half-mast. He pulls me back onto his lap and he pulls my head into him, then he kisses me deeply. His fingers tweak a nipple and I cry out a little in both surprise and pain, but it quickly turns to a moan as he rubs my nipple with his thumb. The hand behind my head drops and begins to fondle the other breast as he kisses me senseless. Both his fingers tweak, rub and pinch my nipples and then he slides down the bed so he's flat.

I move off him and look at his penis, standing up at nearly full mast. I bite my lip.

"Do what you want sweetheart," and he nods as I glance at him. I've never had permission to do anything to anyone, save the one night in Rotterdam two years ago and mostly then, he was in charge.

I lick my lips and then take him into my mouth. He groans in pleasure and arches up but keeps his hands to himself. He tucks them behind his head but he seems to be fighting the need to hold onto me. I bob my head up and down, using my tongue to lick his underside and across the opening whilst using one hand to jerk him.

"Jesus, Ellen!" he gasps and he reaches out to stop me. "Condom," he gasps and I reach across to grab one.

"Let me show you," he gasps and he rips it open, then shows me how to roll it onto him. "Come here," he says and I move up to kiss him. "On my face, beautiful," and I gape. He grins.

"You're on top, the whole way baby," and his hand reaches for me, stroking me gently. "Let me make you come again Ellen," my eyes close as his fingers work me, making me wetter than I thought I would be.

He wiggles down the bed again and I position myself above his face. Then his hands are on my hips, holding me in place as his tongue laps me, his teeth nibble and his mouth sucks. I try to hold onto a sense of reality, but his wicked mouth has me undone and I scream out as I climax, shuddering over his face. I regain my senses and I move off him, to find him grinning at me.

"You taste," I wiggle down onto his stomach, afraid of what he might say. "Fucking amazing," he growls and he sits up a little. Then he pulls me close and kisses me so I can taste myself, which I find rather disgusting but as we're kissing, he's moving me and I can feel his hardness poking at me.

"When you're ready sweetheart," he whispers as if he understands my uncertainty. He holds himself and I slowly take him inside of me. Facing him is very different, especially when I'm in charge. He has one hand on my hip and another around my back. I can't help but admire his biceps, pecs, and abs. He's not a ripped bodybuilder, but he is certainly fit. He groans and lies back, both hands on my hips, his eyes locked onto me.

I can feel him deep in me and I adjust so that my clit is touching his V. I can't take him any deeper, there's no more of him but he's not a tiny man. He's long but thin and I can feel him as he helps guide me to riding him. His fingers play with my clit as I move up and down and already, I can feel the heat, tension, and feelings build up inside of me. A few more moments and I'm coming undone on him, but he doesn't let me stop. His hands have my hips and he's lifting me as he thrusts upwards. It's all I can do to hold onto his biceps and let him buck into me from beneath.

"Ellen," he croaks and I look at him just as he throws his head back and he convulses, sending me into another climax as he rides out on his own. I can feel my inner walls contracting, holding him, almost milking him. I fall onto him and he has his arms around me, stroking my hair and kissing me gently. I hear him tell me I was amazing and that I should sleep. I murmur something and then do as he suggested, flat on his chest.

# Twenty
## Nick

Ellen's responses to me have been amazing. I hold her to me, noting how tiny but how perfectly formed she is. Tiny, bouncing breasts that perk up, a soft roundness to her stomach that makes me want to kiss her all over, an arse I want to see jiggle as I take her from behind and the most responsive part is her pussy. When she came on my face earlier, I couldn't help but demand more from her. That has to be my new favourite flavour.

She lies on me, hair sprawled over an arm and I gently let her body naturally fall off me onto the empty part of the bed. I quickly get rid of the condom, fetch the quilt back and throw it over us, then I fling a leg and an arm over her, keeping her close. Her eyes are closed, her breathing light and frequent. She's asleep and before long, I've joined her.

Something knocks into me and I open my eyes, not recognising for a moment where I am. Then I remember and I look down at the woman wrapped up in my arms. Her breathing is irregular, but she's still curled up into me, like a cat. I smile and pull her to me, obtaining an "oomph" from her as I do so.

"Hey beautiful," I whisper. I hear a soft giggle and she looks up at me. I hold her chin and kiss her deeply. I swallow one of her happy sighs and before long, she's beneath me as we kiss. "Another round? Greedy…" I chuckle as I move to suckle a nipple. She arches up against me and I scoop an arm under her, holding her where I want her. I've never usually been this greedy for a woman before, but with Ellen, I'm turning into a beast.

"Nick," she gasps and she gyrates against me.

I look at her eyes, they're the Grecian blue I've been wanting to see since yesterday. "On your knees Ellen," I commanded. When did I get so bossy? I reach across for another condom as she turns herself over to present her arse to me.

I slap a cheek gently and watch as the flesh bounces. Then I rub where I've slapped and pass my hand over her pussy, feeling how wet she is. Or not right now. I slap the other cheek and do the same. I smack and rub her arse a fair few times before her entrance is slick enough for me to push my fingers into. She arches and pushes against my fingers.

"Naughty girl," I tell her, putting her arse back how I want it. She mewls a little and my penis is throbbing, aching to release itself into her. I slide a finger, then two into her, not just fingering her but stretching her and making her ready.

"Nick, please," she begs in that soft, sexy voice I think she's long forgotten she had. I roll the condom on and then smear my cock in her wetness, but I don't push into her yet. I lean over her and play with her breasts, which hang down like perfect little jewels. She's small anyway but they drop like tears. I tweak one and roll it in my fingers, making her gasp. I do the same with the other and as she gasps, I thrust home, deep into her in one movement. She cries out my name and I can only grin.

Grabbing her hips, I pull back and drive into her again, repeating the slow withdrawal and hard drive home. I set my rhythm and I smack her arse here and there for good measure. Seeing her flesh bounce makes me drive in harder, withdraw a little faster. Before long, she's climaxing and I have to hold her hips to keep her up. I lower a hand to her clit as I increase my pace again and she's screaming out my name, to God, as I plough myself home for the last time.

# Twenty-One
## Ellen

I'm face down on the mattress, Nick on top of me, his hand on my clit, squashed beneath both of us. He's kissing my neck, my ear, and whispering how fantastic I am. He's pretty damn good himself, being honest. That's twice now I've lost coherent thought after sex with him. It wasn't just sex, there was love in there too, I can feel myself beginning to crave him, his touch, his voice, needing him in every way for the rest of my life.

He rolls off me but pulls me to him after a moment of doing something, keeping me close, possessing me. The quilt comes back over us again and I find myself wrapped up in warm, strong arms with sleep once again, tugging at me.

It's later when we awake, mostly because I think I've made Nick's arm dead, but he pulls me close and groans into my ear.

"You're absolutely amazing Ellen," he whispers as he caresses my breasts. "I'd be happy to go again, but your phone has been pinging and I think we need to get up," he kisses the side of my head. "Can we resume this tonight?"

I smile at him. Goodness, I wreak of sex and I realise, I do not care. I grab my phone and notice that I've received several texts from Sam and my phone needs charging. I plug it in and then read the messages from Sam on WhatsApp.

*S: Mum, can I go to Merry Hell?*

*S: Due to lack of reply, Trisha's mom is taking us anyway.*
Several hours pass in time before the next one.

*S: Staying for lunch, then I need to get out of Trisha's hair… Are you awake?*
Another hour passes and I look at the time. It's nearly two pm.

*S: MUM!?*

I hit reply.

*Mum: Sure, head home slowly but carefully, I'll see you in about half an hour?*

*S: You're alive!? Thank goodness! Thought he'd taken you to the underworld or something!*

*Mum: I'm not Persephone*

*S: No, but wouldn't that make you Demeter?*

She has me there!

*Mum: Probably! Anyway, give me half an hour*

*S: You've had lots since I woke up mum! See you soon, I'm packing up my things now.*

Nick leans in over my shoulder and kisses me.

"I'll strip the bed if you want to shower before she comes home," he offers. I turn, kiss him, and head to the bathroom, grabbing a fresh towel on the way.

By the time I'm finished, Nick has indeed stripped the bed and taken the pile down to the machine. I can remake the bed later, with fresh sheets for tonight. Is he staying tonight? It's Saturday, I've not checked in with him about it but he said about resuming things tonight. I curse under my breath and suddenly there are strong arms around me.

"What's wrong, gorgeous?" Did he hear me?

"I was just wondering because I hadn't asked…" I turn to him and look up. "Do you want to stay tonight too?

Nick pinches my chin and kisses me. "I didn't think I'd be leaving until Sunday and I'd like to unless you're kicking me out?" I shake my head in reply.

"No, I'd like you to stay, just we hadn't said when you needed to get back," I squirm as his amber green eyes dance and change right as I'm looking into them. I catch my breath, my heart beats faster and I swear he can hear it. Or is it me hearing his? I'm no longer sure.

"Then I'm staying," he kisses me gently and swats me on the bottom. "You do need to get dressed. I'll make breakfast," he smiles as he heads towards the door. I start to protest but I stop as he gives me a look.

"Be quick," he tells me in a no-nonsense brogue. Then, he's gone, leaving me standing in my bedroom, wrapped in a towel, still in a daze.


I'm at the table, eating some of the tiramisu he's made from a recipe his sister-in-law has given him. When I came down, he'd brewed the coffee, had toasted me a bagel and we indulged in last nights' dessert. We're sitting there, talking about general, mundane things when I hear Sam come in through the front door, loudly. I guess it was in case we were busy, but I should give the poor guy a rest.

"Hey, mum!" I can tell by her voice she's shouting upstairs where she thinks we are.

"In here," I call out, smiling at Nick who finishes off his portion of tiramisu. It's lovely, rich, and fills my sweet tooth craving. My stomach is no longer growling at me for food and the coffee has woken me up.

Sam appears, hesitant in her approach until she realises we're dressed and eating.

"Oh!" she says, eyeing up the last spoonful in my bowl.

"Would you like some?" asks Nick, rising and heading over to the fridge. I watch as Sam contemplates the dessert and Nick's offer. I nod, she'd like this, even with the rich alcohol in it, it's not too strong, the balance is perfect.

"Oh, yes!" she breathes and she fetches out a bowl and spoon. She joins us and I swear she inhales the dessert before Nick's even put the remainder back into the fridge. He giggles and helps himself to more coffee. I think that's his third. He holds the coffee pot up at me, asking in gestures if I'd like more. I shake my head. Two in one day is enough.

"That's not shop bought," she tells him. He shakes his head.

"Lisa helped me make it. She's quite good at making cakes and things. When your mum said she was making lasagne," his comment stops her dead.

"We have your lasagne?" she's practically squealing at me. I nod.

"Tiramisu seemed to be the perfect dessert to go with it," he adds, smiling as she places her spoon in her bowl and burps. The grin on his face makes me smile too. I love how his eyes shine and the crow feet that I see at the corners of his eyes.

"It was," I say. "Pity I fell asleep during the movie," I pretended. Nick shrugs at me and when Sam is looking at me, he winks. He gets it: sex talk with my teenage daughter and my lover in the room isn't ideal.

"You didn't mum," she admonishes. I shrug.

"I was tired," I replied to her. Tired from Nick wearing me out and worrying about what he thought of me as if he were Mark, yes. From the movie? Not so much.

Sam picks up the sound of the washing machine as it fills up. I hadn't realised Nick had put the sheets on for me.

"Could you clear these away?" I ask her, then I go to check on the laundry. I'm surprised when I see that the sheets are on the right wash at the right temperature. I jump when I hear Nick's low voice in my ear.

"I got it right, I hope?" he asks. I nod.

"I've never had anyone," I begin but he holds up a finger to my mouth.

"I'm not anyone," he whispers, then his lips are on mine, softly. Then he moans and pulls away, a grin on his face and he motions back to the kitchen.

"Sam's taken her stuff upstairs. What do you want to do for the remainder of the day?"

I look at the time and it's mid-afternoon, yet I feel like it's early morning. I shrug.

"Hadn't thought that far," I reply. He nods.

"A park? A walk? Some shopping?" I realise instantly that he's giving me a choice. We're not in the bedroom where he commands things and takes control, we're out in the world, living and I have choices.

I shrug. "I'd like Sam to come with us," I tell him, biting my lip. He nods in reply, grabs my hands, and kisses me again.

"Good idea," he replies in a fake whisper. "She's a part of the deal with you and I can't hog you the whole time I'm here." I go to reply, but his kiss stops me and I forget what it was I was going to say.

"Do you want to go and ask her?" he enquired, his voice soft and caring.

I can only nod and he lets me go. There's something about how he holds my chin before he kisses me that has me weak at the knees and confuses my brain.

Sam is heading downstairs as I go to find her.

"What do you fancy doing? How was Hell?" I ask. I've not been there since we witnessed the accident two weeks ago.

Sam shrugs. "It was busy, but nothing you couldn't handle. We've seen it bad down there." She stands on the bottom steps and nearly towers over me. "As for what I want to do, I've had walks with Trisha and I've chilled. I'm good. I have English homework to do," she smiles and I return the gesture.

"We are going to take a walk," I have no idea where, but out of the house is a good idea. Sam nods and heads to the kitchen to grab herself a drink and snacks. She always munches when she's using her brain.

I follow her back to the kitchen and she has already explained to Nick she has homework to get done. He nods and looks at me.

"I know where we can go," I say, remembering a local nature reserve not too far from here.

"Let's go," he says and we get ready to head out for a walk.

# Twenty-Two
## Nick

I wanted Sam to come with us so that we weren't excluding her, but she assures me she's not feeling that way and will join us next time. She has homework to do and as she puts it, mum needs the attention more than she does.

Ellen drives us in her little Fiat 500 to a nature reserve next to a pub. We find a parking space and I take in the "Welcome to Saltwells" signs and the various walks that seem to be around.

I'm glad the ground is still rock hard and dry, I've only worn light trainers. Ellen smiles as we climb out. I smile at her and I take her hand as she locks the car. Soon, she's guiding me through the woodlands, around paths with wrought iron sculptures in the shape of dragons, monkeys, upside-down bats, and squirrels. There are huge metal dragonflies on the side of cliffs where something has been mined. I'm lost in this wilderness but I can hear traffic off into the distance. I can also hear the birds singing and I can see the squirrels forage the scraps people leave behind for them whilst pigeons fly around in the canopy above.

When Ellen guides me back to the car, I realise we've spent over two hours just walking, exploring, holding hands, and idling chatting. Has it really been two hours? It feels so much less than that.

"How are you feeling?" I ask her as we settle into the car. She nods.

"I feel good, thank you!" She turns to me, throws me a smile that lights up the entire car, and then she starts the engine.

"Where shall we go now?" I ask as she pulls away.

"I was thinking we need to remake the bed and work out what to have for dinner, Sam is staying with us tonight." I nod.

"That's good. I was afraid we'd have chased her away," I say. Ellen chuckles.

"She told me she wanted me to get to know you first, that there would be time for you and her to get acquainted," she air quotes with her free hand and she checks the junction again before pulling out. We're heading back and we're at lights when I sense her tense up.

"Ellen, what's wrong?" I ask and I see her check her mirror and look in her driver's wing.

"That car," she whispers. She's gone pale and she moves us forward as the lights change. I ask her to pull into a pub's car park and she does. They follow.

"Pull up and call the police Ellen," I say. "Lock the doors." Then I pop the door and jump out, heading to the car that's just followed us.

Sitting in the front of the black Mercedes SUV is the same man from the accident in Merry Hill weeks ago. I recognise the licence plate and repeat it in my head for good measure. He looks behind him and tries to reverse but there's another car now behind him and I can see his companion get animated. I can hear Ellen's driven into a free parking space but I dare not take my eyes off the men in the car. The car behind the black Mercedes beeps their horn again, long and loud.

I stand and watch as the driver now debates what to do, he puts the car into gear and swings past me, out of the car park and down the street, tyres screeching loudly.

The car that beeped him from behind pulls in and the driver gets out.

"You okay mate?" Their accent is local and I thank god.

I nod. "They followed us," I began.

"Know them, do you?" he asks. He's about the same height and size as me, slightly older as he's greying at the temples.

"Kinda. Witnessed them making someone go into the back of them a few weeks back," I look around for Ellen and I hear sirens approach from the main road.

"They followed you?" He stands and folds his arms. "That's not on," he says. We turn as the sirens stop and the flashing of blue lights swarm around us.

"Too right it ain't. No idea what they were thinking," I say. The officers get out and we each talk to an officer. I see the other guy go to his car and point to the dash cam. Moments later, he's handing over the memory card. I nod towards him and then focus on what I was telling the officer I was talking with. Another unit pulls up and two women in uniform emerge, then an unmarked car pulls up behind them. I see two plainclothes officers get out and head towards us. Ellen suddenly appears at my elbow and I pull her in close. Thank god she's okay and there with me.

The uniformed guys talk with the plainclothes one and then we're introduced to both and again, we're asked to tell them what happened. Ellen stands beside me quietly but I can feel her shivering, despite the warmth of the day. I excuse myself and head to the car, grabbing the blanket from the backseat that Ellen keeps there, folded neatly. I go back to her and wrap her up in it, then hold her close.

"You were driving Miss?" asks the officer. Ellen nods and gives them her details. I pull my phone from my pocket and bring up the crime reference number we were given when they started following her and that of the incident we witnessed. How can a small shunt, even a crash-for-cash one, create such havoc?

The officer nods and then pulls his colleague, an athletic-looking woman, into a small conference huddle. Then they switch and she confirms details with us. It feels like we've gone over this incident four or five times already and for hours, though it is probably fifteen minutes at the most.

"That marker is out," says the male plainclothes detective. The woman DCI nods.

"Marker?" I ask.

"PNCR marker, sir. Thank you both for your time," she nods to us, dismissing us. The other guy who recorded the stand-off nods too.

The two DCI's walk away, taking the marked units with them and I turn to him. Ellen's not shaking anymore. The police cars head off in different directions and we watch them go.

"Are you two okay?" he asks us.

I nod and Ellen shrugs.

"They scared me," she whispers and I pull her close, kissing her head.

"I know sweetheart," I wrap my arms around her as tight as I think she'll let me.

"I owe you a new memory card," I say, looking at our new companion. The guy shrugs his indifference.

"If it'll help bring those ratbags to justice, it's worth the small cost."

I introduce us and offer again, to buy him a replacement, or at least give him the money for it. He waves us off. "No need, honestly, I buy them in bulk," and he grins. We shake hands and then we head our separate ways. Ellen hands me the keys and I just nod, helping her into the car and then I drive us home.

## Twenty-Three
### *Ellen*

Being followed and tailgated like that scared the living daylights out of me. I'm not a confident driver at the best of times. Thank goodness Nick was there. I come to my senses to find Nick on the phone with someone, pacing in the garden. Sam is near me and watches me intently.

"Hey," I whisper, able to find my voice. Sam smiles.

"Nick was worried about you. What happened mum?" Her voice rises slightly but it's still low enough that Nick hasn't heard us talking yet. I look towards the back of the house and he's still pacing.

"That crash we witnessed? They followed us back from Saltwells, I was driving," I shiver and Sam just nods. Then she comes to crouch near me and takes my hands in hers. I should be the adult here and with that thought alone, I'm suddenly feeling bolder. I am an adult. I will deal with this and I won't back down. I can hear Shauna's light Scottish brogue in my head as I think that thought. That's certainly something she'd say if she were here. I know Shauna would have done far more than Nick did, having the skills she does.

I smile at my daughter. "Put the kettle on will you?" I ask and she nods, then rises to go do as I've asked. I uncurl myself from the chair and make my way to Nick.

He stops pacing around the patio when he sees me, his eyes light up and he smiles. Then he holds out an arm and I walk to him, letting him embrace me.

"Cheers Alex, thanks. I'll get that organised for her car." I see him nodding and I realise Alex is his brother. I've not met them yet but that isn't what catches my attention. Get what organised for my car?

He hangs up and puts the phone into his back pocket as Sam comes out with a coffee for him and herbal tea for me. She sets them down on the picnic table and vanishes off inside, leaving us alone.

"Get what, organised?" I ask as I pick up my tea.

"Dashcams," he says, picking up his coffee. "Both ends of the car. It would have helped more today. My car has them, but yours doesn't. My old uni mate in Lichfield can do it for me, he runs his own car electronics company, fixing the electrics on cars and doing car security."

I hadn't thought about having any fitted, until now. I nod. "I need to know how much," Nick shakes his head.

"Your safety is worth it. I'll take care of it." His voice offers no other path and I put my cup down, then fold my arms across my chest. Nick chuckles.

"Sweetheart, I'm not asking. All I need you to do is come over to mine and it can be done in a day. They've already followed you twice, we need more evidence to give to the Police if nothing else. I worry about you, I just want you safe."

"And I don't get a say in it?" I demand in a quiet voice.

He shakes his head. "They scared you, twice. They won't back down until they're caught and that is only a matter of time. However, in the meantime, I want everything that happens to you when you drive, recorded." I lowered my eyes when he was talking. Nick's right, they have scared me twice. I sigh, relenting.

"At least let me pay for some of it?" I offer. He shakes his head

"Liam owes me a favour, I'm calling it in," he says. I raise an eyebrow and he chuckles. "I'll tell you one day," he promises and pulls me close. I drop my arms and wrap them around him as best I can. I sigh and breathe in his scent.

"So come to mine tomorrow. Liam can do it then."

I look at him.

"Tomorrow is Sunday," I say.

Nick nods. "Liam is single, he's been spending time building his business up and I promised him a good review on his social stuff, but as I said, he owes me a favour. He can do it either tomorrow or next weekend," he pauses. "I don't like the idea of you driving around without any dash cam's on," he says. To be honest, after being followed twice, neither do I. I nod.

"Good girl," he says with a smile that seems to be combined with relief. "I'll let you lead with Sam, I'll follow behind as I have the double camera," he's being bossy but I realise, protective. For some reason, my sex clenches, and I pull my shoulders back.

"Bossy," I tell him, just loud enough for him to hear me. He growls.

"Ellen," he lifts my face to his as he takes a step back. His voice is low, controlled and his jaw is set. "This might sound out of date in this modern time, but you're mine. I protect what's mine," his jaw twitches. "That means, you, Sam, your car, everything that's yours is now mine to protect." I go to answer him but he places a finger on my lips. "I don't just sleep around sweetheart, I'm picky. I picked you and I wanted you, even before I knew you were interested. The fact that anyone thinks they can push you around, angers the fuck out of me and I won't stand for it." He leans in and claims my mouth, stepping back towards me. I can feel his erection jam into me as he holds me close.

I resist the urge to call him mine too. Is he? We've hardly been together for any length of time and the memory of Shauna's second wedding comes back to me. I snuggle in close and close my eyes. I might get brave enough soon to say the words I hear him not saying, to say the words on the edge of my tongue, but that moment isn't right now.

Nick checks his watch and he rubs my back. "We really ought to think about dinner, don't you think?" he suggests. I open my eyes and pull back from him, nodding. "Is there anywhere that's good around here? Indian or Chinese?"

I nod. "There are a few good Indian restaurants I like," I offer.

He nods. "Pick one and we'll eat out tonight, the three of us," I shiver at the suggestion. I don't want to go out, I'm safe here and I know my favourite place will deliver to me. He moves into me and pulls me close. "Or we can eat here, that works too." I simply nod in reply and mumble a thank you.

"What was that sweetheart?" he asks in a curious but gentle tone. I'm sure he heard me.

"Thank you," I state, stronger than I did before.

"You're welcome," he replies, then he lets me go and we organise what we're having from the local takeaway.

Saturday nights were made for cheesy, funny television and I'm glad Nick is here. Sam took it in her stride when I told her we'd be going to Nick's tomorrow and why. She said she needs to bring some studying with her but that's not a problem. Given her coursework load, I'm not surprised, though I will try to ensure she doesn't spend hours at it. She needs to give her mind a rest.

The curry arrives and Nick pays, despite my protests otherwise.

"You don't have to pay for everything," I admonish, knowing he's paying his friend for the dashcam installation tomorrow. He kisses me and just smirks. I go to say something else but his look changes, then it relaxes. Sam has taken the food through to the kitchen and the aroma of the food hits us shortly after she does.

"Let's just chill and relax," his voice is quiet, pleading. "I'm not keeping tabs on who pays for what or why and when," he kisses me gently. "I like spending time with you and Sam." His hazel eyes sparkle, changing colours again as he speaks.

"Okay," I nod and take the hand he offers me to guide me to the kitchen.

Sam has plated up the family mixed starter onto a large serving platter we have. The rest of the meal is in the oven on a low heat to keep it warm.

"Did you put the bread on the mesh racks?" I ask as I grab the serving utensil.

"Yep, they're at the bottom," Sam brings out cans of coke for her and I and offers Nick a choice of beers. He selects one and we sit down to eat our first meal as a possible family of three.

As we consume the wonderful food, we talk. Sam and Nick exchange information on their love of music and movies. Sam goes off about what the women wear in some of the movies, or the lack thereof and I have to remind myself that she's only a teenager, a young woman, not an experienced, jilted one such as myself.

"You just be you," he's talking to her like an adult, not a parent to a child. I wonder if I do that, or if I'm always just going to be her mum, the boss, the disciplinarian. "There's plenty of time to get intimate or dress up for a man. A real man wouldn't ask you to do something you're uncomfortable with or to lower your standards. He'd be raising them," he tells her. She's been badgering me for lingerie that's not suitable because the boys she likes at school tell her that's what girls wear. She shares that with him in a mature way.

Nick shakes his head. "They're lying. What they're asking for is a fantasy and to see how far they can push you. I was there not too long ago," he says, laughing to hide his cheeks going red or pink. "Don't fall for their tricks, I can tell you're smarter than that."

She nods confidently and I'm seeing the change before me. She's taking his advice on board as if she needed to hear a man's point of view. As he said, a real man would be raising her standards. He's setting her baseline, something I've tried to do before and I thought I had succeeded. How is it that he can come into our lives and already get through to Sam? Am I that bad a mother? I stop eating and I excuse myself for a moment, then I go to the attic room and quietly close the door.

I need a few moments to think. How can he do something in support of my daughter in a few moments that I can't? I've been there for years, he's been there and not totally, for a few weeks. I run my hands through my hair and I sit on the floor in my usual meditation position.

Suddenly, a pair of strong hands are rubbing my shoulders, my back. He's fitting himself around me, not giving me space.

"Sweetheart, what's wrong?" he's prodding, being gentle, asking. How can I tell him I'm… what? Jealous? Angry? Frustrated? All the above?

"How can you get her to listen? I've been trying for years now," I moan. He sighs.

"It comes down to biology." He sweeps my hair aside on one side so he can at least see an eye. "I can tell her what "men" think because I am one. " He rubs my back a little more which sends a warmth into me I didn't know was missing. "Not that you haven't told her what I did, but I know what teenage boys are thinking, I've been there, unsure of what to do with a pretty girl so they tease her. It's like Oscar asking me what teenage girls think about. I haven't a clue, though I can guess. You and Sam could answer that quite well, I couldn't." He pulls me into his chest and I lean against him.

"You come into our lives, knock down every defence I have like it's not there," I grip his arm. "How did you do that?"

He chuckles. "You're like me. You're ready, I guess, to not be alone. To be with someone who gets you, gives you what you need," he sighs against my head then kisses my temple. "Dinner's back in the oven, keeping warm. Come on, let's go enjoy it."

He takes my hands and leads me down. Sam's watching something on the TV. When she sees me, she mutes it and joins us back at the table. She hugs me tightly as if she's afraid to let go. I kiss her cheek and we break apart, our bond is still strong, though we're making way for Nick to be a part of it. I'm just not sure how fast I want that to happen.

We get around to watching the Saturday evening entertainment on the television and I smile as I head out to the back room and grab a book when it gets very cheesy. I'd usually be sitting in the front room, but the television would be off. I open the book where my bookmark indicates and I pay attention to the detail of it. Shauna gave it to me as a gift when we left secondary school to go to college. It's a metal sheet, embossed with Scottish thistles and a heather-coloured tassel. We each brought the others a personal gift and I smiled as I held it in my hand, remembering.

Life was uncomplicated then, so full of potential and we were so unaware of what life would bring to us. Would I have dated Mark? What about the choices we made? Would I go back on them now? I get so lost in my thoughts, I don't notice that Nick and Sam have joined me and are reading their books. It's not until I look up that I see them. I smile at Sam, she's reading the latest Felix Jones book by the local author, Julian Roderick. He's not internationally known, but his books are quite good and I got the ones we have signed at a launch last year.

Nick I see, has aimed for something far more to his taste, a James Deegan book. The SAS-style adventure I think is right up his street, though I've only one shelf suitable for him unless he decides he likes romances. Then I remember another local author, Angela Marstone, and go to pick out the first of her Kim Stone books for him.

"You'll like that, I think. It's set locally, murder mystery, police and not a kiss insight," I wink and grin at him. His eyes light up and I can just see some crow's feet as he does so. His smile melts me but I refrain from falling into his arms for a tryst and return to my seat. Coming back to the story I was reading, I curl up and get stuck in, forgetting everyone else that's now around me.

I jump when Sam comes to give me a kiss goodnight ages later. The darkness has fallen and Nick is also a good way through the book he's borrowing.

"Night kiddo," I say, letting her go. She waves goodnight to Nick, who bids her goodnight, and then she vanishes. He looks across at me and smiles.

"How are you feeling now?" he asks. I sigh and ponder.

"I'm good, calmer," he nods and marks his book with a bookmark Ruth gave me.

"Fancy a tea?" he asks, standing. I nod and uncurl myself from the chair. He holds his hand out to me and I take it, steadying myself when I rise. He leads me into the kitchen and I watch as he starts making tea. I pour myself a glass of water and drink the whole thing down in one.

"There's some roti left," he says, pointing to the small pile of leftover food. I nod and take one of the thin Indian wraps and nibble on it. Its rich, buttery, bready taste is divine and I must moan slightly as Nick's eyes widen in surprise for a moment, then he comes back to his resting, watching face. He takes the other two, folds them, and eats them quickly. I giggle.

His cheeks pink and he winks at me as one part of his mouth turns up in a sly smile and he leans across the table as the kettle comes to the boil.

"I'll make you moan like that later, just loud enough for me to hear you as I slowly make love to you." I feel my sex tighten and damn it if my nipples don't respond in kind. A wicked grin dances across his face and he moves away to make the tea. Whilst his back is turned, I shiver in anticipation and close my eyes.

"The bed," I whispered, "we didn't remake it." He stops and then nods.

"Let's go do it now," he says, leaving the tea to sit.


We've remade the bed in quick time. This is new to me, a man helping me with the chores. I smile and thank him.

"You've never had help in making up the bed again?"

I shake my head.

"Sam doesn't count, I think,". He leans over the bed, placing his fists in the middle of my king-sized bed.

"Then he was more than a total idiot," he says and in seconds, I'm in his arms on the bed, being tickled and kissed. I laugh out loud, trying to get him to stop and when I mention Sam, it seems to cool his heels a little.

He nods and smiles, then gets up off the bed and helps me pull the covers back into place. We go and drink our tea as we watch an old Buffy episode on Prime, then we head to bed.

I try not to think about how it will be with Nick next to me tonight. He's certainly been attentive, caring and my mind thinks back to what he promised earlier. He stays in his jeans and underpants as he goes to brush his teeth and use the toilet, then I go to do the same. When I get into my bedroom, he's waiting for me at the edge of the bed, the quilt folded back to allow us entry.

"I didn't know what side you preferred," he grins and holds a hand out for me. I close the door gently, place my laundry in the basket and breathe. I'm aware that Sam might still be awake, though I hope she's not. I take his hand and he pulls me to him, into his lap. I had removed my knickers in the bathroom and now his hands were exploring up from my knees, stroking my inner thigh in light, feathery circles. He groans at finding me without coverings between my legs.

"Oh, Ellen," he moans and I shiver as his fingers lightly brush my folds, tease them apart and the tips of his fingers brush against the very edge of me. He turns us and I'm suddenly underneath him, then he's receding down the bed and he winks at me wickedly as he pushes my skirt up.

"Try to be quiet sweetheart," he winks and he folds the skirt back so I can see his head, then his hot tongue is licking me, teasing, his mouth gently sucks and his hands grab my arse cheeks, holding me fully in place.

I bite my lip, trying to hold back my demands, my cries of more, my groans as one hand leaves my arse and his fingers push inside. I can't hold back my final release and I am sure Sam hears me.

Nick suddenly looms over me, kissing me and I can taste myself in his mouth. How can he like that taste? I claw at his shirt, trying to untuck it from his jeans and he stops kissing me, pulls back, and sits up, taking his shirt off. I sit up and pull at his belt, then unbutton him and pull his zip down, freeing him from the confines of his rather nice, tight black underpants and blue jeans. He jumps off the bed and shakes the jeans off. I stand and remove my skirt and just as I'm about to remove my blouse and bra, Nick is at my back.

"I want to do it, sweetheart," he mumbles into my ear, kissing his way down my neck. I let him finish undressing me, his kisses as he reveals each new part of my skin sends shivers down me. A moan or two escapes me and he quietly hushes me but grins at me as it becomes obvious, he doesn't want me to be quiet.

He vanishes for a moment to the bag he's placed by my dressing table and he pulls out a condom. Then he grins at me and lays down on the bed, motioning for me to join him.

"On top, Ellen," he mutters as he rolls the condom onto himself. I can feel my mouth drop open at his command and he guides me to sit on him.

"I want to see you as you come, sweetheart," he mutters as I slowly line myself up with him and descend upon his long dick.

"Fuck" he groans, not all that quietly, as my pubic bone meets his. "You feel so," I lift myself off him and slide back down, then I swirl my hips as I land and he throws his head back. His hands grab my hips and within moments, we have a movement going that suits us.

His hands touch me all over, fondle my breasts and his fingers tweak my nipples as I crash down.

"Play with yourself too," he groans, watching us where we're joined, one hand holding a hip. I reach down and I can feel him but I do as he asks and suddenly, I'm riding the crest of orgasm and so is Nick. I can feel my inner walls clamp down on him, but he's slender and he's still able to move in me as I go headfirst into oblivion. Moments later, both his hands are on my hips and he's holding me as he bucks up into me from below, grunting and calling out my name in a growl as he convulses.

## Twenty-Four
### Nick

I never thought having a woman on top would be as good as it just was with Ellen, she gets more intense every time. She crashes down on top of me, her form slight, limp, languid. I kiss her head, brush away her hair and utter that she was just amazing. She was. I've never bucked up into a woman before her, there's so much I could do with her that I've never done before.

My hands stroke her sides, feeling the lines of her ribs, the softness of her arse, and the curve of her hip.

"Fuck, Ellen, you're bloody perfect," I growl at her. She lifts her head and I pull her head to mine, kissing her deeply. The taste of her is my new favourite thing and I'm never going to get enough of her.

"Even with," she begins and I silence her with a kiss, then turn us over so that I'm on top, in charge, in control.

"Even with what?" I demand, stroking the side of her face. I lean down and kiss her deeply. "You're perfect, every inch of you is divine, exquisite," I kiss a breast, "perfectly formed," I kiss the other, "responsive," she squirms a little and I smile. Then I kiss the valley of her ribs down to her soft stomach and kiss around her belly button. "Divine," I mutter, loud enough for her to hear me. I bestow kisses from her pussy, to her rib cage, and then up to her mouth, laying myself in her hot, sweet, open valley.

Her eyes are open and she's smiling. "You're fucking perfect sweetheart, that I can promise you."

"If you say so," she replies in a tone that is somewhat disbelieving of my words. I move so that I'm covering her and growl into her ear.

"Do I have to fuck you so hard that you can't think of anything else but how perfect you are for me?"

She responds with a squeak and her hands push against me. I grab them, pin them above her head and kiss her again, demanding her full attention. Her legs wrap around me and she begins to buck against me, making my half-mast cock stand to attention. I haven't removed the condom yet, though I know I should but I don't want to let her go, to let her insecurities continue to take hold.

"Wait," I growl and she stops. I slink back, removing the spent condom and quickly replacing it with a fresh one. She's dropped her hands and I grab them, putting them back above her head.

"I'm going to compliment you Ellen, a lot. I'm going to tell you exactly what I think of your hot, lithe, tiny, perfect body and you," I kiss her, taking control, biting her lips, and commanding her attention. "You are going to believe that you are because of how I'm going to worship you." I am already lined up and I plough straight into her again, right to the hilt. Her eyes go wide and she mouths the word "fuck" as I take control of her mouth and begin thrusting in and out of her as hard and as fast as I can.

"You're," I say, thrusting home to punctuate every word I'm about to tell her. "A fucking Goddess. Start believing it, sweetheart." She bucks against me as she comes for the first time this round, but I'm not stopping, not until I have her blissed-out again. Her second climax hits her harder still and her inner walls clamp down on me and I hold myself back, I know I can give her more. Her third takes over as soon as the second is dying back and I lean into her ear and roar my own climax, shuddering and going stiff as my cock pulses within her.

I raise my head and find her mouth, but she's hardly responding. I pull my arms under her and turn us so she's on top, then I somehow get the cover over us and I fall asleep, still inside Ellen who is now asleep on me. Blissful and perfect.

We awake hours later, just as the dawn has struck. It's still silly o'clock, too early to actually get up. Ellen goes to move off me and I let her slide to my side, then I turn and face her.

"Morning sweetheart," I tell her in a low whisper. She smiles. "Did I sleep on you all night?"

I mumble an agreement, an "Mmm-hmm," and she squeaks. It's so darn cute.

"I didn't mean to," she says. I lift her chin and look at her.

"It was perfect," I told her. I can just see her eyes in the light. "Go back to sleep, it's too early," I watch as she decides between snuggling down or going for round three. Then I remember about the condom and I swing my legs over the edge of the bed to take it off. It rips as I do so and I hope it wasn't ripped before. Fuck, I never checked if she was on the pill or taking any other preventative contraception.

"Something wrong?" she asks, her low voice and frightful.

I discard the used jonny and bin it. "It ripped, at least I hope it ripped as I was taking it off and not while I was…" I let the sentence hang.

"Inside me?" She smiles. "I'm on the implant," she says, rubbing her arm. I reach out to feel where she's rubbed and it feels like a little bumpy line under the skin. I nod.

"Thank fuck," I mumble, reaching down to kiss her.

"You don't want kids?" she asks when I pull away.

I snuggle down to face her. "I do," I begin and her face falls, "but not yet. I've only just found you," she giggles and sighs, a smile spreading across her delicate features. Her hair is tousled and I brush it away from her face.

"Did you want any more kids?" I ask. She isn't that much older than me, five years is nothing but then, I'm not the one that's going to be giving birth to any potential children.

"I honestly haven't a clue. I did, at one point. Then Mark left and I've not really had a reason to think about it," she whispers to me in the ever brightening gloom.

"We'll think about it later, okay?" I kiss her forehead. "I need more sleep, I think you do too," and she smiles at me, nodding gently.

She turns away from me, her back to me like a little spoon and I pull her in to hold her close, my limp cock snuggled into her arse. It doesn't take either of us long to get back to sleep.

# Twenty-Five
## *Ellen*

Nick and I talked very briefly far too early in the morning. The ripped condom I hope was a result of him staying in me too long after he'd fucked my brains out.

I awoke a second time to find him spooning me, his breathing steady behind me. His cock is thankfully limp. I'm not sure that I could do with him telling me how utterly gorgeous and perfect I was a second time today. I smile and close my eyes again, remembering what he told me and how he told me. I don't see me as he sees me; to me, I'm not tall enough, my boobs are tiny and I have plain hair. But, he doesn't see that. He told me I was bloody perfect, divine, exquisite, hot. I want to believe him. Can I believe him?

Nature prods me to untangle myself from his embrace and make my way to the bathroom. I check the time, it's just after eight and I know Sam will sleep in a little more. I smile and wrap my pink floral dressing gown around me, then visit the bathroom.

I head quietly downstairs to make some coffee. I open the backdoor and let the sounds of nature flood though. The weather is getting colder, but it's still warm throughout the day. First thing in the morning though, it's chilly. It doesn't take me long to pull the door closed quietly once the coffee is brewed, I make it up how I remember Nick having it at the cafe and the motorway services, then I head back to my bedroom.

Nick is just rubbing his face awake when I enter with two steaming mugs of coffee.

"Morning," I tell him, my voice a loud whisper.

I place his coffee down on the table nearest him and he beams at me.

"Morning sweetheart," he moves the pillows so he can sit up against the headboard and I go around to my side, joining him. He holds an arm out for me and I snuggle in, still wearing my dressing gown.

"Oh, silky number," he quips and I grin. It is, for now.

"I prefer a heavy one for winter though, I get cold easily," I tell him. I'm sure he knows that anyway.

"I'll bet you're a furnace in the winter," he tells me, taking a sip of the coffee.

I shake my head. "Not really, I struggle to stay warm, being as slight as I am," I pull the quilt back over my legs and smile. This is cosy, this is… home. Is this what I've been missing all these years? Does Harek do this for Shauna? Fons for Helene? I need to check in with them all very soon.

"You've gone somewhere," Nick mumbles. I focus on him and smile.

"Just thinking about my friends," which is true. "Helene and Shauna are settled after all they've been through just trying to either find romance or make a long-distance relationship work out," I shrug. "I was just thinking that this," I motion between us, "is perfect. It's nice, it's home."

Nick grins like a child on Christmas morning, his smile going from one ear to the next, the light dancing in his amber green eyes.

"It feels good, doesn't it?" he asks. I nod and sip my coffee.


An hour later, we're dressed, the bedsheets are again in the wash and the bed has been remade. Nick won't be coming back with me tonight, which makes my insides ache a little, but we're dressed and packed for the day.

Nick takes my phone and types in an address in Lichfield.

"That's Liam's house. I'll follow behind you," he nods and kisses me lightly on the lips, then helps me get into the car. Sam is in the front seat, her usual place. A bag behind her and an audiobook in her ears. I put in my earbuds so I can hear the sat-nav, then we're on the way, Nick behind us.

The traffic to Liam's house is light and we're there in little to no time at all. A man is on the drive of a house not too dissimilar to mine and guides me onto it, his van on the road out front, advertising his business.

"You're clearly Ellen," he says, extending a hand towards me. I shake it and I try not to appear nervous when meeting new people.

"Liam, I assume?" I shake his hand gently and Nick appears at my side.

"Liam, this is Ellen. The lady I was telling you about." I wonder how spaced out I was yesterday. I know he called Alex, but when did he call Liam?

"I can see why you're keeping her a secret," he smirks at me and I blush and Nick stands up taller if that was even possible.

"How long do you need?" asks Nick, standing at my shoulder, a hand gently touching me, letting me know he's there. It grounds me.

"About three hours, but I'll need the keys," he says, holding his hand out to me and grinning. I hadn't realised I'd tucked them back into my hand. I purse my lips together and I feel my cheeks go hot.

"I'll drop it around to you, there's someone I want you to meet when I do," he tells Nick.

"Oh?" I can sense the electricity from him, clearly, this is new for him and something of a surprise.

Liam just nods. "Later, lovebirds!" he calls and he points a fob at his van, which pings and unlocks.

"Cheers bud!" calls Nick and we're whisked away to his house.

As we approach his house, I see a sleek black Mercedes sports model sitting on the drive with two occupants in it.

"Mum and dad," whispers Nick. He swallows. "I guess you get to meet the folks," he says as he turns the engine off on his car. I go wide-eyed and look at Sam, who jumped into Nick's car when I handed mine over to Liam.

"It's okay, I'm here," she whispers. I sigh, hating that I dislike myself at meeting new people. I nod.

Nick's come around to open the door for me and take my hand.

"They'll love you, don't worry," he says to me, quietly. Then he helps Sam out of the car, like the gentleman he is. It's not the fact that I'm older than Nick, it's Sam. I'm a mother, I have been a wife, and all the insecurities Mark installed in me almost make me freeze.

"Breathe," whispers Nick as he closes the door behind Sam.

He turns to his parents, who have alighted from their car. His mother has a kind smile on her face and his father is embracing Nick.

"Mum, dad, this is Ellen, the lady I've been talking about," he wraps an arm around me, possessively and then he motions to Sam.

"This is her daughter, Sam," Sam leans forward as his mum extends a hand.

"Oh, forget handshakes," she says and hugs Sam. Suddenly, I am being hugged and not by Nick. His father has his arms around me.

"So," he booms. "You're the lady that has my Nick all in a twisted knot, eh? I can see why," his voice is light but deep and his eyes shine.

"You're lovely," his mother says. "I'm Laura and this is Martin," she says, stroking the back of Nick's father.

"Let's go inside," suggests Nick, who is grinning.


Nick opens the door and lets everyone in.

"Feel free to look around Sam," he says as he steps into the kitchen and begins to open up a large Amazon box that's been left on the table.

"You've made this look really nice, Nicholas," says his mother and he winces.

"Mom, what have I said about you calling me by my given name?" He gives her a look and she just grins. She did it to wind him up and I grin.

"I don't quite know your full name," I utter amazed that my voice worked. It usually doesn't happen for a while when I meet new people.

He stops and smirks at me. "He's Nicholas Oliver Taylor," says his mother proudly. "He has his father's middle name as his first," she explains. So his father is Martin Nicholas Taylor.

The kettle whistles and Nick takes it off the boil, empties it, fills it, and puts it back on the hob. Another few minutes later and it's ready. It's not an electric kettle, it's a hob one, cream in colour that whistles when it's ready. I had no idea those things still existed. I don't recall seeing it the last time.

"The electric one broke and I got this one," he explains, flattening the box it came in in a few swift movements. I watch as his arms flex just doing that simple task and I recall how caring they could be when holding me. I smile at him, hiding the fact that my heart already knows what my head is slowly catching up with.

Nick makes everyone what they usually drink and I smile when he hands me a mug of herbal tea.

"You got some in?" I ask. He didn't the last time when I came over when I was followed to Lichfield. He nods.

"For you, anything," he quietly tells me, but it's loud enough that his mother hears.

"Let's take these through to the lounge," says his father. I can see Nick in him and his mother. Though Martin is older, he's a silver fox with hair that's about the same length as Nick's. It's swept back and his beard is like Nick's, short but now mostly salt with the sprinkling of pepper. He's handsome now, goodness knows what he was like thirty years ago when Nick was born.

We move through as Martin instructs and Sam grabs a corner seat, curling her legs up. It's her usual position of choice when she's nervous. I wink at her and she smiles. I know she'll uncurl when she gets to see what Martin and Laura are like.

I check in with myself, something I do a lot when I'm in new situations with new people. I find I'm not anxious, or fearful. Which is somewhat surprising.

"What is it you do, Ellen?" Laura looks at Nick then me. "Please tell me I got your name right, I often don't, until I've spent some time with new people."

I smile at her, seeing that her smaller nose was gifted to Nick. "You got my name right. And I work at the Central Library in Birmingham," I reply, remembering my manners. "Tell me more about Nick," I grin, handing the conversation reigns back to his mother.

Nick groans and shakes his head. "Don't, mom, please," he begs, though it's half-hearted and his lips are curling at the edges.

But, she does. She begins with stories from when he was a boy, just walking and talking and eating worms, to the somewhat unsavoury girls he and Alex brought home to meet them in their teenage years. He sounds like he was a typical teenage boy.

"Perfectly normal," I tell her at the end of her regaling. Sam is in her chair, chuckling with her eyes bright.

"And you have a lovely daughter," Laura tells me, making Sam go red in the cheeks.

"I do," I quietly admit. It's been her and I for so long, I've forgotten what it's like to be with someone regularly. I look at Nick and he winks at me, casually.

"It's not been easy, with just the two of us," I begin and Laura pats me on the hand.

"You don't have to tell us if you don't want to," she tells me. I suspect Nick may have told them, but I want to tell them too.

"I'm not sure what Nick's told you," I say.

"He told us he had a lady interest, that she had a daughter already," Laura looked at me. "He didn't tell me she was very pretty and capable though." I find myself sitting up a little straighter, a little bolder. All because of her gentle compliment. I can see where Nick gets his tenacity and gentleness from.

Her blonde hair is a contrast to Nick's and I can see why he is the darker shade of blonde, his dad must've been darker to take Laura's lighter colouring down a notch or two. His mother's smile is similar to Nick's and suddenly, I'm comfortable with these people. I notice Sam uncurls a little in her chair and it makes me happy.

We spend another hour just chatting away, idly, comparing notes and learning more about each other.

"So what do I owe the pleasure, mom?" he asks his mother.

"We haven't seen you outside of work," she begins and smiles at me. "I can see why, so we thought we'd come and drag you away to Sunday lunch," she announces. She turns to me and Sam. "You are, of course, both invited. We'd love to have you join us," she smiles and it's there, in her eyes. She's sincere and... nervous I think.

"We didn't dress to go out," I begin, hoping that they've not picked somewhere expensive or that won't let us wear jeans. Sam wears nothing else, but at least today these are clean.

"Don't worry, The Owl isn't known for an ultra dress code," replies Martin, standing. "I'll get the extra seats added, be right back," he says and removes his phone from his back pocket as he leaves the living room. I can hear his voice but I can't make out what he's saying. I look at Nick who moves across from where he is sat to where I am and he takes my hand. I relax as soon as he does so.

"We didn't mean," I begin and Nick turns to me, then kisses me gently.

"Trust me, it'll be fine" he whispers as he breaks off the kiss. I sigh and nod, then close my eyes and lean into him for a moment. His dad's voice booms out as he comes back into the living room.

"They've reserved us a table for five but it'll be half an hour later than we planned love," he says more to Laura than anyone else.

"That's fine," she replies. "It'll give us a chance to get to know each other a little better before we all eat," and she smiles.

"Shall I make more tea?" I offer. I need somewhere to breathe a little. Drinking tea and answering questions is one thing; eating a meal together in a public place with newly met people sets me on edge, though I do try to not let it show.

"I'll help," Sam pipes up, and together, we head to the kitchen, Sam having gathered the mugs. I fill the kettle and get the stove lit whilst Sam washes the mugs. For a few moments, I lean against the counter and breathe.

Nick joins us a few moments later as we're letting the tea brew in the tea-pot he had out. The coffee machine is just about finished when his arms wrap around me. He pulls me in and offers an arm out to Sam.

"Mum and dad want to get to know you both," he starts and I turn to watch him. "I've never brought anyone significant back to meet them. Okay, so they kinda ambushed us with this, but that's okay." He pulls us both close and sighs.

"We can do this," I say, loud enough for Sam to also hear. She nods.

"Sure," she says, one of her arms wrapping around me too. "We've got this."

I nod, gathering confidence from Nick and Sam, then breathe in deeply. My daughter is right and again, I can hear Shauna's voice as well as Ruth's in my head. We have this.

## Twenty-Six
### Nick

My parents suddenly turning up is a curveball I hadn't expected, neither was the sudden lunch date. Ellen leaves the room with Sam, who has taken the dirty cups to the kitchen.

"Mom," I half growl through my teeth. "What's going on?"

She sighs. "We honestly just wanted to invite you to Sunday lunch. We didn't expect your girlfriend and her daughter to be here, though they are welcome." The look on mum's face is genuine but I sense that there's something else going on.

"What else?" I prompt. I never have to get aggressive with her, I just have to be honest. "I've told you before she's painfully shy," I remind her.

"You've not called this week, not once," my mother moans at me. I sigh.

"You can call me too mom," I reminded her. I touch her hands and smile at her. "I'll go and calm Ellen down a little." I stand and glance at my father and his face holds its usual kindness. "What time is the table booked for?" I ask.

"One now," my father replies. I nod.

"Back in a moment," I say, rising and heading to the kitchen.

Ellen is leaning against the counter, her back to me and I pull her in for a hug. I hold an arm out for Sam and we talk, which galvanises Ellen.

As Sam leaves, I hold Ellen a little longer. "You don't have to go for lunch with them," I tell her. "You have the option not to go," I remember that giving a shy, introvert like her, choices helps with her processing of new situations. I really ought to send a huge thank you to Oscar for that website link.

She looks up at me. "They're your parents," she tells me. "They've been gracious enough to offer," her eyes search mine. She's really trying here, despite the fear I see in her eyes. I nod.

"They are and they did. If you're sure," I give her one more chance to back out, but she doesn't.

"I'm sure," she tells me. I nod and kiss her forehead.

"Let me text Liam," I tell her, "to let him know he has a few more hours."

*N: Parents are here. We're going to The Owl; you've got longer.*

*L: Good! I'm having… issues.*

*N: Such as?*

*L: Big hands, small car. Good job I've got an apprentice. Tell you about it later.*

*N: Okay.*

"Okay," I say, lifting my head to look at her. She's smiling gently and I can sense someone at the kitchen door. It's mum. "Liam says he's having fun because of his big hands on your small car," I stop mid-sentence as both Ellen and my mother laugh out loud, my mother snorting as she tries to stop herself. I'm about to ask what when I realise what I've said and I too, begin to chuckle. The noise brings dad and Sam to the scene. We're laughing so hard, we can't tell them why for five minutes.

When we can stop laughing, I repeat it for dad and Sam's benefit. Sam covers her ears and starts saying "la-la" over and over and heads back to the living room. My father booms out a laugh and we join in again.

By the time we're finished laughing, it's time to head off to the carvery to eat.

The meal was excellent. Dad and mum got to spend time with us all and for the first time, it didn't feel alien to have a woman by my side who, once she got over her initial shyness, joined in and communicated like a pro. The selection at the carvery was up to its usual high standard; nothing overcooked, undercooked, cold or bad and the service was excellent too.

Sam puts away as much as I do, which causes Ellen to smirk.

"High metabolism," she comments as we watch Sam devour a huge chocolate profiterole sundae to herself, whilst Ellen and I share the same.

During coffee, I get a message from Liam saying he's done and I tell Ellen.

"Why do you need them?" asks Mum.

"I keep being followed," Ellen replies before I can interject. "It's been happening since the accident we witnessed on our first date and Nick here, decided I was having them."

I nod. "I did say, I'll protect what's mine," I look at her as I speak but I can feel my parents' eyes on me.

"That's right, we do," agrees my mother, reaching out for Ellen's hand.

"Always," adds my father, emphatically.


We finish our coffee and dad pays the bill. Ellen whispers in my ear as we slowly make our way to the cars. "I want to contribute to this, your family has paid for everything today," she sounds frustrated.

"They invited us, it's not a problem," I began. Then I see the look in her eyes and an idea strikes me as I get where she's coming from. "But, dad will forget to tip the waiting staff," I hint. She gets it and kisses me on the cheek before she darts off to find the lady who waited on us throughout our meal. I see Ellen give her a healthy tip and she comes back to me, smiling. Dad gives me a quizzical look and I mouth the word "tip". He rolls his eyes and nods. Yep, he forgot again.

"Thank you," whispers Ellen as she folds herself into my arms. Sam is talking with my mum and dad is between both sets of us. This is how it should be; good times with family, building memories, being important to those who love us and who we love and care for.

Why has it taken me so long to figure that out?

I hold Ellen a little closer before we part ways, dad taking mum home in his car and me taking Ellen and Sam back to mine so that Liam can bring her car. I text him to say we'll be home in about ten minutes and that I'll have the coffee on. He replies with a simple thumbs up and in no time at all, we're back.

The coffee has just finished brewing when Liam and his apprentice arrive, though I suspect she's anything but an apprentice. The huge rock on her hand and Liam's arms around her shoulder, suggests she's far more.

"Congratulations!" I tell Liam happily. Out of the two of us, the odds were on me getting married before Liam. But I know who I want now, and she stands beside me with a grin on her face, congratulating his now-fiancee and admiring the huge rock.

Liam leans into me, lowering his voice so the girls can't hear. "Steph's a firecracker, dead handy to have around. She's got her thoughts and she enjoys a good debate." I look at the woman and see she's quite similar to Ellen in height. Steph has tattoos, short pixie hair, and is wearing Doc Martens. They're very different women.

Steph is also clearly more outgoing but they seem to be getting along well enough, which is good.

"I have got a favour to ask," he says, looking at me. I steal my face, knowing that he's about to ask one of the most important questions one close friend can ask of another. "Be my best man?" he asks.

I nod. "Sure, I'd be honoured," I reply and I get a bear hug from him.

"Great!" he says. "Now that's out of the way, let's show your girl what we've managed to do, and it was a bitch."

Steph has already grabbed Ellen's hand and guided her to her car. She talks Ellen through all the cabling that they had to do, the tight spaces in the engine compartment, then Steph asks Ellen one question.

"Can you see where the rear one is?" she asks. "That was a proper smeghead." As brash and as direct as Steph is, her Red Dwarf references just made me like her a heck of a lot more.

I watch as Ellen looks around her tiny 3-door Fiat 500 and I can't see where it is either. Then I spot it but Ellen doesn't. I smile and point to the licence plate and it takes her a good few moments more before she spots it where the licence plate light used to be, and it's doubling up as the licence light and the camera.

"Wow!" she guffs.

"If she didn't see it easily, others might not either," Liam comments loud enough for Ellen to hear. She turns and smiles.

"Sneaky," she quips and Steph starts showing her how it all works. Sam pays attention too and being honest, it's straightforward. It starts when the engine does, the camera controls are on the facia for the rearview mirror, which is where the front one is. There's a button to press if she wants to save any recordings whilst they're driving and it's not a small button either.

"You've done a fabulous job mate," I comment to Liam as we head in to sort the drinks. I know Ellen won't drink any more coffee, so I make her a herbal tea. Liam turns his nose up at it.

"For Ellen," I say, pouring out the three black coffee's. I watch as he heads to the fridge to grab some milk and he pours a healthy amount into one of the mugs.

"For Steph," he says, winking. I grin in reply.

"So, she is the one?" he asks whilst we have a few quiet moments. I nod.

"It's come-on fast, but when I'm with her, I feel…"

"Contended" Liam offers. I nod.

"Unbelievably so," I confirm. "Like I'm home no matter where I am with her," we turn at a sound and Sam appears at the door. Her cheeks are pink and I know she heard us.

"Shall I take these out?" she offers. I nod, thanking her.

Liam gives me a "whew" look but I'm not certain it was a near miss. I know Sam would have heard me but I haven't a problem with that. I haven't told Ellen yet. I need to, but only when I know she's even reading the same book I am.

"How'd you meet?" I ask him. He tells me he fixed some weird electronic cabling on her car and they got chatting, met up for drinks and they've been together since. He asks me about meeting Ellen and I'm telling it as all three girls walk in.

"My butt was still hurting the next day," moans Sam. I grin at her but there's a smile on her lips and in her eyes. "I won't let him forget it," she tells me.

"Liam, thank you so much," Ellen gushes and comes to snuggle into me. "It's so simple to use and not a cable in sight!" she beams and my heart swells. I so want more of that, with the benefits of her being with me every night. Or more than we're getting right now.

"Not a problem," he tells her, pulling Steph in close. "We had fun but I couldn't have done it without Steph here, some of those gaps…" he says and I chuckle, remembering his message and my bad repeating of it. Ellen laughs too, shouldering me gently, reminding me.

"We need to be going back, I'm afraid," moans Ellen. I find it hard to believe that it's early evening, but it is. I know it takes at least an hour for Ellen to return home, but I'll be slightly less nervous now about her driving back with Sam.

"We need to be off too, catch ya later Nick, and thanks mate," he says.

"Not a problem and thank you," I reply, feeling grateful he has the skills I needed for sorting Ellen's car.

Liam and Steph head off, which gives me a few moments to say goodbye to Ellen and Sam. Sam is curled up on a chair now, her English book in her lap. I watch as she reads the words using her little finger. Ellen taps me on the arm and motions for me to follow. I do.

"Do you know she uses her finger?" I ask. Ellen nods.

"Her eyes jump lines if she doesn't trace, it's normal," she says. I blink.

"She didn't the other day…" I begin, which makes Ellen smile.

"She needs to do that with the textbooks, as she reads them slower to absorb their teaching. With fiction, she doesn't have that problem. In fiction, you can skip a paragraph and it'll still make sense, but it could be that important, revealing paragraph you happen to skip in texts, so she slows down and needs to trace." Ellen's voice is a matter of fact, quiet but determined. What she says makes sense and Sam is old enough to know how her brain works.

"It's strange to me, that's all," I say, backing down a little.

Ellen nods. "It was to us at first too, but that's how she needs to read the textbooks," she shimmies up to me, "But that's not why I dragged you back here," she licks her lips, and then she's pushing herself up onto her toes to kiss me. I bend down and meet her halfway, claiming her warm, small mouth.

My tongue pushes against her mouth and she opens up, our tongues dancing, a hand in her wavy hair and one on her hip. I feel her fingers dig into my biceps and I hold her steady. Eventually, we slow and if Sam wasn't here, I'd be taking her upstairs. God, the woman can kiss and my jeans are very uncomfortable now.

She sighs as I kiss her forehead and pull her to me for a hug. I want to tell her that I love her already, but I hold back and close my eyes, enjoying the feeling of her against me.

"Let me know you're home and safe?" I ask as she pulls away from me. She nods.

"Thank you, for the cameras," she smiles at me and I bend down for another kiss.

She pulls away after a moment and I know I have to let her go. She calls out for Sam, who is with us in short order, her book closed and the marker showing, her backpack slung over a shoulder. I walk them out to their car and help both inside, then I watch as Ellen drives away from mine for the second time. I look forward to the day when we don't have to do this.

# Twenty-Seven
## Ellen

I hold it together until we're out of sight of Nicks, then I pull into that same petrol station and Sam hands me a tissue.

"He's in love with you mum," she tells me. I dry my eyes and look across at her.

"Is he?" I look in my rearview mirror and I know I've left a piece of my heart there.

"Yep. He told that Liam guy that he feels at home with you," she shifts and faces forward. "Content. If that's not love, I really haven't a clue what is," I dry my eyes with a second paper tissue and breathe deeply a few times.

I can't tell her how I feel about him. Can I?

"I feel the same," I tell her.

"I guessed that. Otherwise, you wouldn't be sitting on a petrol station forecourt, crying." She pats me on my knee "Come on mum, let's get home."

I nod and continue the journey home.

On the way home, I check the camera a few times, but there's nothing in my mirrors or in front of me that I need to record. I concentrate on the drive when I get to the A38 and then onto the M6. I relax the further I go, knowing that if anything happens, there is going to be evidence of it.

The motorway flows and we're back home in just under an hour, even with my stop-off point at the start. I'm still processing what that means when Ruth sends me an SOS text. She's coming over. I send her a thumbs up and warn Sam, who has just taken her books upstairs. Then I quickly text Nick to say we're home, thanking him for the dash cam's again and that Ruth is visiting.

"Do you want anything to eat?" I ask Sam as I put the kettle on. She pulls down three mugs to help. She always takes a tea and crisps up to snack on whilst she studies.

"Just the tea, thanks, mum." She turns to look at me and I sigh heavily. "You like him?" she asks me

I nod. What else can I say? I do.

"I know he likes you. I thought he was going to tell Liam he loved you, and maybe he does," she sees me going to interject but she rattles on past it, not giving me a chance to add to it. "You should follow your heart mum, you didn't want to leave. I'd have been happy staying there overnight, a weekend is okay too. I like him, he is funny," she giggles at the memory of earlier. "He's also attentive to your moods, your needs," she hugs me as the kettle finishes boiling and I go to make the tea.

"See what Ruth has to say," she says, grabbing a packet of crisps from the cupboard and she finishes making her tea the way she likes it. Then, she kisses me on the cheek and she vanishes off upstairs with her tea and snacks in hand.

Ruth appears through the front door shortly after. I left it unlocked, knowing she was on her way over. After bringing in the tea and a selection of biscuits, I sit in my favourite chair in the living room as Ruth switches between pacing and wringing her hands out. Usually, that's my tell.

I sit back and wait, knowing she'd do that for me. After about five minutes though, I can't stand it. "Roo, what's happened?" I ask her, gently. She throws herself onto the sofa, buries her head into her hands, and begins to sob. I move across to her, switching between hugging her and rubbing her back.

"I've fallen for him, Len. We agreed at the start that we wouldn't, but if we did, we were to speak up." I place a box of tissues before her on the table and sit next to her, rubbing her back as she wipes her eyes and blows her nose. On the fifth tissue, I get up and grab the small bin, then bring that to her too.

She finally gets herself together enough to tell me about the agreement she and Daniel made. If either developed feelings for the other, they were to speak up. Ruth is afraid she'll lose him if she does.

"If he can't figure out what a great woman you are," I tell her as I finally get the chance to pass her the tea, "then that's his issue." I sip my tea. "When you tell him you've got feelings for him, he either has to man up or sit down so you can see the man behind. I've seen him on Insta," I tell her as she turns to look at me, her eyes red and swollen.

"It was a good chase," she tells me.

Oh.

No.

I know what she's doing. She's deciding and that's it, poor Daniel won't get a say, even if she is what he wants, she's locking her heart away and there's nothing I can do to stop her.

"Ruth, don't do it that way," I plead. "You need to talk with him," I pleaded with her. "He might feel the same way but perhaps he just can't tell you."

She looks at me and shakes her head. "He was clear that he broke up with his ex, that's why he was in Brum that night; downing a few to say goodbye to her, get *her* out of his system. I've met her, we've foster kids in the system with better attitudes and manners than she displayed." Ruth shivers and finishes up her tea, then snaffles a shortbread finger and devours it in seconds.

"I'm the rebound girl, Len. Again." She stands and I can see she's getting angry now, her temper kicking in. I'm just glad that it's not Shauna pacing before me, her temper is worse and more volatile. "I'm not being the rebound girl," she turns to glare at me. "I am not," she tells me. I can only nod, remembering that Dirk was not the first time she'd been the rebound girl.

"You don't deserve to be," I tell her as confidently as I can, feeling for her.

"You're right, I don't!" She's getting fired up now. "I do deserve so much better." She stops pacing and turns to the mirror.

"I'm going to talk with him," she tells me and I jump up to hug her before she runs out of my home. She hugs me, then makes use of my bathroom to freshen up and reapply her makeup. When she comes out, she still looks like she's been crying but she has her fight back.

We hug and she leaves, then I crash on the sofa, exhausted.

I use the chat group to wish her good luck, which brings replies of :

*H: Why does Roo need luck?*

*E: She's going to see Daniel and tell him how she feels about him.*

*S: He'd better listen...*

*E: I agree! She deserves to not be the rebound girl.*

*H: Good luck Roo!*

Shauna sends through four blowing kisses, tagging Ruth. The rest of us do the same. There's nothing more I can do for Ruth now but wait.


It's nearly midnight when Ruth sends the group a simple text:

*R: Not the rebound girl anymore. I'm not anything.*

Following that small proclamation are half a dozen broke heart emojis and my heart sinks for her. Shauna replies in an instant.

*S: Then he's an ejit! I'm going to bat for you...*

We can see Shauna is typing, but it's not to our group. Oh no! Shauna's tearing Daniel a new one via WhatsApp? At midnight?? She wouldn't... But I know she has.

*R: Shaunie, please don't! We've said what we needed to, please don't...*

*S: Too late. I'm not having my friend upset and not saying something. I'm hormonal, the twins are giving me gyp and I'm awake, walking them around Rosen so I can maybe sleep at some bloody point. He's getting the bad end of me tonight.*

I smile. Even pregnant, Shauna's a force to be reckoned with.

*R: You're having twins?!*

*H: When did you find out?*

*E: Congratulations!*

*S: Earlier today. Not sure of the genders, not sure I want to know this time. Harek hasn't decided if he wants to find out as we have a girl already and the boys, so...*

"Double trouble," I whisper into the darkness.

*S: Mum and dad and his parents, our sibs are all ecstatic! It's just... taking a little time to digest in my head.*

*E: I'll bet! I'll send YOU something this week, please do try to relax*

I'm usually the peacemaker, the calm one.

*R: I'll be okay, girls. Thanks! Heading to bed to try and sleep. I think I'll book tomorrow off if I have a bad night*

I've known Ruth to work through a stinking hangover from hell, so she must be feeling terrible if she's taking a day off.

*E: Here if you need me!*

Ruth sends back a thumbs up, then the chat goes quiet.

## Twenty-Eight
### Nick

I get a message from Ellen, telling me she's home but she's got her friend coming over unexpectedly. I send a quick message back, telling her I'm glad she's home and safe. Then I text the guys.

> *Nick: You guys up for a beer? The first round is on me*

Liam replies first. *Not tonight, busy…*

I can guess in what way, since he's now engaged. I didn't ask if Steph had moved in, I can only assume she has, or about to.

Phil takes his time to reply, but eventually, he does. Being a postman, he's probably heading to bed.

> *P: Not now, could have earlier though. Work tomorrow.*

I curse. I need a guys' night out with someone I can talk with. The other two on the list, Jonathan and Chris, hardly ever respond, although we'd help each other out if they needed it.

> *J: I can. Red Lion, half an hour? Not staying for long, but a swift pint would be ace!*
>
> *C: I can't, sorry. Mrs will kill me if I go out tonight too.*
>
> *N: Mrs? You're married now?*
>
> *C: No, but starting to feel like it! Next weekend?*
>
> *N: Will have to see, that's why I want to meet up.*
>
> *L: You know what I think already mate.*
>
> *N: Yeah, I do. Thanks for today!*
>
> *L: You're welcome!*

I quickly pull on some shoes, grab a jacket and my wallet, then I head to the Red Lion to meet with Jon.

Jon is outside, waiting for me and it doesn't take us long to get our drinks and find a quiet corner in the courtyard.

"So, what's occurring?" he asks as he downs half of the pint that's before him. I don't down quite as much but I go into the brief points about Ellen and the situation.

"I want it all, but this is moving fast, even for me."

Jon nods and sups some of his ale. "I reckon you need to talk to her about it mate. What do you want though?"

I pause. "Her."

"She comes with a kid," Jon reminds me. I nod.

"Yep, Sam's nice, smart too." Jon nods.

"So, what are you waiting for?"

I sigh. "Ellen's... super shy. If I tell her how I feel, she might run."

Jon chuckles. "So, you chase her down. Or," he says, taking another swallow of his beer to finish it off. "You start telling her how you feel, slowly. Drop semi subtle hints, or start telling her that you love it when you two... spend time together, go out together, stay in..." He looks at me and winks. "You just need to be honest. Women can smell a lie at one hundred paces Nikky," Jon pats me on the back and moves off. "I fancy another if you're up for it?" he asks and I nod.

He comes back a few moments later with another two and we talk some more, mostly about women in general and how confusing they can be.

"So if you know so much about women, why aren't you married?" I ask him, reminding him he's more lonely than I was.

"I haven't found the one I want to annoy, fuck and be the mother of my kids yet," he tells me, quite simply. "But, I do enjoy looking!" He grins at me and sips his pint, slower this time. We're idling chatting away and he steps to the side and swears.

"Shit," he rubs a hand over his face. "Don't look now, but Bobbie has just walked in." I don't turn around but I can tell by his sudden put-on smile, she's right behind me.

"Nick, how lovely to see you," she chirps. She drapes her hand over my shoulder and I shrug it off.

"I'd say it was nice to see you Bobbie, but it's not." The half drank pint before me has now lost its appeal and I push it away. Jon finishes his and cocks his head, suggesting we leave.

"That's not nice Nick," she states. I look at her and I feel nothing for her taller figure, bigger but fake boobs, and flat stomach and I cringe at what she's wearing. She's got nothing on Ellen. Ellen is genuine, warm, caring. Bobbie was never any of those characteristics.

"Truth hurts," I say, nodding to Jon. He nods back, we're leaving but I have something I want to get off my chest first. "You walked away. You," I make sure Jon can at least hear me, I can feel that he's at my back and I feel the eyes of others around me, on us. "screwed around with someone else behind my back for months. Don't come near me again," I state.

"He's being pretty clear Bobs," and I can see her throw him a look that could kill.

"And that's another reason we're not together," I add. "You hate everyone that isn't what you want them to be."

"I do not," she begins, but I hold my hand up.

"You do. You have. You're shallow, you're fake and you're damn hard work." She backs away, recoils. The anger I have long since felt at her betrayal and having found Ellen, knowing that she's genuine and the woman before me is not, makes this last comment to her delightful.

"I'm not being cruel, I'm being honest. Something I should have been with you from the get-go. You hurt me. You don't get a second chance." I nod again to Jon and we leave her standing there in whatever she has managed to drag onto herself. It's certainly not flattering.

We leave the quickest way possible and we walk towards mine. Jon lives the other way but I offer him a coffee.

"Naw, you're okay. Shit wasn't expecting her to turn up. Thought you'd said your piece to her a year ago?"

"I thought I had too, but since I've met Ellen, I know now she's all I'll ever want."

Jon nods. "Then, start telling her that. Every damn day," he sounds remorseful.

"Something you're not telling me mate?" I ask him. He shakes his head.

"Nothing I wanna go into right now. Just, take the advice Nick, yeah?" He slaps me on the shoulder, then turns and starts to walk home.

"Night Jon!" I called out. He waves a hand in acknowledgment, then stuffs it into his jacket and he carries on stalking away. I make a note to check on him in a few days, then I head into the house.

When I've settled onto the sofa with a coffee, I work out a text to send Ellen. It's past midnight now; so do I send it now, or do I wait? I didn't tell her how I felt yesterday, so I will today. Now. If she doesn't respond right away, that's fine, it's quite late.

*N: I loved spending time with you this weekend. Can't wait for next. Let me know what you would like to do. Talk soon!*

I put the phone down and I sip some coffee. The caffeine won't keep me awake, but the six hours of sleep might mess me around for tomorrow. It pings and I'm wondering who, then I see it's Ellen. She's still up?

*E: I did too. Just heading to bed. We can talk about it tomorrow, after work? Good night Nick.*

My heart skips a beat and I smile. It's the first time she's said good night to me via text. I finish my coffee, tidy up, and head to bed, dreaming of her in my arms on a more permanent basis.

# Twenty-Nine
## *Ellen*

The text last night was unexpected and after Ruth's revelation that she and Daniel are no longer together, though we still don't know more than that, I had to tell him how I felt. I get more determined to ensure that Nick doesn't slip through my fingers because of my fears and insecurities.

We've been together two weekends and he's asking for a third. I need to get braver and I know that comes with getting to know him better and more deeply than I do right now. I know how he likes to be physically loved, I'm learning new ways for us both every time. Then I remember the snuggles, the kissing, the touching, the hugging.

All the ways he's shown me he cares, how I've been blissed-out, then become aware of myself again during these moments and I've not felt abandoned, neglected. Him fetching me coffee in the mornings is a part of it. I feel a lot better knowing that he's establishing a trust with me. Then I realised something. Nick needs this connection, this trust he's building, he's asking me to trust him, to believe in him. Has he been hurt before? He's not said; I quickly sent him a text.

*E: looking forward to chatting with you tonight.*

His reply is instant.

*N: Not as much as I am! What are your weekend plans? Have a think, we can discuss tonight. I have to work, but will text when I'm free during lunch; if I can manage it!*

There it is again. He's asking, he's giving me time to think. He's trusting, he's setting boundaries, expectations. I love that about him and it's so different from my ex-husband.

I ponder and then lose myself in my personal Instagram accounts until I reach my stop. My brain catches up with what my heart already knows: he will be there for me. I smirk as the Friends theme tune pops into my head and I'm humming it as I enter work, with a smile on my face and a spring in my step.

"Morning perky!" Lisa sings out at me as I bounce into the staff room. I grin at her.

"Oh, you got some at the weekend, huh?" she coo's at me. I grin and blush. "You did! Lucky girl!" She goes to hi-five me and I join in, giggling like a schoolgirl.

"Details!" she demands, sitting at the table like she's interviewing me. I shake my head.

"No… but he's good," I drool. Her eyes go wide and she grins at me.

"You lucky git," she says, grinning broadly. "Enjoy! Not many decent men around these days," she adds. I nod, I know.

We each grab a hot drink and start the day. It's getting cooler now that we're in late September. Another three weeks and we'll be on half term. I need to make arrangements to go see my parents and I make a note on my phone of what I need to talk with them about. I want to introduce them to Nick, tell them all about him. I lock my phone into the desk and head off for the staff meeting, then we're let loose on the floor. Again, I have the Instagram account to update and I head outside to photograph the library in the late September sunshine.

My day goes by quickly. A few local authors I know come in to borrow books in their genre or from the history section, research purposes I guess. Before I know it, it's lunchtime and I check my phone. There's no reply from Nick today, not yet.

I eat a light lunch of a chicken salad and some fruit since I count breakfast as my first coffee. The barista holds out my usual herbal tea as I approach and I throw her a huge smile. As I'm heading back up to my floor, a voice I recognise is calling out my name, a voice I know I shouldn't be hearing, makes me stop dead.

"Shauna?!" I go wide-eyed as one of my best friends makes her way over to me. Already, her pregnancy bump is noticeable, far more than it was the last time. We reach each other at the same time and we embrace.

"What on Earth are you doing here?" I demand of her.

"I had to come to check on Roo. And see Dan," I gape. Shauna's doing more than just ripping him a new one.

"Is that wise?" I ask her. With Shauna, because of the length of time we've known each other, I can speak my mind.

Shauna shrugs. "Harek and Johan have the kids for a few days. I go back tomorrow on the afternoon tide. Being up at three to come across makes for a very quick drive from Hull," she grins at me, her accent has changed I noticed.

"I was hoping to catch you for lunch, but I think I've missed you?" she's asking. I nod.

"Sorry," I offer. She nods.

"How about tonight? I'm famished, but being pregnant with twins means lots of small meals often," she rubs her already extended stomach and grins.

"I'd love to. Indian?" I suggest. She nods. "You go eat, there's the cafe on the ground floor and they do a lovely salad," I suggest. She grins but rolls her eyes.

"More rabbit food," she scoffs. I go wide-eyed. "Harek's being a little more… attentive this time around," she rubs her bump again. Twins, of course he's cautious. "He doesn't get that sometimes, I just want the fatty, greasy, fry ups or the unhealthy stuff. So I'm pigging out here a little. I know I won't get it when I go back!" she giggles and winks at me.

"What time tonight?" she asks as we start to head off in different directions.

"Seven?" I suggest. She nods, then she comes and kisses me on the cheek, sighs into my hair as we hug and I feel that she's missed us. She's closer to Helene in Rotterdam, but with them both having young ones now, they can't be seeing each other as often as they'd like I'm sure.

"Seven," she confirms and we part ways. I grin as I walk back to the station I am at for the rest of the afternoon. I grab my phone and text Nick that one of my oldest, closest, and best friends has popped across from Rotterdam and I'd like him to meet her.

*N: The scary one that is a badass? Your words! I'd love to. Board meeting still ongoing, stopped for lunch. What time and where do I need to be? Might come straight from work, apologies if I do.*

*E: You can start leaving things at mine, if it will help?*

*N: I was going to suggest that tonight! You've read my mind.*

*E: You know what they say; great minds and all that!*

The fact that he was thinking what I was just thinking, shows we're at least on the same floor of the same library in the same town. I sigh happily and text him back the name and location of our usual Indian restaurant.

*N: I've got it. I'll be there as soon as I can get out of here. Take care sweetheart.*

The end of his text shows a pink heart. Pink. I blush, purse my lips and lock away my phone, my head buzzing.


At the end of the day, Shauna is at the staff exit of the library waiting next to the huge Q7 we know Harek purchased for her when her car blew up.

"Need a lift?" she grins at me. I smirk back, knowing that this was intentional. My phone pings and it's from Nick.

*N: Leaving now. Bringing a fresh shirt. Can I shower at yours?*

*E: Of course! There will be a Q7 on the drive. I'll leave the front door unlocked for you.*

*N: Perfect! I'll see you soon sweetheart.*

I look at my watch, it's just after half five. Nick might not make it on time for seven and I mentioned it to Shauna.

"That's okay. The restaurant isn't open until six, so we can't book it right now even if we wanted to. We can always just turn up when everyone is ready. What will Sammy have?"

Shauna assumes Sammy will come with us. "I have no idea if she wants to come," I say.

Shauna scoffs a little. "She's not going to miss out on curry, is she?!" Shauna looks across at me as we sit in traffic. She's driving and despite the fact she now drives on the other side of the road, she's handling the Q7 and the traffic as she always has. Like a pro.

"I don't know, I've invited Nick," I say. "She's been giving us space to get to know each other," Shauna nods.

"Always been empathic, that daughter of yours. Well, she's welcome to join us, and Harek's paying, so…" Shauna throws me a wicked grin and I laugh.

"What else have you had to tell him off for buying you?" I ask. Harek's wealthy and very able to take care of Shauna and her entire family and then some.

"Nothing else, he likes his bedroom rites," she's watching the traffic but I can hear the grin in her voice. As rich as Harek is, Shauna was able to give him the one thing he had always wanted. Children. He's protective, that much I do know, but he's charming with it.

"I'll bet he does," I reply.

"So, tell me more about Nick," she asks. And I do. It takes us the thirty-five minutes of travelling home to tell her everything, including the trust he's building and the blissed-out state I've found myself in a few times.

She only nods. "Harek's sent me there a few times, going by what you're saying. It's intense when he gets animalistic like that, though he's far gentler at the moment," she rubs her bump and I can guess why he's much gentler.

"So it's not just Nick that can…" I struggle to form the words.

"Fuck a woman's brains out, properly? Hell, no… I'm sure I've sent Harek there too. Or at least made him see stars. That much," she parks the car up and turns to look at me. "He has told me. Especially at the start. We'll have to wait for a while until these two are a few months old," she grins and rubs her tummy again, then omphs as she climbs out of the car.

We head in and Sammy's already home. She's ecstatic to see Shauna and they hug, Shauna asks her about school and homework, boys and potential boyfriends. Sam shakes her head.

"We're heading out for dinner," I tell her. "Curry. Shauna's paying," I tell her.

Sam nods. "Great! I had PE today, so I'm starving!" Shauna grins at her comment.

"You're as bad as Mickey," she says. "I'm surprised he's not eaten Mune Rosen some of the time, he seems to eat everything else! I'm also glad it's not made of gingerbread," she winks at me but grins at Sam, who laughs.

We hear a car pull up and a door slam, then another door is shut. I hear footsteps just outside the front door and then Nick appears, carrying his clean shirt and jacket.

"Hey sweetheart," he says, ignoring anyone but me until he's kissed me. I don't hear the top stair creek and Shauna doesn't interrupt. "Hell I've missed you," he breathes at me when we break apart. It's loud enough that Shauna chooses to make a noise.

"Ah, sorry, forgot you had company," he says, blushing and stepping to my side.

"That's quite all right," replies Shauna, extending her hand out. "My friend here deserves what you're offering, be good to her, aye?" Nick takes Shauna's extended hand and despite Shauna being several months pregnant and inches shorter than him, I can tell she's giving Nick a very firm handshake. He stands taller as their hands fall apart.

"I have every intention of doing that, and more," he states. Shauna just nods confidently.

"Good to hear. I need a drink of water," she smiles at me as she waddles past us and Nick lets out a small sigh.

"Scary," Nick whispers at me when she's out of earshot.

"Protective, just like Harek," I whisper back. "Go, shower, you know where it all is," I tell him with a smile on my face. He nods, kisses me again quickly, then heads off upstairs.

"He's a good one," Shauna tells me as soon as I enter the kitchen. She's placed two of the cushions on the chair and she's not sitting on it straight.

"Are you okay?" I ask her. She nods.

"They're wiggling around, wee tykes," she says.

"But, yes, Nick is great," I reply. Shauna chuckles.

"Hey, Belle," she chuckles. "He's no beast but that rose is wilting away. When are you going to admit it to him?" she asks, sipping a tall glass of iced water. It's not that warm and I feel for Shauna.

"When I'm sure he's on the same page," I tell her.

Shauna snorts.

"Honey, you're both on the same paragraph, same page of the same book in the same damn library. Trust me," she winks at me and I can hear Nick make his way to my bedroom from the bathroom.

"Are we?" I ask her, quietly. She nods.

"Same everything Len," she holds out her hand as I sit down with her. "Go for it," she squeezes my hand. "I didn't think I'd find what I have after Matt died. Hell, Harek didn't think he'd get what he was looking for either. Now look at us," she rubs her bump. "He's got one daughter, two adopted sons, and another two on the way." She sips her water, then lowers her voice.

"We're busy, we're tired but we wouldn't have it any other way," she smiles at me. "We took a chance that night at Helene's wedding and it paid off. Grab this one, please?"

I nod. "I intend to," I say, perhaps a little louder than I intended to. I go to hug my pregnant friend and the creek of the second to bottom stair reaches our ears. Shauna winks at me and Nick appears with Sam at his back.

"We're ready," he announces and he comes to us both, helping Shauna up off the chair. "I can drive," he offers. Shauna shakes her head.

"I'll drive. I can't drink anyway, I have to drive back to Hull for the afternoon tide. Harek will drag me back himself if I don't make that tidal crossing," she chuckles and rubs her bump at the same time and I know he probably would, even though his catamaran is probably docked in Hull. It would go back to fetch him if he ordered the captain to.

"You do worry him," I offer. She shrugs.

"He knew from the outset I was never going to do as I'm told, especially when I've set my mind to things. Providing I don't hurt myself doing it, he's okay. Though, the last time, it cost him a nanny and a girl-friday for me. Though, I think Bryce got the better end of the deal," she chuckles. Nick has a confused look on his face and on the way to the restaurant, Shauna explains about having a funny turn when she was up a ladder putting some shopping away because she didn't want any additional help. He nods as she explains how Tanja got to be employed by them and that she's now engaged to Bryce, her younger brother who is living not far away.

"Wow. What a connection," he breathes. We talk about her boys, Sam asking questions about Michael and Andrew. At dinner, Shauna shows Sam how the boys look, photographs that were taken a few days before. Aisla looks so cute in her little dresses and Shauna laughs.

"She found a mud puddle the morning after we took that photo. We'd put her in that dress again. It's ruined, we can't get the mud out," we tuck into the stack of poppadoms that have been placed on the table. "She's a wee terror, copies the boys. She wanted her own gaming controller, so Harek brought her one, in pink. It's not connected to the console yet, but she plays with it when the boys are on their games. She's their permanent shadow and I think they're glad to go to school a lot of the time."

She regales us with the kids' achievements, praises Sam for hers, and listens to Nick about all his activities. She updates us on what happened with Harek's ex and her sentence, we hear about Cait's wedding and when we're back at mine, Sam heads up to finish some homework she needs for tomorrow before bed.

I nod and we settle in the living room.

"How's Ruth?" I ask Shauna's sighs.

"She's hurting. Dan's hurting just as much, though he's being a stubborn arse about it," she shakes her head. "He's almost a Netherlander in that regard; or a Scot. Not sure which one wins with him, I'm sure he's Swedish blood in his family line. But, until he works out what he wants, who he wants, they're going nowhere. At least I know Ruth's okay and not going to do something silly."

I nod. "Would she?! I should have gone over," I say. Nick grabs my hand, squeezing it gently. "You still could, but perhaps at a more sociable hour," he suggests and glances at the clock. It's later than I thought. I nod.

"Yes, that would be wiser," I agree.

"Speaking of a more sociable hour, I better head back. I'm spending tomorrow morning with mum and dad before I go back," she says, rising from the chair.

"Are you going to be okay?" I ask. Shauna nods.

"Yeah, I'm going back to Bryce's. Tanja's done a heck of a job with the place as well as doing her Uni course. I have a comfy bed, and she'll wait on me hand and foot." Shauna grins and then hugs me tightly.

Shauna pulls out a business card and hands it to Nick. "In case you ever need me too," she says. Shauna's acceptance of him warms my heart and he tucks it away into a back pocket. We stand on the step and watch as she drives away into the night.

"I should go too," Nick says, his voice heavy as we close the door.

I turn to him and smile, locking it. "You don't need to," I say. I wasn't able to jump him earlier, but seeing him in a tailored suit, fresh shirt with the sleeves rolled up showing his forearms, his collar open, is hot. "Leave in the morning," I suggest, a coy smile on my lips. He pulls me to him and kisses me deeply. Our tongues dance and he tastes of the curry, and the one beer he indulged in.

"Bed," he whispers to me.

"Need to lock up," I reply and we do so, quickly.

It doesn't take us long to get ready for bed, that is, getting naked and under the covers. Nick is half spooning me, his cock nestled between the cheeks of my arse and I wiggle against him. He growls in my ear and nibbles it.

"I don't want to frighten you," he whispers, "But this, right now," he kisses my ear, "is perfect. I want it all the time." I turn over to face him.

"Same here," I confess. "But Sam has to finish school, I can't just get up and move." He kisses me and our tongues dance a little.

"I know, she's a priority. The commute daily would kill me too, so, how about a compromise?" I look at him in the darkness and I can't see a damn thing.

"Go on," I reply, gently, twirling a finger in his light fuzz of chest hair.

"We do as we have been, but half the time I'm here, the other half I'm back in Lichfield. We work out where we want to live, together, when she's passed her exams. You come over some weekends, I come here some weekends."

"Oh Nick," I breathe and reach up to his face, rubbing my hands against his stubble. "I'd love that," he kisses me and rolls me onto my back. "That will be about eighteen more months though," I remind him as he nestles between my legs. His cock knows where it wants to go and I can feel that my core already wants to welcome him.

"Condom," he whispers and I pull him back.

"You're clean?" I ask him.

"Yes," he whispers.

"We don't need them then," I tell him.

"And that thing works?" he asks me, stroking where the implant is.

"Yes," I whisper. My period was short and quick this time, lasting only a few days last week.

In a second, he's in me balls deep, bare and so delicious. I groan and he kisses me, absorbing it. He breaks the kiss as he slowly begins thrusting in and out of me.

"Jeez, Ellen, you feel so amazing!" he growls into my ear. I wrap my legs around him, my arms around his neck and as he kisses me, he slowly makes love with me and I to him. The pressure in me builds at a delicious rate and he moves my legs so that they're upon his shoulders. His hands pinch my nipples and I have to bite my lip to keep my screams quiet so we don't disturb Sam.

His V is hitting my clit and the angle he has me at is hitting me right where I need it. I feel the tension building and I whisper that I'm coming. His thrusts get more intense, frequent and I arch against him as the first one hits. He rides me to the second one and the third, then stops. He pulls out of me and turns me, then he lifts me, runs a finger through my wet sex, and thrusts into me from behind. Whilst he's doing that, the finger that I assume he coated, pokes at my dark passage and he gently presses it in as he's thrusting into me like a piston.

I can only bury my head in a pillow and scream out another orgasm as both my holes are filled. I can feel my insides clamp down on him, trying to hold him in one and repel the finger in the other. The sensations are unbelievable and I climax again, this time, taking him with me.

# *Thirty*
## *Nick*

I manage to not squash Ellen as we collapse into a heap in her bed. I check to see if she's still with me and she partly is. I pull her to me and hold her, then I remember where my finger just was and I kiss her temple.

"Be right back," I tell her and I pull on my briefs so I can go and wash my hands. I come back as soon as I'm done and I pull her to me, kissing her, holding her. When I hear her sigh I know she's back with me.

"Hey, you," I say, kissing her. "Unbelievable, fabulous you," I whisper to her again.

"I've never," she begins and I chuckle.

"Every night, I want to make you scream like that," I tell her.

"I want you to make me too," she whispers at me. I snuggle her close and kiss her.

"As often as we can sweetheart," I tell her, letting my eyes close. Her breathing evens out quite quickly and before long, I'm asleep with her in my arms.

Her alarm goes off at six, which is too early but I have to get going. I grab a shower and wear the same shirt that I wore to the curry, knowing I'll change it when I get home before going to the office.

"You should really leave some things here," she tells me as she kisses me goodbye at the door. She's brewed me a coffee to take with me so I can drink it on the way.

"I'll bring some next time I'm here. I've left some of my wash things," I tell her and look up to where the bathroom is. She nods.

"Shall we come to you for the weekend?" she asks as I unlock the car and load my few things into the backseat. It'll be the first time she and Sam have stayed over.

I pull her to me and I kiss her. "I'd like that. I'll make sure there's a comfy bed for Sam," I tell her. "We can kit it out so it's home from home," I suggest. She nods and gives me that cute, dainty smile I've come to love.

"Sam will need to study," she tells me. I nod, understanding that Sam's education is paramount right now. She's at a crucial point in her education and whilst we're seeing each other, this is how it has to be.

"I can organise a desk into one of the bedrooms for her, so it's like a den?" I know we've spare odd desks at the office. I just need someone clever to make it fit where I want it to go.

"That would be great," she tells me. Then I kiss her one last time and head off, pleased as all hell that I came to meet one of her closest advocates.

As I travel on the M5 towards the M6 and Lichfield, the direction signs on the gantries give me an idea that takes hold in my head and I grin. I head home, change shirts, put the two into the wash, quickly measure up where that desk might go, then I head to work.

As soon as Hayley is in, I get her to send a message to my office manager to visit me as soon as they can, though it's not urgent. Twenty minutes later, Gavin is knocking at the office door and I invite him to sit down.

I tell him what I'd like to do, using the older desks from the company, and give him the idea of utilising them for staff. I'm sure Ellen's not the only one with teenagers who need office kit. We're due an upgrade on everything ergonomically anyway to keep one of our operating standards, so I found out yesterday. Gavin's face lights up when I tell him my plans and ask him to get it written up formally, but as his proposal.

"Why as mine?" he asks, rising from his chair.

"I don't need the reward for improving the services," I told him. "And this was something you mentioned to me months ago." Gavin's going to benefit from this. His partner and he are raising a child together who heads up to secondary next year, the improvement bonus will be nice for them. I don't think dad has figured out Gavin is with another guy. Not that it would bother him anyway.

Gavin's grin makes me smile. "Go, make it happen for us," I tell him. Gavin heads out with a spring in his step and I get on with my day.

Five hours later, he's back with a twenty-two-page proposal, documenting where we get it all from, how it'll look and what he needs to make it happen, timescales, costs, everything. I quickly skim-read the report and it looks great.

He shifts nervously as I look through the report. "How did you get it together so fast?" I ask him. This is a few days of information gathering right here and there's no way he's done it in five hours.

"I've been drafting this for a few weeks," he tells me and I nod. He was coming to me with this anyway, though goodness knows when.

"I'm going to read through this again tonight," I informed him. "Shouldn't be an issue getting dad to sign off on it." He gets up and grins at me.

"Thanks, Nick," he says, shaking my hand.

"Thanks for the idea, Gavin," I counter. Hayley smiles and winks at me. She knows what I'm doing; looking after my people.

I read the report again over dinner. I'm using it to distract me from not being near Ellen and Sam and so far, it's working. I read it again, I quickly text Ellen, and then I call dad. It takes an hour for us to run through it verbally. He wants to see it and I suggest I bring it over tonight, have a cup of tea with mom and we chat about it again tomorrow in the office with Gavin. Dad agrees and I head over. I'm doing everything I can to distract myself from the loneliness I currently feel when I'm not with her.

Two hours later, I'm home and getting ready for bed. I fired off another message to Ellen. She hasn't responded to my first one and I frown a little. Then the dots appear and I smile.

*E: Sorry, been helping Sam with some history homework.*

*N: No need to apologise. Sam's education is important. Did the Internet help?*

*E: No; but books did! We went into work before they closed to borrow the really big reference books she wanted.*

Did she travel into work? Damn.

*E: What have you been doing?*

*N: Been looking at an ergonomic report our office manager has produced. We'll be upgrading the offices in the next few months if dad will agree on the expenditure.*

*E: Oh, exciting!*

*N: Going to be chaos, but it's needed. How was your day, apart from the extra trip back to work?*

*E: It was good. House is quiet. I've made some cards, about to post them up on my Insta page.*

*N: Great! I'll get you to make my parents' anniversary card from us. They married on Christmas day. Dad's forgetful with dates...*

*E: They had a Christmas day wedding? How?!*

*N: Vicar was a good friend. It was the late 70's...*

*E: How romantic!*

I made a note of that for Ellen. What does she find romantic? Rose petals on the bed? I'll say yes to that. I begin to wonder what else. My eye catches the fairy lights in the living room. I need some for my bedroom.

*N: Never thought of it like that, they've always told me that dad's just terrible with dates.*

*E: Even so, Christmas Day... did it snow? Please, tell me it snowed, even a little?*

*N: I'll have to check with mom.*

I do and it did, whilst they were having Christmas Day dinner with the vicar who had married them. I relay that back to Ellen.

*E: Oh, that's just... amazing!*

*N: I guess it is. I never knew that about their wedding.*

I wonder if Alex did, no doubt I'll bring it up with him next we talk, probably tomorrow during our weekly call.

*E: I need to talk to you about the half term. We usually go to Hull to see my parents for a few days.*

The dots continue but there's no message for a few moments.

*E: I'd like for you to meet them.*

I look at the screen. She's met my parents, perhaps sooner than either of us would have liked, but that's okay. The least I can do is return the favour.

*N: Sure! Let me know the dates and I'll organise a few days up with my brother and family.*

*E: Great, thank you! Good night handsome*

She sends me a kissing emoji and I smile, sending her a kissing one back. I'm going to meet her parents.

## Thirty-One
## Nick

We fall into a routine where Ellen and Sam spend a weekend at mine, then we swap and I head to hers on a Friday night. Sometimes, the motorways play nice, but it's not often. Whoever is travelling, the other cooks. Ellen has had no further issues with the people who caused the accident we witnessed, and I'm glad.

Tonight is the last night before we head up to Hull for four days. I've offered to drive us all as my car is bigger and since we're staying with my brother for most of the time, it made more sense.

The weather's turned and the days are cooler. Sam is settled at school and the boys that were giving her grief have backed off from what I can tell. I smile as I pull into Ellen's drive and spot her car is more tucked away than usual. I swing mine around and reverse onto her drive. We're leaving early and I'm making it easier for us to do so.

Sam's standing at the door and she smiles. Ellen must be busy doing something and as soon as I walk into the house, I can tell what she's been cooking. Our favourite. No wonder Sam greeted me, the girl would live on the stuff if Ellen would let her.

"Hey, Garfield," I tell her as I drop my bag and close the front door.

"Garfield?" she asks. She's dressed in her usual torn jeans, t-shirt but today, she's thrown on a cardigan of sorts. Not the traditional things my nan would have me wear at her age, but some modern floaty thing that wouldn't look out of place on Ellen. I wish I could have introduced Ellen to my grandparents, but they've passed on now.

I nod and remove my coat. "Yeah, you know, the ginger fluffy cat that eats lasagne," I try to keep myself from grinning at my own joke, and maybe for a few seconds, I succeed. When I can't hold it in anymore, she laughs with me, then she whisks my bag away.

"Mum's in the kitchen," she tells me as she points the way. She zooms off upstairs and I know she'll drop the bag into her mum's room. A room that I'm fast calling ours.

"That you Nick?" Ellen's voice reaches me from the kitchen and I can smell the garlic bread cooking from here.

"Sure is!" I call out, toeing off my shoes as I head towards her voice. Ellen left my usual slippers at the door. I always feel that I'm home when I'm here.

The kitchen is warm, homely. The table is already set with a beer for me, wine for Ellen, and a can of pop for Sam. It's our usual Friday night routine. I smile at Ellen and hug her as soon as I can, holding her close and kissing her deeply. I'm sure this is why Sam disappears for ten minutes no matter who goes to whose house.

Ellen groans as our tongues dance. We haven't seen each other since quite late on Sunday evening as they stayed at mine last weekend. It's always a long five evenings without each other. I look forward to the day when we're able to be in the same house every day, though that's a conversation for next year, maybe even twelve months from now.

"You taste like lasagne," I tell her when we break apart. She grins at me.

"I had to try the filling as I was cooking it," she licks her lips and I join her, licking her lips for her.

"Haven't you two finished that yet?" teases Sam as she thumps into the kitchen. She can be as loud as an elephant, or as quiet as a lynx. Usually the former if we're together, though she's good at sneaking to the bathroom once she's supposed to be in bed or asleep.

I chuckle and Ellen blushes. Even now, weeks later, her daughter can make her blush a soft pink. I refrain from whispering something naughty at her but I wink and Ellen's pink blush goes redder as she gets my meaning.

"Not yet, no," I tell her. I like verbally sparring with Sam, I think it helps build her confidence. Something Ellen's mentioned before she's worried about for her daughter.

Sam just rolls her eyes and the timer goes off. I chuckle at our timing and I take the lasagne out of the oven for Ellen, placing it on the heat mats in the centre, just like the first time I visited.

We eat, talk, catch up with what's going on with each other's lives, even though Ellen and I text every day and chat every evening.

At the end of the meal, Sam helps tidy up then she vanishes. I hear her go halfway up the stairs, then come back down.

"Nick?" she asks tentatively from the hall.

"Yeah, Sam?" I turn to face her as I roll up my sleeves so I can wash the lasagne dish tonight.

"We're leaving early, aren't we?" she asks. I nod.

"Six am," I tell her. "It takes hours to get to Hull, the earlier we set off, the more reasonable the M1 is likely to be."

She nods at me. "I didn't get to say last week, thanks for my desk in your house," she leans against the door frame. "It's better than my one here."

"Do you want one like it here, but with white wood?" I ask her, knowing how Ellen has her room here decorated. We have a few desks that still need a remodel and home.

"Is that possible?" she asks. I turn to Ellen, who shrugs.

"Her current one isn't as sturdy as the one at yours," Ellen says as she makes up the sink with hot, soapy water. I nod.

"I'll see what I can organise for you next week. My office manager is sorting out the last of the refurbishment this coming week, but I don't want to bother him over the weekend."

Sam bounces over to me and throws her arms around my neck. Then she snuggles in close.

"Thanks, Nick" she whispers. Then, she vanishes off up the stairs, as quiet as a lynx.

I turn to Ellen, who is as wide-eyed as I probably am. This is the first time Sam's hugged me since I started seeing Ellen or spending time with them both. I make sure to include them both, not just think of Sam as a tag-along.

"She's accepted you," Ellen whispers as she dunks, then wrings out the cloth from the bowl of hot water.

"Wow!" is all I can say. "I didn't expect that," I admit.

Ellen glances at me over her shoulder as she wipes down the worktops.

"I did. You might find yourself fielding awkward dad-like questions soon enough. You're the only significant adult male she's in contact with, grandpa apparently doesn't count," Ellen grins at me. What she says makes me feel amazing, though I can't quite put my finger on why I'm so proud of that fact.

"I'll do my best to guide her," I tell Ellen, then I kiss her neck and hug her before I go and wash up.

Due to our early start the following morning, we chose to retire early. I've already been to the bathroom and settled into the bed when Ellen joins me. I smile as she changes out of her clothes, showing off her perfect form. Her arse has to be one of my favourite parts of her. She snuggles into me and even though she was dressed a moment ago, she's freezing!

I jump back in shock and she giggles.

"Sorry," she grins.

"No, you're not," I tell her.

She nods. "Can't help it, the bathroom floor isn't heated." I put a heated en-suite bathroom floor on my mental "want" list for when we look for a joint house.

"We'll have to get one when we get our house," I blurted out. She looks at me with her eyes wide.

"When we what?" she asks, timidly. I kick myself mentally.

"When we move in together. That is where we're headed, isn't it?"

I watch as her eyes change from shock to something else.

"You?" she starts to say something, then stops. I watch her swallow and I reach across to touch her face.

"Yes, I want you. Always. This travelling back and forth is necessary for now, but I am looking forward to the day we're living together. Please tell me that's what you're wanting too, sweetheart?"

I'm suddenly swamped by her arms as she leaps at me. Her mouth crashes into mine and I waste no time in pulling her onto me, resting her right above my now hardening cock and playing nipple to nipple tag.

She pulls back, breathless. "Yes!" she hisses at me, her mouth holds a huge smile, and her eyes are wet. I reach up and dry them.

"Why the tears?" I ask her, kissing her gently as I dry her eyes.

"I wasn't sure if you wanted that," she tells me. How can she not know how the heck I feel about her?

"Let me tell you this. I love you. I want you, Sam, and I to live together. I want to marry you and if you're willing, to bless us with a child. If not, we've other options. You're a great mum already."

She covers her mouth and sobs and I pull her to me. Has she been worried about how I feel all this time?

"Ell?" I push her away a little to look at her. "Talk to me, what's been going on?"

"I didn't know if you felt the same," she tells me between sobs. I pull her back to me and snuggle down under the quilt with her in my arms.

"You didn't know that I leave a piece of myself behind every time I leave? Or that a piece of me goes with you when you have to leave with Sam? A piece I want to come back and claim every damn night?"

She shakes her head against me. "Then I'm sorry. I should have told you so much fucking sooner," I hardly ever swear, I'm articulated enough to get my point across without it, but damn, this time it needs it.

How can I have been so neglectful as to not tell her what my heart already knows? I'm so glad hers is on the same page.

"I just haven't heard you say it in one go," she whispers as her fingers dance over my pecs and chest hair. I turn and roll her so she's half on her back, but my arm is still under her.

"Then listen well, because I now mean to tell you, show you and remind you somehow, every day we're together. You're mine. I'm yours. I want you in my life until one of us is put into the ground. I'll stand on the highest mountain in the country and shout it out for all to hear if that's what you want."

She lifts her head and plants a kiss on my lips. "Or I can fuck you senseless and remind you that way for as many times as I can until I'm worm food."

I kiss her deeply, our tongues dance and she shifts a little, so I move so I'm right between her legs. I break our kiss to kiss her ears, her jaw and she moans into my ear, loud enough for me to hear her, but not loud enough for Sam to do so over the hallway.

I make my way down her body, paying attention to her perfect breasts and I hear one of my favourite types of moans from her. I kiss down her stomach and I realise she's trimmed everything.

"Mynx," I tease her, and my tongue darts between her folds. I watch her as she runs her hands through my hair, digging her nails in slightly as I make her writhe. I can tell her pressure is building as she starts to arch up on me. I clamp her hips down with my hands and in moments I can taste her honey as it begins to drip into my mouth. I suck one more time on her clit, then I move up to be over her and fist myself a few times. I swipe myself at her entrance and call her name. As she looks at me, she grins and I slide into her until I'm balls deep and I can feel her walls contract a little.

Bracing myself over her, I begin to move and I kiss her as I make love to her. Her legs wrap around me, pulling me in closer but I want to go deeper.

"Going to make you scream Ellen," I say and pull back to pull her legs up onto my upper arms. She whimpers as I change the angle I have her at.

"Don't stop," she breathes at me and her tiny, perfect hands grab my biceps as I thrust deeply into her again and again. I can see and feel her climax building again, the blissed-out look on her face, her fingers digging into me, her walls contracting around my length and her moans are perfect, music to my ears.

"Len," I whisper out. She opens her eyes as I thrust slightly deeper. "I love you," I tell her.

"Love you too," she manages to say as the start of her last climax hits her. I know I can get her another time and I move my hand to play with her clit as the second climax fades. The third hits her and she arches up, my balls draw up and I climax with her, emptying myself into her in thuds and convulsions as her walls milk me for every last drop.

I gently drop her legs and brace myself over her again, kissing her deeply. I can tell when she comes to, her kisses become more engaging, her tongue dances with mine and she moans softly into my mouth. All indicators that she's sated, happy, aware.

"Mine," I tell her as I slowly break our kiss-off.

She moans at me in agreement and I move to her side, then pull her to me.

"Love you," she mumbles at me as sleep takes her.

"Love you more," I tell her. She doesn't reply, so I cover us with the quilt and wrap her in my arms, letting sleep and the warmth of holding my woman take me under.


The following morning, both our phone alarms wake us and we groan. It's still dark out, but I know we have to get moving.

"Shower," I whisper to Ellen and I get up, wrap a dressing gown around me and make my way to the bathroom. I'd been given these for presents but because my house has an en-suite, I never needed them.

Until now. I shower quickly and Sam is outside the bathroom as I finish.

"Morning," I quietly tell her and kiss her on the head.

She grunts, or groans in reply and heads into the bathroom. I grin and make my way back to our room. Ellen is awake but hasn't moved to get showered or dressed.

"Nick?" She calls me and I turn to her.

"Yes, sweetheart?" I go and crawl to her, pinning her under the quilt as I loom over her. "What is it darling?"

"You meant… last night?" she asks.

I nod. "Every word, action, kiss, suck and drop I buried deep into you. Do I need to do it again?" I ask. She giggles.

"No, just making sure in the cold light of day," she tells me.

I lean in and kiss her. "I'm not going to up and leave you," I kissed her again. "Not now that I've found you."

She gives me a happy, contented sigh. "Come on, you need to shower and I want to get going, it's a long assed drive," I say as I move back and sweep the quilt off her. She squeals as the coldness hits her. I lean down. "If you're really good, I'll do that with you again tonight and we can stay in bed tomorrow morning until the coffee is brewed," I wink.

She jumps up and puts on a dressing gown, a fluffy light grey thing, which hides all her perfect curves and form.

"I'll be ten minutes," she tells me. Enough time to brew a half pot of coffee. One for now, one for the road.


Twenty minutes later we're on the road. It's still dark and will be for a while longer yet. Sam is curled up in the back, headphones on, her head resting against the support, eyes closed. She's chilling which is great. The bags are in the boot and we've double-checked every lock. At this time of the morning, the motorway plays nicely and we're headed towards the M6 and M1 in no time flat.

Two hours later and we've still an hour to go, I can hear all our stomachs growling in hunger. Dawn was a grey, but dry affair. Ellen had dozed off, so had Sam and thankfully, I used my earbuds to listen to the stations I usually listen to when I'm alone. It let the girls sleep and the soft snores from both just made me smile.

I see the signs for the Doncaster services and I indicate to pull in, calling to the girls as I do so.

"Breakfast," I tell them. It wakes them up and by the time I've found a parking space (I do have a few to pick from today) they're rubbing the sleep from their eyes. We do what we need to and I am the first one of us into the eating area of the services. I placed the order for a Full English, two half English, tea, juice, and coffee. I'm just paying and getting our table number when the girls find me.

Sam grabs the condiments and we find one of the nicer tables at the window. As we eat, I check the upcoming traffic reports and see that we should have a clear run to my brother's place.

"Remember that we're going out with mum and dad tonight," Ellen reminds me as she bites into a piece of crispy bacon. I nod.

"Haven't forgotten darling," I wink at her. That meal is hours ahead and if I am going to drive another hour, I need this fuel.

She nods, smiles at me, and blows gently on her tea. One thing I've noticed about her, she doesn't rush her food. Sam, chews and gets the food thing over with as soon as possible. Ellen takes her time. There's been a few times I've seen the cogs working, then she's dashed off, written something down, then gone about her day as usual. I've never asked what she writes down or why and I make a note to do that next time.

As usual, Sam finishes first, then I do. Ellen takes her time and I'm on my second coffee before she's done. She sits back and finishes her tea with a sly smile on her face.

"What?" I ask, thinking there's something on my chin. She giggles and Sam just rolls her eyes.

"Mum's just been checking you out, that's all," Sam shakes her head and begins to clear our stuff away.

"Oh yeah?" I tease her, leaning over the table at her. Ellen's cheeks go pink and she purses her lips together. She nods but her sparkling eyes are revealing the smile she's trying to hide.

"Later," I whisper as Sam returns.

We gather our things as soon as Ellen has finished her tea. Another visit to the bathroom for the ladies and we're on the way again. I text Alex with our new ETA and why. He tells me that he's the only one up so far and now I don't feel so bad that we took a little longer here at the services.

I glanced around and whilst it was the southbound side we met up again on the way home that first time, this place is somewhat special to us. I wonder if Ellen realises.

I decide not to mention anything and I concentrate on rejoining the motorway and following the SatNav for the last leg of our journey.

# Thirty-Two
## *Ellen*

Nick is quiet as we set off of the last leg for our trip to Hull. He seems tense but I won't ask why when he's driving. Then I cast my mind back and realise that this set of services is where we bumped into him after all those accidents on the first trip back home we both had to do.

Sam's lost in her world with her headphones and whatever she's reading. I get motion sickness if I try to read whilst travelling, even on a train. It's annoying. I look at Nick who has his earbuds in. He notices me glancing at him and removes the one nearest me.

"You okay, sweetheart?" He asks as he checks his mirrors.

"Yeah. Do you want some music on?" I ask.

"I don't, but you can if you wish. I'm listening to an old podcast," he checks everything as he changes lanes. Always observant, I feel safe with him driving and his car is far more comfortable than my little Fiat.

"No, just wanted to know if you did. It seems like a lifetime ago, doesn't it?" I ask him.

He looks at me for a second, then turns his eyes back to the road.

"Do you remember the services?" He asks, slightly hesitant.

"I do. I remember the coffee, the table outside. You being there and holding space for me after what we'd seen in the accident," I shiver slightly, I haven't thought about that overturned car or the cutting gear the fire service was putting away as we drove past.

"It was bad for a lot of people, I'm sure you and I weren't the only ones shaken up with what we saw," he tells me. He throws me a quick smile and signals to come off at the next junction. We're closer now than I thought, the rest of the journey is A-roads with lights.

"You didn't seem affected by it," I told him. He was calmness personified that day.

"I thought about it a lot. I asked Alex about it afterwards during one of our chats. He says that the people were hurt but they were all due to make a good recovery. They had a tyre blow out at high speed," he explains as he eases the car to a stop at some lights. I don't recognise this part of Hull and for my parent's place, I'd go up another junction.

"That was scary for them. I'm glad they were all due to get better." He nods.

"Yeah. I'm glad too," he reaches across for my hand and gives it a quick squeeze before it's returned to the gear stick. I let him drive the rest of the way to his brother's in peace, getting lost in my own thoughts about that day.

As he signals to pull into a quiet road on a newly built estate, I watch as he maneuvers the car into his brother's driveway like a pro. I am not that confident behind the wheel, but it's something I have to do if I want to get anywhere, especially to see my parents.

"Here we are," he tells me. Has it been an hour since the services? I checked the time and it's about fifty minutes once we left, which means we've made good time.

"Nick!" exclaims the man who stands in the entire doorway of his house. He's slightly taller than Nick, but they have quite similar build and structure. Their faces are similar but not exact. Their eyes though are identical and it's clear that they're brothers.

"Alex," Nick hugs his brother enthusiastically.

"Good trip up?" asks Alex as Sam and I emerge from the car.

"Better than usual," Nick replies. "Alex, bro, this is Ellen, my girlfriend and her daughter Sam. Tell me Oscar's up?" and there's a huge grin on Nick's face at the mention of his nephew.

"Is he heck as like," he scoffs with a huge grin. "Lisa's only just getting dressed too. Her little decorating advice has taken off, thanks to your make-over images on Instagram," he tells Nick. Alex ushers us into the house and grabs the bags from Nick.

"Let me show you to your rooms," he tells us. He takes us upstairs and gives us a quick tour of who is in what room and where we'll be staying. Sam has the single room opposite Oscar and is using the JackNJill bathroom with him. Nick and I have the room across the landing with the main bathroom for our use.

We're escorted downstairs and it's lovely, homely. New, but well used and loved, almost calming.

"It's beautiful," I tell him. It is.

"I love the modern look," Nick tells me.

"I don't mind a modern look, but I do like houses with character." Nick nods and throws Alex a look I can't describe.

"Have you seen this lady on TikTok who has done videos on her modernising her Victorian six-bed London home?" asks Sam as she crashes into a kitchen chair. I scowl a little at her and she frowns, mouths the word "sorry" to me and smiles at Alex.

"Just like Oscar," he says as he fills up the kettle. "Tea?" he asks as the kettle quietly boils. I've never heard a kettle be that quiet.

"No thanks, some water would be great though," I ask. Alex nods.

"Nick tells me you like herbal teas, so Lisa got a few in. She's been trying it as the tanning is playing havoc with her vitamin D levels. Doc told her to back off the black tea," whilst Alex is looking at his brother, I have a feeling this is also for my benefit.

"Really?" asks Nick. Alex nods.

"Yeah, the amount she's drinking is stopping her body from absorbing the vitamin D. That and we're in the North," he smirks. The North of England does get sunshine, but not anywhere near as much as the south coast.

"I never realised," says Nick and they go through how they found out Lisa needed to get off her Granny Weatherwax level of tea. Itchy, dry, almost constant pale skin. I never knew either.

"No secrets, eh?" asks a woman as she comes through from the hall. I hadn't heard any stairs creak.

Nick stands and hugs her. "Lisa, this is Ellen, my girlfriend and her daughter, Sam." He stands taller, chest prouder as he introduces us.

Lisa doesn't go for the handshake, she comes in for a hug. I wasn't prepared for it but after a second, I hugged her back. She reminds me of Ruth and Shauna combined.

"Did you make me one too hubby?" she asks Alex. He nods and passes her a mug with the teabag still in it. She fishes it out and places it in a food caddy, then she motions for me to follow.

"They'll spend ages catching up about the blooming football, or something else to do with Nick's work. Or Alex's," she grins at me and leads me out to the conservatory. Everything in her home is neat, has a place.

"You have a nice house," I tell her. She really does.

"We wanted a new build, less maintenance," she tells me. "Though, the stop cock flying off one night and flooding us out was not planned," and she goes through how the ground floor was flooded a few inches deep until the water company shut off the water to the house, five hours after the internal stop cock leaked. She used the chance to get the place redecorated how she wanted it and it's far less vanilla than Nick's place is.

"I hear you helped Nick," I told her. "You have a wonderful eye for detail," I praise. She pulls out her phone and shows me her clients before and after on Instagram. Each post is about ten images long, a before, the progress, the after.

"You're good at this!" I said to her, I want to show her my cards and book reviews but I hesitate.

"Nick says you're good at making cards," and I nod. For the next little while, we go through the cards that I've made. I never thought about doing a progress profile on each card I make. Lisa's engagement is amazing so there's a trick I've learned both for me and work.

We talk about everything, the guys, the kids. I wonder about Sam for a moment and I go to check on her, to find she's nowhere around. I throw a quizzical look at Nick who points upstairs and mouths: Oscar at me. Ah, she's with him.

"I just want to check on them," I tell Lisa. She grins and nods. I already feel at home and safe here. We find that they're on the Xbox, chatting and playing a game. I'm grateful that they're fully clothed and not up to anything. Sam was really taken with Oscar when we first met and I know they've been chatting as Nick and I slowly found our way to this point.

"They're good kids," Lisa tells me. "How you've raised her on your own," Lisa shrugs and shakes her head. "I guess you had no other choice."

I sigh. "I did, but I didn't want to move, I could have come up to Hull with my parents, moved in with them. But I wanted to stand on my own two feet," we descend the stairs and find our way to the comfy sofa in the living room. Lisa closes the doors so we have some privacy.

"And I didn't want to move Sam. Her friends got her through that first year, just as mine and my parents got me through. I thought I wanted him back, at first," I look at Lisa and she is so like Shauna. She's just holding space, nodding, acknowledging. "As time wore on, I realised he would never come back and I figured out, eventually, I didn't want him to either. It's been Sam and I for so long, until Nick."

"And you're happy with Nicolas?" asks Lisa. It's the first time she's used his full name. I nod.

"I am. When someone tells you that they want you, only you, how can you not be?" She smiles broadly at my statement.

"At last!" she exclaims and I frown. "He's been like a ship without a rudder for a few years, I was getting worried about him."

"You don't have to worry about me anymore," Nick's voice makes me jump as he appears from the hallway door. He comes and perches on the arm of the chair and Lisa scolds him. He just chuckles and leans in. I look up and then he kisses me, full-on tongue tango as his sister-in-law watches. She coughs and slaps him on the shoulder as she leaves to find her husband.

"Wind up merchant," I tell him. It's a phrase Shauna used to use and it fits. Nick grins.

"Yep," he says. "Fancy a walk in one of the parks, stretch our legs?" he suggests. I can hear Alex calling for Oscar and Sam. I nod. Some fresh air would do us good.

We spent the afternoon just chilling out after an hour's walk at a local park with a lake. Walking around it took a good forty-five minutes, and then we're preparing to get freshened up and visit my parents for dinner.

"Mum, can I stay here?" she asks. I frown.

"Mum and dad are looking forward to seeing you," I tell her. "So, no. Go and get ready please," I tell her. She's wearing what we travelled up in.

"I'm good to go," she tells me. I shake my head.

"Sam," I caution. Nick appears behind her and hears my warning tone.

"Come on kiddo, I need my wing-girl with me tonight, hurry up" he cajoles her. She rolls her eyes, mutters, and stalks off.

"Wing-girl?" I ask, raising my eyebrows. He winks and leans into me.

"If it gets her ready so I can meet your parents," he whispers. I smirk at his deviousness. Twenty minutes later, Sam skulks downstairs but Oscar tells her something on the stairs that puts a spring in her step. She's not changed her jeans, but she has put on a pretty blouse and her cleaner trainers. Her hair is slightly damp, so she's at least had a shower. I smile at her and she smiles back.

"Come on then, slow coaches!" she teases as she puts on her warmer jacket. Nick and I roll our eyes and get ready to go and meet my parents.

We're meeting them at their house before we go to their favourite restaurant. Nick has prepared a small bouquet for mum and he's brought dad a small bottle of his favourite American bourbon. I smile at his ingenuity and Sam is in the back seat, being her usual happy self.

"What did Oscar tell you?" I ask as Nick sets up his Satnav to my parents' house.

"Just that we'd play more Halo when I'm back," she tells me. I glance at Nick who shrugs. I don't think I'll ever figure teenagers out, especially my own.

We're only fifteen minutes from mum and dad's, which is handy. Whilst they can cater for Sam and me, adding Nick to the household means we're a bed short. Nick's brother has the room, hence why we're not at mum and dad's.

Dad greets us at the door and I introduce him to Nick, who is immediately charming and charismatic. He shakes dad's hand and ushers us in before him. Dad raises an eyebrow and nods at me as we walk past, I'm not sure if Nick sees it. When we get to mum, she's presented with the flowers and Sam's already off to get a vase. A few minutes later, they're on the kitchen table. I don't tell Sam off for just plonking them in the vase and setting it down. She's being helpful and trying, so I'll hold back my OCD. I can hear the kettle being put on but dad asks her to turn it off as we won't have time for a drink before we have to go.

"I can drive us all, let you have a drink," Nick offers to my dad. Dad nods in appreciation and I give dad the front seat so he's more comfortable. I squeeze in next to Sam and behind dad. In a few minutes, we're on the way and within ten, we're at the restaurant, being seated. Mum and dad are nice about it but they ask Nick a lot of questions, then dad asks the immortal one as the main course is presented, despite a nudge in the ribs from mum.

"What are your intentions with my daughter and granddaughter young man?" Dad ignores mum tusking him. Sam giggles.

"I do intend on marrying Ellen," he looks at me and I reach for his hand. "But letting Sam finish her exams and stuff before we move in together is important." Dad nods at him.

"So have you decided where you want to move to?" he asks. Then he looks at me. "You sell the house for what you're comfortable selling it for honey. Use the money to help build a life with this young man," he nods to Nick. I must have my mouth open because Sam reaches across and pushes my jaw closed.

"That's very kind of you sir," Nick tells my dad.

"You just take care of her and Sam, okay?" Dad commands Nick.

"I have already and I intend to do so going forward," he smiles across at me and dad raises an eyebrow.

"You have? How?" he asks.

"I haven't told you as I didn't want you to worry," I begin. Dad sits back and holds mum's hands as they learn about the accident we witnessed, how they have been following me, Nick putting dash-cameras on my car.

Dad nods. "You should have told us, darling," mum says before dad can add another word in.

"I didn't want to worry you," I quietly replied as Dad huffs in disagreement.

"Not the point Ellen" my mother scolds, but dad looks at her and she backs down from a public telling off. I'm glad now I'm not staying at theirs, though I'll hear about it when we talk during the week.

"It's in hand," he confirms and Nick nods. The rest of the conversation focuses on our plans. Which we've not made yet.

"When we're ready, we'll take the next step," Nick tells my dad when he asks about us moving in together. "We've not started looking at areas or anything yet. I don't want to rush or push Ellen, I know she needs time to adjust and," he looks at me. "The wait is worth it."

I try not to lean into him but I must do as his arm is around me, pulling me close and he plants a kiss on my temple. I get nods again from Dad, who clearly approves and mum's gazing at Nick in a motherly kind of way.

We order dessert and the topics get lighter, thankfully. Dad invites us back but Nick declines as we're at his brother's.

"I'd like to meet up again for an afternoon before we go back home," he tells them. He's good at managing expectations. He's not saying no, just 'not right now'. It's more than I usually do, I often go along with things that others want just because it's easier. Not Nick. I admire that about him.

"How does Monday sound?" he asks and Nick puts it in his phone calendar. I know that if he doesn't put it in there, it just won't get done at all. He sets all the reminders he needs and then we're taking mum and dad home before we go back to Alex's.

Sam dashes off to find Oscar as soon as we're back and I take a few moments to chill on the sofa. Nick hasn't asked me why I didn't tell mum and dad about being followed, though I know that conversation is coming.

We chill out with Lisa and Alex. The kids see themselves to bed, letting us know that they've retired for the night and into their separate rooms. We retire before Alex and Lisa and as we're lying in bed, the dreaded conversation about why I didn't tell mum and dad begins.

"You didn't tell them. Why?" His voice isn't angry, it's concerned, wondering.

"I didn't want them to worry," I tell him, honestly. "Dad would have, and given his heart condition." It's a feeble excuse but it's the only one I have.

"Oh, Len," he whispers and pulls me close. "Think about if Sam was dealing with this and not you. How would you feel if you found out after the fact? Or when she got hurt?"

I shudder. "Exactly," he whispers into my ear. "You'd be afraid for her, as they are for you. But you don't have to do it alone," he tells me. He's kissing my temple and holding me close.

"No more secrets, please?" he begs of me.

"I haven't hidden anything from you," I tell him honestly.

"From those we love. If you don't tell them and I go put my foot in it," he explains.

"Then that's on me," I turn my head to try and see him in the darkness, but Lisa has blackout linings up on the windows, so I can't see a thing.

"It's the same with you, not telling your parents everything, or Alex and Lisa. If we put our foot in it, we do. Though it wasn't done maliciously. I didn't want daddy to worry. They had enough of that when Mark left us," I sigh.

Nick kisses me. "I can only guess," Nick confirms. "But, from now on, no secrets unless you and I have agreed to it before?" His voice is questioning but commanding.

I smile. "Okay," I say and wiggle back against him. Before I can acknowledge if he's kissed me again, I'm asleep.

I awake to the door swishing against the thick carpet and Nick appearing with some mugs in his hand. He pushes the door closed with one foot and makes his way to my side of the bed. I can't tell what time it is and I'm without coffee, so I can't see or make anything out.

"What time is it?" I ask him.

"Just after seven," he tells me. Then he leans over me and kisses me on the forehead. "Good morning gorgeous," he sings to me in a low voice so that we don't wake anyone else up.

"Good morning," I chirp back, blowing on my coffee. He climbs back into bed and I smile at him.

"What's our plan today?" he asks, still keeping his voice low.

I shrug. "No idea. Chill out? We're spending the afternoon at mum and dad's tomorrow," I ponder and I squint in protest as Nick lifts the blackout blinds a fraction.

"Now we can see," he tells me and he comes back to bed.

"Is there anything you wanted to do today?" I ask him. He shakes his head.

"Not really, no." He sits back in bed and places his coffee on the bedside.

"Let's see what Alex and Lisa want to do," I suggest. He nods and for an hour, we just sit, chill, chat about what kind of house we'd both like, and snuggle. Whilst we both want to go further, there's no insulation in these new houses to hide the noise so we daren't do more than kiss and cuddle. I'll be glad when we're back home.

We get up when we hear Lisa and Alex quietly descend the stairs and we're at the kitchen table eating our breakfast when the kids arrive, half rumpled, semi-asleep, and yawning.

"Morning," I greet Sam in a friendly tone but she grunts at me. Lisa places down a glass of orange juice, a bowl, and two boxes of cereal. I watch as Oscar half fills Sam's bowl of one cereal and then mixes it with the other. I watch, almost in horror as he adds the milk for her and encourages her to try it. She shrugs, munches and I watch as her face lights up.

"No way!" she says. Oh my gosh, I shove some toast into my mouth as she eats the mixed-up cereal.

"Told ya!" Oscar exclaims and he does the same for his bowl, mixing them up before adding the milk.

"Oscar!" scolds his mum, but she doesn't stop it. I don't think she can and it's probably one of those many teenage battles you just let them win.

"Alex, what's good to go do today?" Nick asks.

"Oh, I wanted to know if Ellen wanted to come shopping with me?" Lisa pipes up. I look at Nick and smile.

He nods, smiling. I turn to his sister-in-law, who I know will one day be my sister-in-law.

"I'd love to!" I reply as Lisa swings in behind me and whispers; "book shops?" I giggle and nod.

Lisa is driving us into town just over an hour later and we're comparing notes between Alex and Nick. It turns out they're quite similar in some ways but so very different in others. Lisa pulls into a multi-story car park space and I gingerly step out.

"You're with me, we'll be fine," she tells me and wraps an arm around mine. Nick had a little chat with her away from my earshot and I guessed he told her that I don't do well in crowded, new places.

"Where to first?" I ask and she guides me to an independent bookstore on one level. I want to get the start of a series for Nick to keep at mine and his.

"I'll be over here," Lisa whispers as she heads over to the romance section. I browse the action and mystery section and pick up the start of J.B. Turner's books about Jon Reznick. I then spot a SAS book by James Deegan and grab that. I look down and see I've got about six books and I look around for a basket. A clerk smiles at me and offers to bring me one and in a moment, they're stacked neatly in the basket as I add two more to the collection. Splitting those between our homes means they'll come together when we do move in but it should keep Nick busy for a little while.

Lisa joined me as I got to the counter to pay, deciding that we'll take these back to the car. We do and then Lisa takes me to a dessert shop, where we indulge in an afternoon tea.

Lisa fires a text off to Alex and grins. "The boys can take their turn, we're having a girly day," she tells me. I laugh but I feel happy to have made a new friend so quickly, even if she is going to be family. Perhaps that is the best part.

Once we finished the afternoon tea, we headed to the nearest Ann Summers but I'm not brave enough for any of the risky stuff, or any of their items in general. Lisa shrugs and picks up a matching bra and knicker set in a deep red, winking at me. I go and look, then motion that I'm going to wait outside, or nearer the door. It doesn't take Lisa long to buy her items, there's hardly any queue. She smiles at me and leans in.

"It's our anniversary on Halloween," she tells me. I smile.

"Lucky," I tell her. Though, I'm not sure who is luckier, her or Alex.

"You don't want anything to wear for Nick?" she asks. "It's amazing what happens when one strips before your husband or partner and they start drooling like Roger Rabbit," she grins and I chuckle. I remember that movie, though Lisa certainly has a very Jessica-like figure.

"Not got that far yet," I tell her but I head to the lingerie department of M&S, picking out something that's a little more my taste. Lisa shrugs and holds up the black version of the pale pink one I've picked out. I check the tags and I can afford both.

"My treat," Lisa says, insisting that she pay.

I shake my head. "You did lunch and brought your own," I say.

She winks at me. "I'm not technically paying, Nick, is," she says. I stop.

"He asked you to do that?" I ask her. She nods and holds a finger to her lips.

"I told him I wanted a girly day out with you and he wanted me to ensure you got something but on him, so," she smiles. I hang the garments I picked up back. Lisa gives me an astonished look.

"Back to Summers," I tell her, and I can hear her footsteps catch me up as I head back to Ann Summers.


We're leaving the shopping centre and heading home when Lisa starts checking her mirrors. We've been driving for a few minutes.

"Ellen, phone Nick will you?" She takes charge and I glance behind, then even I swear.

"How the hell?" I ask. I put the phone on speaker as Nick answered.

"Nick, it's us. They're behind us," I tell him.

"Who are?" he asks. I can hear shuffling in the background.

"Lisa, you okay babe?" asks Alex.

"Got some assholes following me in a black SUV. They've been following me since the shopping centre." Lisa presses a few buttons on her car and she can read out the licence plate of the car behind. A number plate Nick and I know too well.

"Keep calm babe, I'm getting you some help," Alex barks out. The SUV slows when we slow, it accelerates when we do. "Lisa, honey, where are you?" Lisa tells him exactly where we are in Hull and in which direction we're going.

"There's an unmarked unit on its way babe," he tells her. "Just remember what I taught you, okay?" Lisa nods.

"She's concentrating, but we understand," I tell him.

"Good, now, stay on the line for me okay? Ellen, tell me what you see," I hear some beeps and I keep talking.

"Ellen, this is the police. We have an unmarked car approaching you with its lights off. I'll let you know when it is in position. When I tell you, I want you to find a space to pull over and tell me when you're doing so."

I foolishly nod then stutter out, "Yes, we understand." A few moments pass and Lisa drives us in a straight line.

"He'd better get into position soon, we're nearly at the dual carriageway," Lisa growls.

"That's okay. That's what we want. We've blocked the road and we have our second unit coming into place now. Ladies, follow the flow of traffic and do as you normally would do when you're in a traffic jam. Keep extra distance from the car in front, in case he rams you to try to get out."

"Got it," replies Lisa. I glance at her and she doesn't have her usual, sparkly grin on her face. My hand reaches across to where hers is on the gear stick and I grab her wrist. That gives me a small smile from her mouth. I look ahead and I see the traffic slowing.

"We're slowing down now," I relay. Lisa checks her mirrors and I can see an unmarked police car to Lisa's right. He waves a slow-down motion, then I realise he's not looking at us, but the guys behind us.

"We've stopped," I tell whomever happens to be listening and, then suddenly all hell breaks loose. The police that were to the side of Lisa, jump out and aim tasers at the SUV behind. To my left, police with guns, which I've only ever seen at airports, point their guns at the SUV. There's some shouting about getting out of the vehicle and then Alex's voice booms out of the phone.

"Lisa, Ellen, unless they're talking to you, stay exactly where you are!"

There's a uniformed officer to my left and he's motioning for us to stay. I simply nod.

"What the fuck Alex?" Lisa demands of him.

"They're wanted, long before they tangled with Nick and Ellen. I'll explain what I'm allowed when you're home, I should know more by then too. There's a PC Pugh there who will get you, ladies, home. I'll see you both very soon. We love you both!"

Then, there's silence in the car. There's nothing but Lisa, myself, our shopping and a lot of noise outside the car neither of us wants a part of.

It takes twenty minutes before the officer who motioned for us to stay now motions for us to slowly get out. There's no carnage, there's the black SUV being swarmed by the kind of people you see on Luther or NCIS in lab coats. Certainly not something you expect to see in the North of England.

"Are you ladies okay?" he asks us. We nod.

"I've saved my dashcam footage for you," Lisa tells them. Her swanky electric huge Volvo has them built-in. It is a beautiful car and right now, I'm glad for all its technology.

"Great, can you email it to me?" He asks. Lisa pulls up her phone and in moments, has the video files being sent to PC Pugh directly. Now that impresses me.

"I need to take some statements from you both, then you'll be free to go."

I hear Lisa mutter about thanking the Lord and I smirk, then let out a huge sigh.

Half an hour after we're allowed to get out of Lisa's car, we can go home. The crime screens are up now, stopping people from being nosy. We've given our statements, been wrapped in emergency blankets, gently questioned, and really, there's nothing left to see or say.

Lisa thanks the officer that's been looking after us and asking us questions, then he tells us he's escorting us home. Lisa doesn't argue, though I can tell she wants to. PC Pugh checks in with someone who turns looks at us, see's Lisa, smiles, and nods.

"Good, we can get the heck outta here," she mutters as she climbs into her car, waving at the other officer. I follow suit and let Lisa lead the way. If it were me, I'd still be here long after all the police had left.

Lisa pulls her car into her driveway half an hour after we were let away from the scene. Alex and Nick are the first two at the door, the engine isn't even off when Alex has the car door open and he's hugging Lisa. I'm similarly greeted by Nick and I'm glad now I purchased the lingerie Lisa suggested.

"Large one," Lisa tells him and Alex laughs.

"Already prepared babe," he tells her as he hugs her tightly with a shower of kisses. I throw Nick a questioning look and he smirks, kissing and hugging me just as tightly.

"Come on, let's get you both inside and fed."

There's takeaway pizza being kept warm in the oven, with mozzarella sticks and cheesy garlic bread, and I can see now what Lisa meant. The largest G&T glass I have ever seen is waiting to be prepared on the side.

"That's something I never want to fucking repeat," Lisa exclaims, sitting down.

"I agree! How did you keep your cool?" Nick hands me a glass of wine whilst Alex hands Lisa that large G&T she ordered. Lisa downs half of her glass and Alex chuckles as she does so.

"I knew two of them, thanks to Alex. As soon as I saw Andy on my right, I knew I'd be alright." She lifts her head to Alex as he leans into a kiss. She pulls him down more by his shirt and Nick laughs as their tongues dance the tango.

They eventually stop and Alex leans his head against Lisa's. "That's the most scared I've ever been in my life," he hoarsely tells her. He then takes a seat next to her as Nick sits in behind me, pulling me close. I lean my head against him, suddenly tired but ravenous. We hear the thud of footsteps on the stairs and seconds later, Oscar and Sam are bounding through the door. The kids hug each of us tightly and demand to know what happened.

Lisa tells the story and I feel Sam shiver as she realises before Oscar does, who was in the black SUV.

As we talk, we eat. We drink. The kids vanish upstairs once Lisa's finished her second G&T. I'm still on my first glass of wine but I'm feeling calmer now that I've eaten.

"Your colleagues were scarily impressive," I inform Alex.

Alex conveys that there was more than the vehicle of interest out from when they followed me out of Saltwells, it was part of a fleet. They'd been tagged from London to Devon, to Bath, the Birmingham area, Nottingham, Lincoln, Manchester, and now Hull.

"Their fraud goes into the millions, it was a matter of time before we caught them but they didn't expect to have Ellen and Nick step forward to counter one of their fraud claims with an insurance company. It's all being part of the case against them including the intimidation of other witnesses."

I look nervously at Nick. "Will we have to give evidence?" I ask. Alex shakes his head.

"Highly doubtful, the insurance companies are out for blood. Theirs. The amount of paperwork the CPS will have to go through... I doubt those boys will see daylight this decade and that is if the trial starts in the next twelve months. They'll likely go on remand at Her Majesty's pleasure," he takes a swig of his beer. "And what's even better is, it's not my case," Alex chuckles and he pulls Lisa into him.

"So that's it? We're… it's over?" I ask him. Nick plants a kiss near my ear.

"Yes," he whispers at me.

I begin to cry, more from the relief than anything. Then I begin to laugh and cry some more, Lisa joining me. The guys don't quite know what to do with us, but them being there is enough.

# Thirty-Three
## Nick

Seeing Ellen let the stress out last night was a relief. Lisa too, once the gin took hold. I thank God it was Lisa driving and not Ellen, though I wish it had been Alex or I. Alex pointed out, once police control cut the call, if it had been us, they'd not have followed the Volvo. Thank goodness Alex had all the toys fitted to their car when he ordered it.

I've left Ellen asleep in bed. I can hear movement downstairs and I can tell it's Alex. I pad downstairs quietly in bare feet in my jeans and a t-shirt, taking in the underfloor heating. Yep, I think I want that for our house too.

That still gives me goosebumps, thinking about buying a house with Ellen. Nerves get overridden by the intense feeling that this is exactly who I am meant to be with, so nerves be damned.

"Morning," I say quietly to my older brother. He nods.

"Is she still asleep?" he asks as he quietly pulls a chair out and motions to the open kitchen door. I nod, closing it and he sighs.

"Yeah, thank fuck Lise was driving," I tell him.

He nods. "Yep, she said the same thing. I am glad Ellen was there though, Lisa can go a bit Lettie-like behind the wheel," he takes a huge swig of his coffee. "I've been told they've lawyered up, so it's going to get very interesting. The bail hearing is set already, next week."

I raise an eyebrow. "Think they'll get it?" I ask.

He shakes his head. "They've got a history of absconding from bail before, there are two outstanding bail warrants in London alone. This is going to go to the High Courts I reckon," I let out a breath I hadn't realised I was holding.

"Coffee?" Alex asks as he heads to the machine. I nod.

"Yeah, I'm gonna need it," I tell him. "Spending the afternoon with Ellen's parents, getting to know them."

"Can we watch Sam?" Alex offers. "Or rather, she can keep Oz occupied," I note the nickname for my nephew and chuckle.

"Her call, though she might take you up on it if there are crisps and tea involved," I wink. I know what she's like when she's at home. She's not a chocolate fanatic, she's more into her savoury snacks, just like me.

That's when it hits me.

"Well, damn," I mutter.

"What?" asks Alex, placing the coffee down before me and sitting back down.

"How did you know you wanted to ask Lisa to marry you?" I lean forward as I ask him, lowering my voice. These new houses are ace, but they amplify the sound.

"When you realise you can't wake up without her, or go to bed without kissing her, or more."

I nod and grin. "I'm already there. I just thought of Sam as *my* daughter," I tell him. Alex grins.

"You're there brother. Ask her when you know she's ready."

"And I know that how?" I'm ready now, even though it's only been a few months.

Alex shrugs. "There's no one perfect time Nick. Carpe Diem," he tells me. I roll my eyes.

"That shit again?" I comment. He got into his empowering Latin phrases in school and he used them when we were growing up far too much.

He nods. "Got a better answer?" He teases me. I open my mouth to retort that I do. Then I close it again like a venus-fly-trap. He's right. I don't.

So now I get to work out when and how I'm going to propose to Ellen and get Sam's help to boot.

Ellen and Lisa get up at around ten am. Oscar and Sam have already devoured a weird breakfast, another of Oscar's concoctions of mixed cereal with banana and chocolate spread sandwiches. Where they put that amount of food makes my mind boggle. I hold fire on talking with Sam just now, it's more than enough that Alex knows I want to ask Ellen to marry me.

I tell Ellen that Alex has offered to supervise Sam today, leaving us the whole afternoon to sit and talk with her parents. She hums and dallies.

"It means they can ask anything and everything they want," I tell her. She nods.

"Okay then," is her quiet reply. She's not looking forward to this and it sets me slightly more on edge, even though I've met them.

She looks super gorgeous in flowing trousers that sit just above her ankles but pinch in at her tiny waist, a crochet top in a pale, almost Grecian blue that matches her eyes, and light makeup. We can hear the rain lashing against the windows and pound on the conservatory roof. This is the North of England in mid-autumn. The weather is guaranteed to be horrible.

"You might want more robust shoes," I hint and she nods.

"Boots," she quietly tells me with a grin. I watch as she goes off to find them and I turn to see my sister-in-law in the kitchen doorway.

"Mission was accomplished before we got followed," Lisa tells me. I grin and nod. Ellen might be afraid to wear the lingerie here, but at home, I hope that's a very different story.

I hear Ellen come down the stairs and I take in the sight before me. She's changed her outfit slightly to a denim skirt, and the boots just add to it. Two-inch stiletto heels give Ellen's demure height a boost, shape her legs just perfectly and I suppress a groan. I might just ask her to wear only those later on.

"Ready?" she asks, donning her coat. I nod, grab mine and swing it on, then we're off to her parents for the afternoon.

# Thirty-Four
## Ellen

I know it's my mum and dad, but after the fiasco with Mark and how he left us, I'm nervous about what they'll think of my younger boyfriend. Adding to yesterday's events, I'm more nervous than usual.

That lasts until dad hugs me and mum kisses me and I'm sitting on the sofa, Nick's arms around me.

"How are you, love? You look tired," mum begins.

"After yesterday, I'm not surprised," Nick answers. Mum raises her eyebrows and I sigh. Nick nods to me, giving me space to tell them in my own words what happened. Slowly, I do, even though it's my parents, I nervously and slowly relate what happened after Lisa and I went shopping.

Mum and dad sit and join Nick in holding space and letting me tell them what I need to tell them, how I want to. Mum gasps a few times and covers her mouth in shock and dad goes quiet.

"You helped Lisa do what she needed to," dad tells me. Dad looks at Nick, but I can feel his eyes on me and I turn to look at him. He smiles at me and plants a kiss at my temples.

"She did. Lisa was saying last night, she'd have lost it if Ellen hadn't been there," Nick may be answering my father, but he's not stopped watching me.

"If I wasn't there she wouldn't have been followed," I admit. Then I purse my lips together. I hadn't told Nick, Alex, and Lisa that last night, the thing that I thought. My blame, my guilt.

"Oh, hold on right there, that's so not true," Nick tells me.

"It is," I tell him. I don't want to fight him on this, but I know this is true.

Nick takes my hands and sighs into me. "Ellen, did you not hear what Alex said last night? They've been following people around all over. It wasn't just you, but they picked on a copper's wife this time. More fool them," he tells me.

"I…" I stutter, for the first time since I met Shauna, Helene, and Ruth. I didn't even stutter when Mark left me alone with Sam, killing me as he did so.

I'm enveloped in a warm hug, Nick pulling me in, whispering that it's okay.

"They would have followed someone else and turned them into a nervous wreck. They picked on you and Lisa. They were on a road to hell when they did that, Lisa would have seen to it, faster if you weren't there."

I look at him. "She drives like a demon when she's on her own, or Alex is with her. Think Lettie from Fast and Furious, that's more her style," he grins at me. I know he's trying to make me feel better.

"I'm glad you were there, in that regard. Alex has only just started paying for that V90. She had to be more careful because you were with her." I look at him as he informs me and I don't know what to make of it.

"Lisa's an overly confident driver, hand-break turns, the whole thing. She'd give Clarkson a run for his money, and take it." He kisses me on the forehead. "You made her calmer and for that, we're grateful. She'd have gotten herself into A&E, or worse, we're sure."

I smile and let his warmth envelop me. I didn't notice mum going out to make tea, though I notice when she comes back in.

"Sorry mum," I go to push myself away from Nick, but he doesn't let go.

"I'll help," he tells my mum and me, then he leaves me to sit and chill with dad.

I look at dad, who just holds his arms out for me. I go to give him a hug and the last of the worry leaves me. I'm drying my eyes again when Nick comes back in with mum, a plate of mixed biscuits and enough milk and sugar to fill Sam.

I smile weakly at Nick and he just gives me a cheeky wink back, then he sits back where he was. I join him and the conversation with them gets easier. I'm glad he made me do this and with him by my side.

We head back a few hours later but not before Nick and my dad have vanished off somewhere, his tool shed most likely. When they did come back, Nick was smiling and dad was beaming. I didn't want to ask, until we're in bed later, the last night we're in Hull.

"How ya doin'?" Nick asks, copying Joey's voice from Friends.

I giggle. "Better now, I'm really glad you got me to talk at mum and dad's, even though I didn't want to." I wiggle against him, which makes him groan.

"No fair, Len, unless you can keep quiet and I mean, quiet."

"I'll be quiet," I whisper back and in seconds, I'm on my back. Nick lays between my legs and I lift my hips. Nick lifted the black-out roller blind an inch so we could just see when we came to bed. Now, I'm glad he did. He pulls my knickers down and off me, then shucks his briefs off. Then his lips are on mine, his arms on either side of my head so he can support himself and not crush me. I lift my hips again and I can feel him poking at my entrance.

"Going to take you slowly, quietly, deeply," he whispers into my ear.

"Yes," I whisper and then he's sliding into me, slowly. Then he's backing out and pushing forward again as our tongues dance. Slowly, we make love, reconnect. I wrap my legs around him, my nails scratch his back slowly, deeply. He breaks the kiss off and he holds his forehead to mine, our breathing rapid, but still he thrusts into me slowly, deeply. Then his kisses start again, the nibbling of my ear, my jaw and he claims my mouth whilst still slowly making love to me as much as I am to him. His V hits me repeatedly, and he sweeps my legs up from around him to be on his chest. I can feel him deep inside and I grab a pillow to muffle the sounds I can't stop escaping as his thrusts pick up the pace. Before long I'm screaming into the pillow arching up against him as I climax, then he's shuddering into me as his hits, sending me over the edge on a mini-tornado.

He lets my legs go and they fall to either side of him and then he's between my legs again, removing the pillow and kissing me deeply.

"You," he kisses me, almost laughing. "Under the pillow, can come out now."

I wrap my arms around his neck, keeping him close.

"I love you," I tell him before I can stop myself. I've said the words before, but not since we left mine and not since yesterday's incident.

"And I love you," he whispers in my ear as he moves off me. He pulls me closer and I snuggle into him, which is the last thing I remember.

Dawn comes too early, but we have to leave today. I open my eyes, see that I'm still snuggled into Nick, then I close my eyes again and smile, contentedly.

Nick sleeps on and I doze until we hear Oscar and Sam heading downstairs from their respective rooms. I move off Nick and stretch, but he pounces on me and kisses me until I'm breathless.

"Good morning, gorgeous," he breathes at me when he finally stops. I grin.

"Morning handsome," I tell him. "Kids are up," I state. He nods.

"I noticed," he whispers as he kisses my ear lobe. His kisses make their way across to my mouth and his tongue enters my mouth, dancing with mine. I could spend all day in bed with him.

He moves off me and sighs. "As much as I'd love to have you again," he tells me. "Everyone else seems to be up," he leans in, kisses my nose gently, then moves off me to get up.

"We ought to shower," I tell him. He nods.

"You go first, I'll strip the bed," he tells me. I nod, then jump out of bed, grab my clothes, and head to the bathroom to shower and dress. By the time I'm back, the bedsheets are nowhere to be seen, the mattress is bare and Nick is in his jeans. He gives me a lingering kiss, then he walks to the bathroom to do what I've just done. I pack my things away and put my bag on the bed. Glancing around one more time to check I've got everything packed away, I head down to breakfast.

Lisa and Alex are sitting at the table but there's no sign of Oscar or Sam.

"Halo," Alex explains and I realise, they must have gone back up whilst I was in the shower.

"Did you sleep okay?" Alex asks me. I nod.

"We did, thank you," and he smiles with a nod. I wonder if he heard us, heard me, but I don't ask. Alex pours me a herbal tea and I'm blowing on it as Nick comes in.

"Coffee?" Alex checks, though it's being poured as he asks.

"Yep. Got the drive back today. Why'd you pick a pain in the arse location to live in?" he asks. Alex just chuckles.

"Because I have a gorgeous reason to be here?" Alex retorts as he kisses Lisa.

"Good save!" Nick teases him and Lisa just pulls a face at him.

"What time are you planning on leaving?" Alex asks. "Fancy some lunch first? M1 is busted and will be for a few hours. Caravan overturned, crews have shut lanes one and two." Nick just nods.

"Guess we are now! We could have stayed in bed," he winks at me. Yeah, I know exactly what we'd be doing too. I grin and try to hide my smile, but I can't.

Lisa and Alex chuckle and grin at each other, their understanding needing no words. We tidy up the kitchen once we've eaten and then Lisa and I crash on the sofa with books. Nick and Alex head off somewhere and for a few hours, so we indulge in some quiet time.

Lisa and I lift our heads a few hours later as we hear noises from the kitchen.

"Ah, toasted sandwiches," she tells me.

"How can you tell?" I ask.

"I know the sound the grill-press makes when he takes it out of that cupboard," she grins. "I'm letting him get on with it" and I smile. I like Lisa, I like his whole family.

We chill out until the guys call us for lunch, Alex yelling loudly for the kids.

We eat, we chat, we tease the kids, laugh and it feels great. Lisa and I clear up whilst Nick and Alex load the car and go to refuel it.

"He really likes you, you know?" she asks me as we're clearing away.

"I know," I smile.

"Think you're ready to be Mrs Nicholas Taylor?" she asks.

I stop. "If he asks," I reply. Lisa beams like a lighthouse and comes over to give me a bone-crushing hug.

"I'd love you for a sister-in-law. Now, Bobbie," she shakes her head.

"I don't know who Bobbie is?" I tell her, then Lisa blushes.

"Someone he'd be divorcing about now if he'd picked her. You're much nicer and genuine than she ever was," Lisa spits out. She squeezes my arm. "You're much easier to get along with," she whispers.

"Oh," I mumble.

"If what happened to us on Sunday had happened to her and me, I'd have pushed her out and let them have her." Lisa scowls.

"And she's his ex?" I ask.

Lisa comes over and touches my arm gently. "She was long gone from his life before you turned up lovely," she tells me, her northern accent warming me. "Thank the Lord!" she exclaims as she puts away the grill.

Lisa turns to me. "Look, she screwed him over. He found out. He booted her arse out of his life and hasn't looked back since. Now, he's got you, he's already protective of Sam and is starting to think of her as his own. You're in girl, and I'm glad it's you." My heart warms and swells at Lisa's words.

If Nick were to ask me, how quickly could I say yes?

I think about it as we leave and by the time we're at the services on the same side as we bumped into each other that day, my mind is set. When he asks, for Lisa's less than subtle questioning, I know my answer already. I just need to prepare Sam for it.

At the services, we head to the ladies and we share a stall.

"If Nick were to ask me to marry him," I begin. Sam squeals. "You'd be okay with that?" I finished what I was planning to say. She nods like a nodding dog that you see on the parcel shelves of cars.

"Oh yes, mum, yes!"

We swap positions and we carry on chatting. "He's not asked yet, but I'll be answering for us both," I tell her. "I needed to make sure you were okay with that?" I ask as she flushes.

"Oh, heck yeah!" she exclaims. I nod.

"Okay, well, just act normal when we leave. I don't want to give him the heebies or second-guess anything, or back out," I let my nerves show. Sam hugs me.

"Mum, that's not something he'll do," she tells me as we wash our hands. I raise my eyebrows. "He's not left yet and you've freaked out plenty of times," she reminds me. I think back and she's right, I have and he's still here.

"True," I smile. "Let's get going," I tell her and we make our way back out to Nick.

The weather has turned and the rain is lashing down. Nick is standing watching the rain and he smiles at us as we approach. He must have seen us in the window's reflection.

"Come on," he tells me and grabs my hand, pulling me outside. Sam trails back and gives me a thumbs up. I don't have time to send a gesture because Nick has us back out to the tables outside, under the shelter of the building and the table we sat at months ago.

He stops, turns, and pulls me close to him. I can hear his heart beating like a drum and I feel him breathe me in. The next thing I know, he's kissing me, deeply, slowly, sensually, his tongue making love to mine.

He breaks the kiss off and I'm dazed for a moment, then he's gone.

"Down here, gorgeous," I look down and he's on one knee. He's going to ask me. Here?! I cover my mouth and I'm not sure what sound I make.

"You," he tells me and I madly swipe away whatever is making me not be able to see. "You're my sunshine. I don't want to be without you, I want to wake up every day and love you, touch you, be there for you and Sam. I want to hug you when you're sad, make you laugh when you need it. I need you to complete me, Ellen. Will you marry me?"

He opens up a black velvet box and shows me a ring, a solitaire. When did he get time to get this?

"Yes," I manage to breathe out, somehow. He slips the ring onto my finger and suddenly, there are cheers around us and I see people under umbrellas, standing in the pouring Doncaster rain, watching us and wishing us luck. Sam rushes over to me and bounds into me, hugging me tightly.

"I get a dad," she whispers to me, loud enough for Nick to hear but not the swarms of people now wishing us well.

"You knew?" I ask her. She nods, her smile almost breaking her face. I don't think I've ever seen her this happy.

"Nick told me his plans this morning as you showered," she tells me. I shake my head as Nick pulls us both into a hug. So that's why Lisa was asking. She also knew.

"Did everyone but me know?" I ask. "And where did you get the ring?"

"Your dad gave me the ring yesterday. It was your nan's. Your parents had the gold reused and the stone reset into what you're wearing now."

"You asked daddy?" I'm crying again. He nods.

"I was going to ask on Christmas Day, but Sam here suggested this. That's when I got Lisa to ask you about it this morning," he grinned.

I can't decide if I need to laugh or cry, but both seem to be winning. He kisses me.

"Come on, future Mrs. Taylor. Let's get you home."

# *Epilogue*

## *Ellen*

Tomorrow is Christmas Day. Nick is hiding in the spare bedroom where we've set up the folding picnic table and wrapping paper. I've not seen him for hours. Sam and I wrapped everything up days ago, but Nick's been here since mid-morning and he's had to leave it all until the last moment due to work.

Sam perks her head up. "He's done!" she exclaims, a little surprised it's not another three hours of wrapping. I grin.

"Be nice," I tell her. She gives me a grin that tells me she's teasing. Their relationship has gone from strength to strength over the last year. The travelling between both of our homes is murder though, but we've said we won't move whilst Sam's in her GCSE phase. She will sit her exams this coming summer and then, we can look at a potential home for us all.

Nick stomps down the stairs and Sam vanishes, no doubt to make him a coffee or fetch him a beer. Since he arrived she's been his errand girl and I only dread to think what he's got planned for tomorrow.

He smiles at me as he appears in the doorway and I wonder what he'll make of my surprise present when it strikes midnight. We did this last year. We each give the other a present at midnight, something that's personal. So far, it's been sex toys, but this year, I hope and pray he likes my gift.

"You're finally done," I tease as he leans down to kiss me.

"Some of them were pains, I thought boxes were meant to be easy to wrap?" he tells me as he sits next to me on the sofa. I rearranged my reading nook to the sofa so that he can sit next to me when I read. He's gotten into reading but he's got me into watching some television, more so than before I'd met him.

Sam appears with a beer for him and he smiles, thanking her. As far as her school is concerned, he's her step-dad. He's on all the emergency contact forms, parental emails and has stepped up into that role.

"I'm off to bed," Sam declares. She's in her Norwegian frosty white and red pajamas and I'm in mine, though what I have on underneath is for Nick's eyes only.

"Good night sweetie! See you in the morning!" I sing out. She kisses me, then kisses Nick on the cheek and heads off to bed.

"You look exhausted," I tell him. He nods.

"Wrapping things up production-wise this week was harder than usual, one of the main pressing machines malfunctioned. We're having to replace it, which is a blow."

His father has taken more of a back seat and Nick's stepping up to the challenge. Alex has been promoted in the Police force. The trial for the massive insurance fraud is due to start soon and I hear that's been fun and games for the lawyers.

"But, you got it done, the order. And here you are," I remind him.

He leans across to me. "There's nowhere else I'd rather be," he tells me. I close my book, dropping it gently onto the table behind me, and he leans in over me. I slide down so that he's over me, kissing me. I moan slightly as he lets his weight sink onto me, like a blanket. He rises and I take the chance to unzip the Norwegian Onesie I'm wearing over my Ann Summers lingerie.

I watch as his eyes take in what I'm wearing and I hear a satisfied moan. His lips crash into mine and he's feeling a breast with one hand and supporting himself above me with the other.

"Nick, I want to give you your present, now," I tell him, even though it's two more hours until midnight. He stops and pulls back.

"This isn't it?" He asks as a sly grin appears on his face. I Shake my head and can't help but grin back. I reach down between the cushion and pull out a wrapped package. Nick gives me a quizzical look and sits back where he was. I zip up the onesie for the moment, knowing that it might be ripped off me once that present is opened.

I giggle as Nick shakes it. It makes no sound. He squeezes it gently, but it doesn't crinkle. He frowns slightly and slowly begins to open it. I hold my breath a little and watch as he unwraps our new future.

He gets through the pretty wrappings in a moment, then comes to the box. It's a Clear Blue box and he looks at me with his eyes wide.

"Keep going," I encourage, praying he's going to be okay with the news he's now holding. I've known for days. He opens the Clear Blue box and removes the stick inside, then he reads what it says. He looks at me, then the stick.

"You're pregnant?" he asks. I nod. "Really?!" he cries out, but I don't get a chance to confirm it as I find myself being kissed and he's holding me. Then, he's touching my stomach gently.

"Fuck Ellen, I thought it would take months after the implant got taken out?" he asks me about ten minutes later. It might only be two.

"I didn't think it would happen this quickly either," I quietly replied.

"I'm going to be a dad," he says. Then, he's laughing and I'm being hugged, kissed, stroked, and caressed. "Fuck!" he says again. "Does Sam know?" he asks. I shake my head.

"Only you and I," I tell him.

"I was going to… Wait here," he tells me. Like I'm going to go anywhere. He darts off me and I hear him bound up the stairs to the back bedroom. He's stomping down the stairs again moments later like a small elephant. He closes the living room door, then he presents me with a wrapped, flat parcel.

It's in the red and white Nordic theme I've picked for this year. It's my turn to wear the puzzled face, but he sits there and waits as I carefully unwrap it. He's taken care to get the folds neat, the edges straight. No wonder it's taken him hours. The bow and ribbon on the top make me nearly not want to open it.

"Come on woman," he encourages. I take the colourful paper off to reveal a document holder, containing details of a house. I go wide-eyed and look at him, then back at the documents in my hand.

We've been looking at houses and areas for over a year. Nothing has agreed with all of us. Either because of travel to Lichfield for Nick's work, the centre of Birmingham for my work, Sam for school, the age of the house (I didn't want a new build and Nick didn't want a fix-me-up) nothing fitted. I look through the document and I'm in love with what I'm looking at.

It's a house in the Warmley area of Sutton Coldfield, with easy access into Birmingham on either the train or the bus, easy access to Lichfield, and with Sam doing her exams in the next five months, that area suddenly holds possibilities.

It's an older house, with the characteristics of the Edwardian era on the outside but thoroughly modern on the inside, keeping the period features I love. The bedrooms are huge, so adding in the walk-in to ours isn't an issue. Two of the bedrooms are like Lisa and Alex's place, a jack-and-jill between them. The master bedroom has an en-suite I see and there's a spare room almost joining it for something or anything else. The nursery.

"Did you see the attic?" Nick asks as he comes to sit next to me. I shake my head and he turns the page to draw my attention to the attic. It's unfurnished with just plasterboard in the walls but there's a huge amount of light from the Velux and a picture window in one end. "Imagine that as your personal library," he tells me. I gasp.

"Can we afford it?" I ask. He nods.

"Just about, if dad helps and he says he will. The kitchen needs doing, it's stuck in the eighties and one of the owners has developed Alzheimer's, so they can't continue the build. They want a quick sale. I just need someone to replace the kitchen," I kiss him.

"I know a company that will help out," I tell him and I immediately think of Adam and Ben.

"You do?" he smiles at me. "Fabulous! We have a viewing arranged for the twenty-seventh," he tells me.

"How?" I ask. That's between Christmas and New Year, most offices and services are closed for the holidays.

"I made friends with the estate agent, thanks to dad. She's one of dad's golf buddies' daughters. She's been searching for me all over and hit across this two days ago," he looks at me intently. "We can get the house ready and as soon as Sam has done her exams, we can all move in. I can sell my place to act as a down payment and move in when it's ready. Dad will bridge the mortgage until you sell this place and you pay him back. Then it's ours to pay off," he grasps my hands gently. My silence must be deafening.

"Wow!" is all I can say. "I want to view it first before I agree to any of that!" I say.

Nick nods. Can I do that, take on a huge new house, a baby and marry Nick?

## Nick

The morning of the twenty-seventh arrives very fast. We've told Sam that she's going to be a big sister and she was ecstatic. We showed her the house and she was jumping up and down about it, which is good.

We've also said we're not moving in totally until she's finished her exams, that her studies and her revision come first. She told us that she understands, but she's as keen as we are to see the house. Ellen's called in a favour from her old school friend who runs a construction business. Ben said he was going to meet us there and measure up the kitchen whilst we looked around, though it's costing me a bottle of Malt for his efforts.

We're there early, but so is the estate agent, Andrea.

"Nick, glad to finally meet you. And this is the lucky lady who you've been doing all this hard work for," she greets Ellen who blushes.

"You've been doing all the work Andi," I confirm. This is about the twentieth house she'd sent to my email.

"That's just my job Nick. Now, where's the builder?" she asks.

"He's on his way, he will let me know when he's here," Ellen says. Andrea nods and we head into the house. The hallway is laminated in a dark oak wood with plain cream walls, period features in the ceiling but done superbly. Every inch of the house appeals to me and I can see the sparkle in Ellen's eyes too. Sam walks around the bedrooms, noting which one is for who and allocating them out in her mind. She probably won't be too far off.

"The kitchen is one of the last four rooms the owners didn't get to finish," she tells Ellen. She's already told me all this and though I've relayed it to Ellen, we let Andrea do her job. Ellen's phone pings and she checks it.

"Ben's here," she says and Andrea nods.

"Perfect timing," declares Andrea. "I'll guide him in whilst you three look around," and she walks off to greet Ben while we check out the kitchen. Suddenly a figure appears in the kitchen and hugs my fiancee with vigor.

"Ben, meet Nick, my fiance," he shakes my hand vigorously at Ellen's introduction.

"Good for you Len! Now, tell me what do you want to do in here?" he says, looking around then back to Ellen. Ellen walks through the plans that have come into her head and I nod. She can have whatever the hell she wants as far as I am concerned. Ben listens and I'm impressed that he doesn't cut her off once.

"They're old friends, they were a year apart at school. He was a best friend to Shauna's first husband until he died on his bike. They've known each other for decades," Sam whispers to me. I nod. That's a good twenty years or so then. I know who Shauna is too, so that helps.

Andrea motions for me to follow her and Sam and I oblige. I motion for Ellen that we're going this way and she just nods. I smile.

Andrea shows us the basement and I immediately think of a private gym. We're taken up to the attic and that's where Ben and Ellen join us. Ellen falls in love with this room like I knew she would.

"Could you give us a quote for laminating this and fitting in bookshelves all around?" I ask Ben.

"With space for my table here," says Ellen as she stands at the picture window. Ben grins.

"Still making cards, Len?" he asks and she nods. "I should get you to make the family's ones for the year, save me the hassle," he says.

"Give me the dates, what it's for and I'll do it," she agrees.

"Done," he tells her, and then he gets Sam to help him measure up.

I go back through to the basement with Ellen and Ben whilst Sam steps into the room she hopes will be hers. An hour later, we've gone through everything and I tell Andrea to put mine on the market and give her a decent figure for this. It's in a sought-after location and estate so I expect a quick sale. Andrea makes a call and she nods, giving me the thumbs up. Our offer just got accepted.

"I'll get yours up this week for you and get the buying paperwork started," she smiles at me. We've already had the sales photos for mine taken, I was anticipating this. Ellen hugs me close and I kiss her temple. We're going to do this.

***The End.***

# About The Author

Growing up, I was writing stories or making up stuff in my head. It often came out as fibs or tall tales. My imagination was active and anything could (and still does!) set my muse off. pInterest is a classic platform for allowing me to visualise the characters that live in my head. Instagram is doing the same and I'm grateful for every follower I have there & on my other platforms.

I spent many years studying martial arts and I've used it with Shauna, (more so in my darker duet, which will be out in late 2021/2022) I have three children (one is already taller than me) and I've been married for nearly twenty years now. Add in a cat, dog, chickens, friends… I'm a busy gal!

I spent one summer of my youth hooked on Mills & Boon, then YA, then fantasy. Playing Dungeons and Dragons when the hubby and I got together didn't help my muse, the poor lady went into overtime

I came back into writing after reading many good books and the lockdown of 2020 was certainly a platform to do something for me, creatively. So, my thanks to Karen Lynch (Her Relentless Series) for a huge muse, to Sandra Hill for her erotic Vampire Viking Series (honestly, if broken Vikings chosen by the Archangel Michael can find love, anyone can) and for her rekindling my love of romance books.

Thanks too, to recent authors that have helped, guided, pointed and had me enthralled with their series of books: Jolie Vines (Marry The Scott series and all that she's created beyond Storm The Castle), Catharina Maura (The Tie That Binds, Forever After All), Elle Thorpe (Her Cowboy series), Delta James (Tangled Vines & now her Ghost Cat series) and many others whose books I've picked up, enjoyed, met and reviewed on Amazon & Goodreads. (With these ladies, you bet I'm on their newsletter list!)

If you enjoyed this, feel free to stay in touch! Here's how:

My website: www.louisemurchie.com
Newsletter: louisemurchie.com/newsletter
Instagram: @louisemurchieauthor
Facebook: https://www.facebook.com/louisemurchieauthor/
Twitter: @murchie_louise

Printed in Great Britain
by Amazon